GROOMED FOR MURDER

VIVIAN RHODES

A laid-back
L.A. mystery
with two fast-paced
New York sleuths

Ballantine / Mystery / 30732 / $2.50

WHO GAVE THE HAIRDRESSER THE ULTIMATE PERMANENT?

ALISON COLE
His baby sister, who may have loved him too much and was beneficiary of his $65,000 life insurance policy?

TRACY SIMMS
His ex-wife, the dazzlingly beautiful movie star, before she met the same fate?

JEAN PAUL
Born Harvey Lipski of the Bronx, owner of the beauty salon that stood to lose plenty if Michael set up his own shop?

ELLEN BETHUNE
The rich, beautiful wife of a prominent politician with a huge, shameful secret only her hairdresser knew for sure?

MEYER S. ROSENBLOOM
The slimy talent agent with the kinky habits that could make even Hollywood squirm?

CINNAMON BLAKE
The "save-the-whales" fanatic with an equally desperate love interest?

ESTELLE FAGELMAN
The over-protective yenta who raised Michael and Alison?

ONLY THE UNLIKELY TEAM OF
SUSAN FINKELSTEIN AND NICK COMICI
CAN FIND OUT WHY
THE SEXY HAIRDRESSER WAS
✂ **GROOMED FOR MURDER** ✄

GROOMED FOR MURDER

VIVIAN RHODES

BALLANTINE BOOKS • NEW YORK

Library of Congress Catalog Card Number: 83-91132

ISBN 0-345-30732-1

Manufactured in the United States of America

First Edition: January 1984

Dedicated, with love, to my mother, Sylvia.
In memory of my father, Louis.

ACKNOWLEDGMENTS

I'd like to thank Craig Anderson, for his determination in getting my manuscript to the right people; my agents, Patricia Ayres and Barbara Blitzer, for being those right people; Joelle Delbourgo, my editor, for her very on-target suggestions; Marineland, for opening their doors to me; my family, for their encouragement; those friends who physically helped me get my manuscript in "readable condition"; and lastly I'd like to thank my husband, Rick, for his love and for his openmindedness about my beginning revisions during our honeymoon.

❧ 1 ❧

My zeal hath consumed me . . .

Psalms 119:139

Before this summer I could honestly have said that I had never known a single human being, personally that is, who had been murdered.

Oh, certainly I'd been touched by suicides and accidents, such as the time my uncle Arthur went up to the roof to fix our antenna, forgot where he was, and walked off the ledge, plunging fifteen feet to his death.

No, I'm talking murder-murder. The kind TV detectives solve. The kind one reads about in the *National Enquirer*, where the accompanying photo so distorts the features of the murderer that he or she looks almost Neanderthal.

I've always feared being murdered. And my fear conformed naturally to my given environment. Having lived most of my adult life in New York City, I feared being thrown in front of an oncoming subway train by a purse snatcher with a touch of Hitchcock in his soul.

And upon moving to southern California nearly two years ago, I at once adapted to local customs and began fearing possible sniper attacks on freeways or perhaps a Manson-style execution.

But in all my fears and fantasies about being murdered, my would-be murderer has always remained a stranger to me. There would be something unethical, almost incestuous and definitely not nice about thinking in terms of friends and family when contemplating one's own demise. A rapist,

1

a mugger, a madman—these types we may not like but have come to accept, have we not?

But a premeditated murder committed by someone within one's very own nucleus? I never thought I'd come close to one.

As I said, that was before this summer.

Even now I find it incredible that this entire drama evolved in the short span of seven or eight weeks. But maybe it would be fairer to say that that was merely the period during which I first became a pivotal character in the ongoing scheme of things.

I can vividly recall walking down Rose Street in Venice. Venice, California. This was not the more affluent section of Venice, mind you, the part that borders on the posh, swinging Marina area where new condominiums shoot up as often as junkies.

No, it was down the artier, more free-spirited, and possibly more dangerous streets of Venice that I walked that Wednesday evening in June. How in the world had I allowed Stephanie to talk me into meeting her there that evening?

I had mentioned the day before that I was feeling kind of bored and that I wanted to meet new people. People outside of Marc's claustrophobic circle. Maybe get some new perspectives. Inspiration to start that novel I was always putting off.

As always, Stephanie acted immediately. She gave me an address and told me to meet her the next night, refusing to elaborate. She did, however, say that it would be an experience.

Stephanie, who has lived in Los Angeles for four years now, loves using words like "experience" and "beautiful" and eats her avocado salads heavily laden with alfalfa sprouts. All this makes her feel that despite her Semitic features, she is the prototype of the true California golden girl, and that she and Troy Donahue and Sandra Dee all grew up surfing the sandy shores of Malibu together to the lazy rhythm of the Beach Boys.

There are many New York girls who delude themselves in such fashion.

Sheep in Gidget's clothing.

At any rate, here I was walking down the streets of Venice headed for a destination of which I knew nothing.

As I turned a corner I happened to catch sight of my reflection in a storefront window; I looked twice to make certain it was me.

Ordinarily I am considered to be an attractive young woman. At least that's what I've been told for most of my twenty-eight years. I stand five feet eight inches, have straw-berry-blond hair and gray eyes. I'm lusty enough in build to satisfy construction workers and yet sophisticated enough to catch the more subtly lewd glances of many an executive.

On this particular evening, however, to say that I did not look my best would be something of a gross understatement. At Stephanie's suggestion, for which she offered no reason ("Would you please just do as I say?!"), I had pinned my hair up in braids and had worn a pair of wooden clogs. My bare legs were goose-bumped, and my flimsy trenchcoat covered me only slightly.

Damn, I thought to myself as I hurried along, of all the times for my car to be in the shop! Why did Marc have to drive up to San Francisco this week? Why couldn't he have left me the BMW and flown? Why hadn't I accepted Stephanie's offer to drive me here tonight instead of insisting on taking the bus? Why had I bothered coming at all?

Best question yet.

Why? Why? Why?

"Y's a crooked letter," my aunt Bea, widow of Arthur, used to say.

A copout answer if ever there was one.

Looking down at the address I had scrawled on the back

of a McDonald's napkin, I noticed that I didn't have far to go until I got to 277 Short Street. 273. 275. 277. At first I thought I must have made a mistake. It was then I noticed the steeple. You couldn't miss it.

Two-seventy-seven Short Street was a church, sandwiched between a dilapidated building, which probably housed some high-rental artists' lofts, and a closed haberdashery called Serendipity. I noted the location as being a bit unusual for a church.

As I walked toward the entrance, I heard muted chanting. What did Stephanie have in mind when she asked me to come that night? A church bazaar? A bingo game? I'd have preferred Vegas.

Or was this another "cult" Stephanie had become involved with? She'd already done TM, EST, and TA. I imagine Stephanie has always had a letter fixation. Even in college, the fraternity guys she dated were strictly ZBT.

Upon opening the church door and entering, I looked up briefly, as if to reassure Him that Susan Finkelstein was not going to make a habit of this any more than she had of visiting synagogues in recent years.

As I walked down a corridor, the chanting grew louder. I opened a door, and what I saw amazed me. I don't know quite what I'd expected, but it certainly wasn't this.

Standing in the pews, row after row, were women, and some men, of all shapes and sizes. Each one wore a different costume native to a particular country or region. I looked upon would-be geishas, Bedouins, señoritas, and harem girls, to name a few. All of them stood transfixed, their eyes focused straight ahead on the figure at the pulpit.

Dressed in a hula outfit, grass skirt and all, was a somewhat rotund, middle-aged woman with flaming orange hair. She was leading her followers in repetitious song and cheer. In the midst of all this I spotted Stephanie, dressed to the hilt in gypsy fashion, motioning for me to join her.

No one seemed to notice as I slunk down the aisle and quietly took my place beside her. I had to hand it to Stephanie, layers of skirts, bangles, jangles, and scarves really suited her.

Her dark features and high cheekbones were set off nicely by the scarlet bandana she had wrapped around her long black hair. I don't think anyone would have questioned her authenticity for a moment had she casually referred to her gypsy ancestry, as Stephanie, chameleon that she is, was perfectly capable of doing.

Stephanie Groman and I go back many, many years. We met in our sophomore year at Madison High, in Brooklyn. Stephanie approached me in gym class and without even so much as an introduction came right out and asked me if I'd ever soul-kissed. I asked her what that meant, and she replied that it meant I hadn't.

As our friendship grew, Stephanie taught me how to inhale a cigarette, what to wear on a date, and the way to cover a hickey by properly applying the correct shade of foundation to one's neck. Once she tried to get me to change the way I laughed. She told me I'd get laugh wrinkles if I weren't careful.

To this day I don't know exactly how Stephanie benefited from her friendship with me in high school, but she must have because we've remained close friends throughout the years.

I suffered with her through her pregnancy scares and she with me at the loss of my grandfather, with whom I'd been very close. We shared happy times as well. My acceptance to Syracuse University, her first job in summer stock.

We lost touch briefly when Stephanie came out to Los Angeles to pursue her acting career, but when Marc and I moved here two years later we resumed our friendship where we'd left off.

Stephanie is "from money," as the saying goes. Her

father made it big in doorknobs and has always taken great pride in helping out his only little girl. This is fortunate for Stephanie, because with the exception of a few commercials and one small part on a soap opera, her acting career has yet to take off. Like so many people in this town, she satisfies her need to be in "the business" by working on the periphery in just about any capacity. Stephanie's looks and the fact that she appears younger than her twenty-nine years enabled her to secure her present position as one of Universal Studio's many low-paid tour guides.

Stephanie waved me to her side and kissed my cheek, purposely missing it to avoid smudging a carefully made up Borghese face.

"I'm so glad you could make it, Susan."

Stephanie has called me Susan since I've known her, and I've always appreciated it. I hate diminutives. Sue is bad enough, but Susie and (yes) Su-Su are intolerable.

"Stephanie," I shouted, trying to be heard above the next cheer, which was being sung to the tune of *Happy Days Are Here Again*, "Stephanie, why didn't you tell me you were inviting me to a Tupperware party?!"

"It's a Tupperware rally, Susan," she said as she adjusted a big golden hoop earring, "and if I'd told you, would you have shown?"

A valid point.

"But I don't understand. What's with this sudden thing for Tupperware?"

"It's a long story. I'll explain later. Meanwhile, start singing."

To this day I cringe at the memory of myself sitting in that church in Venice, my wooden clogs and blond braids making me look like a god-damned Fräulein.

Sneaky Stephanie. Very sneaky.

I'll have to confess. I fit in with the lunacy that surrounded me rather well.

With half an hour left to the meeting, I decided to sit back and make the best of things. It had been a long day. I closed my eyes and listened.

"So let's sing a song of cheer again, Tupperware is here to stay!!"

✂ 2 ✂

Habit, if not resisted, soon becomes necessity.

St. Augustine

"Two coffees. Black, please."

The way the waitress looked at me you'd have thought I'd committed a major offense, which I suppose to her mind I had.

Stephanie and I were seated in a booth at The Temple of Health, a natural foods restaurant not far from where the rally had been held. The food was reputed to be quite good, according to Stephanie. Their herb-spice tea, renowned.

But at the moment we felt like coffee and said so.

"All we have is decaffeinated. Will that be all right?," asked the waitress in earnest. She was about seventeen or so, wore no makeup, and had on a plain white muslin dress. Her name tag said Kristy.

"That would be fine, Kristy," I said, okaying it with Stephanie at a glance. Kristy smiled sweetly and walked away.

Stephanie lit up a cigarette and offered me one. Sprouts were one thing, but giving up her Virginia Slims was another matter entirely.

"Okay," I said, trying to clarify what she had told me in her Corvette on the way over. "So you meet this woman . . ."

"Rita Simon."

". . . in Gelson's," I continued, "and it so happens that she sells Tupperware, and over the melons she invites you to a Tupperware party."

"Correct."

8

"And at this party you become so enthralled with her sales pitch that you decide to go out and crusade for Tupperware yourself."

"Something like that," she replied.

"Oh, come on, Stephanie. Think. Surely you must have left something out."

Kristy returned with two mugs of hot water and two packets of Sanka.

"Oh. Did I mention David?"

Noting my blank stare, Stephanie explained.

"David Simon, Rita's son. An orthopedic surgeon. He visits his mother frequently, and since I've been working so closely with Rita on this Tupperware stuff, David and I have gotten to see quite a lot of one another."

So that was it! I was relieved that the missing variable was indirectly related to one of Stephanie's many love affairs and not some crazy new form of plastic idolatry. According to Stephanie, David was like no man she had ever been attracted to, which led me to assume, correctly, that he was single.

"I'm beginning to understand," I said. "But what made you think it would be something that would interest me?"

"Oh, I don't know. I guess part of me wanted company this evening. Rita had to cancel out at the last second, but she insisted I attend tonight for both of us. Rallies are a great morale boost, it seems, and this is serious business to her, Susan. Then, too, you'd mentioned that you were feeling kind of down. I thought you'd get a kick out of it. Besides," demanded Stephanie, "what have you got against Tupperware all of a sudden?"

"Not a thing," I admitted. "It's great. My mother uses it. My sister uses it. *I* use it! I just don't know that I'd care to *shlep* from house to house selling the stuff, is all."

Stephanie laughed.

"You know, Susan, it might not be such a bad idea at

that. I mean, at least it would get you out of the house away from your kiddie books and your typewriter for a while. You'd be meeting people, maybe even gathering material for that great novel you've always talked about writing. Tell me, how can you write about life when you lock yourself away from it each day?"

With that Stephanie had hit home.

The truth of the matter was that one didn't need to leave one's house, ever, to write the books I had written. This is not to say that my editor was unhappy with my work to date. On the contrary, my Kelly Cockroach series was immensely popular with children of all ages. *Kelly Cockroach, Singing Sensation* and *Kelly Cockroach Visits Rome* were both especially successful. And my most recent venture, *Kelly Fights the Loch Ness Monster*, had received excellent reviews. But there were times I did feel that I was limiting myself.

Sensing my uneasiness, Stephanie quickly changed the subject, asking my opinion of Mitzi.

"Who?"

"Mitzi Fynch. The red-headed hula dancer. Our esteemed chapter chairlady."

"Oh, right," I said, remembering the woman. "I'll say one thing for her. She certainly caught my attention."

"She spoke well of you too, Susan."

"What do you mean by that?" I asked defensively.

"Well, before I left, Mitzi asked me to extend an invitation to my lovely friend for our next rally. Said she just knows that you'd be as devoted to Tupperware as I."

Now it was my turn to laugh.

"You've got to be kidding!"

Smiling like the Cheshire Cat, Stephanie replied with a wink, "Would I kid you, Su-Su?"

* * *

Two days passed, and I hadn't given Tupperware another thought. Marc was due home that evening. He'd planned his trip so that he'd be back for the weekend. If there's one thing Marc is, it's organized.

I had been asleep when he left for San Francisco, so as was his habit, he'd left me a list to which I could refer in his absence. I went over the list once more.

It was still attached to the refrigerator where Marc had fittingly secured it with a little bunch of magnetic bananas. The list read as follows:

1. Pick up my charcoal suit from cleaners.
2. If my mother phones, tell her I'm away on business and that I'll call her when I return Friday night.
3. Make appt. with dentist for me.
4. I'll try to call you one night this week.

> Love ya,
> M.

P.S. We're out of Mallomars.

His suit was now hanging in the closet. His mother had in fact called last night, once again inquiring as to when "Marky" and I were going to "tie the knot" and "make it legal" so that she could start looking forward to some grandchildren. I told her Marc would call her on Friday.

His dental appointment was set for next week, and Marc had phoned me as promised on Wednesday night, the night I'd been at the Tupperware rally. I listened to his message off our answering machine.

"Hi. It's me. Where the hell are you?"

Mallomars are chocolately marshmallow cookies and Marc's favorite food next to steak. I figured I'd pick up a

few packages on my way home from the hairdresser's. I
had a ten o'clock appointment for a cut and blow dry.

As I got into my trusty Toyota, just back from the shop,
I realized, not for the first time, one's impotence without a
car here in Los Angeles.

Traffic from the Palisades to Beverly Hills was unusually
heavy. I arrived at Jean Paul's salon at 10:25 A.M. hoping
that my appointment hadn't been forfeited. Jean Paul was
a stickler for time.

Stephanie, a great purveyor of gossip, had entrusted me
with the inside scoop on Jean Paul. In fact it was Stephanie
who first brought me to his shop, a rather celebrated one
in its way.

Born Harvey Lipski, the son of a Bronx baker, Jean Paul
had taken his beauty school degree to England some years
back. There he perfected his craft under the guidance of
Sasoon himself and then moved to Paris where he lived for
several years. He ultimately left Paris for Los Angeles and
under his new name, Jean Paul Altereit, set up shop five
years later in an exclusive section of Beverly Hills. Like
his father, Jean Paul too was rolling in dough, of a sort.

He spoke with too heavy a French accent, was about
thirty pounds overweight, and his prices were as expensive
as all hell, but his patrons always returned, primarily because of his reputation for having the best hairdressers in
town.

Especially famous, or infamous I should say, were the
talents of one operator in particular, Michael Cole.

And what an operator!

Stephanie had prepared me on my first visit.

"Just wait until you meet him," she'd said. "Remember
the role Beatty played in *Shampoo*?"

I rolled my eyes.

"Only Michael isn't playing, is that it?"

Stephanie responded charmingly, "Oh, he plays all right. And quite well, I might add."

"Stephanie, no! Not you!?"

"Me and half the female population of Beverly Hills."

"I don't believe it!"

"Come on inside," she said as she ushered me in. "I'll introduce you to Michael, and you'll see what I mean."

Michael looked up as Stephanie and I approached. He was blow-drying the hair of a girl who looked very much like Cheryl Tiegs. She appeared to be enjoying it.

Stephanie placed her arm affectionately around his waist.

"Michael honey, I'd like you to meet a friend of mine, Susan Finkelstein."

She pronounced my name in the more anglicized way, with a long "i" rather than a long "e," though how anglicized a name like Finkelstein can actually be is debatable.

"Susan, this is Michael Cole, the hairdresser's hairdresser."

Well, I could certainly see what Stephanie meant. Michael had wavy, sandy-brown hair and blue, no, turquoise-colored eyes. And his facial structure was exquisite, something like that of a young Tyrone Power. Great build. A melting smile, eager to please.

Yes, apparently this man had a little bit of everything for everybody. Still, there was something a little less than genuine and almost too quick about that smile. Something elusive that didn't sit quite right with me. But truthfully it was the sort of thing that a woman might not easily detect until she awoke beside him the next morning, if she detected it at all. If I'm to be honest, I must admit there had been times when Michael's smile and other parts of his anatomy had found their way into my personal fantasies.

On that particular Friday morning, however, Michael Cole was the furthest thing from my mind. In fact, the only thing I recollect thinking was how I was going to be caught in prelunch-hour traffic, combing the city for a box or two of Mallomars.

I opened the door, and my senses were immediately assaulted by the usual beauty-shop scents and sounds. The hair dryers, the blowers, the senseless chatter. The mingled aroma of shampoo, ammonia, and Halston. The rock music blaring out of stereo speakers. No Muzak piped into Jean Paul's hip salon. I looked around for Jean Paul and was grateful to note that he was not in the shop just then.

Before stopping at the reception desk, as was the usual procedure, I went to Michael's station prepared to apologize for being so late. But Michael didn't even notice my arrival. He was on the pay phone, his back to me. I slipped into the chair and leafed through a magazine while waiting for him. Since the phone was less than two feet away from the chair, it was impossible not to overhear some of the conversation, at least his end of it.

Michal's voice sounded different than usual. Cold. He spoke almost with condescension.

"Look, I've told you my terms. Take it or leave it."

He paused, then went on.

"Really? Well, that's a damn shame, but it's not my problem, now is it, babe?"

I was caught between trying not to eavesdrop and at the same time trying to satisfy my natural curiosity. I couldn't even figure out the gender of the person he spoke with since here in Tinseltown the term "babe" loosely covers everyone from one's agent to one's mistress.

"You wouldn't be threatening me now, would you? Well, there's no accounting for tastes, if you dig my meaning."

He laughed. A horrible, wicked laugh. A laugh that was abruptly cut short when he caught my reflection in a nearby mirror.

"Look," he said into the mouthpiece of the receiver in a very businesslike manner, "I've gotta run. I'll expect to see

you in the shop later, so I suggest you think about what
I've said."

Then he hung up. No good-byes or see-you-soons. Not
even a quick *ciao*.

He turned around and quickly composed himself. Flashing me a dazzling smile he said, "Susan, if my mutilated
body is found floating face down in the Pacific one of these
days, don't be too surprised."

He said this jokingly and laughed as he led me over to
the shampoo bar.

Only something about his tone on the telephone made
me think that he was half serious.

Who hated Michael Cole enough to want to see him dead?
I wondered.

A dissatisfied patron? Someone whom he had under-
permed or overblown? A dissatisfied lover? Someone he
had not blown sufficiently?

Perhaps it was someone for whom he'd neglected to buy
a box of Mallomars. Definitely grounds for murder in Marc
Beaumont's book.

✂ 3 ✂

Is not marriage an open question, when it is alleged that such as are in the institution wish to get out, and such as are out wish to get in?

Ralph Waldo Emerson

"Your mother phoned last night. She wanted to know when we were planning to 'tie the knot.' I got the distinct impression she's getting itchy for the pitter-patter of little Beaumonts."

"That's nice," Marc replied as he attacked his burnt steak. Like many Jewish men I have known in my life, Marc has a blood phobia. He insisted that all his meat be cooked beyond recognition and, incidentally, beyond taste.

"That's all you have to say? 'That's nice?'" I asked, picking at my salad. "I mean, with our being together nearly a decade, the woman's question is not at all unreasonable."

Marc put down his fork. He meant business.

"Sue, I've just walked in after being away for an entire week. Give me a break, for Christ's sake."

"Sorry. It wasn't my mother who inquired, you know."

"Since when do you care about what my mother has to say? Or anyone else for that matter. I thought you were such an independent thinker. Besides, we've been over this before; we'll get married when the time is right, not before."

With that he picked up the bottle of Heinz and smacked its bottom until the ketchup flowed freely, enveloping his potatoes.

"Jesus, Sue," he continued, "I never thought you'd be so insistent on conventionality."

16

When we flew out to Los Angeles on account of Marc's job offer, we moved almost immediately into this sprawling home of ours in the fantastic Pacific Palisades. A home, I might add, that was well above our means at the time. It was Marc who had insisted on the neighborhood, the house, the Jacuzzi, and the 320i, which he'd lately talked about trading in for a Jaguar XKE.

It seemed that conventionality was just dandy when it suited Marc.

"And when do you think the time might be right? Any thoughts on the subject?"

It was true. We had been over this territory before. In fact, a lot lately. Only this time I was reluctant to let it drop.

"Look, Sue, I know how you feel. But we're comfortable, right? And it's not that I have anything against marriage. I just want to play things a little loose for now. We've got plenty of time before settling down to the typical marital rut. You understand."

"I understand," I lied. What I understood damn well was that deep down Marc was a chicken shit.

"Good. Now what's for dessert?"

"Häagen-Dazs."

"Rum raisin?"

"Uh-huh."

"My suit back from the cleaners?"

"Uh-huh."

"Dentist?"

"Next Thursday."

"Good."

No siree, no marital rut for Marc Beaumont.

I had met Marc while studying journalism at Syracuse University's Newhouse School of Communication. I was twenty. He was twenty-one, a junior in the university's School of Business.

We were set up on a blind date by a girl who lived in my dorm, someone whose name I've forgotten, oddly enough.

The timing was right. I was just getting over a two-year involvement with a wiry, angry young man of the sixties. As a matter of fact, Russell not only sang Dylan, he composed his own Dylan-type songs as well.

Mistakenly I had interpreted his silence as sensitivity rather than dullness. His self-absorption, I mistook for introspection. So at the tender age of eighteen, I had given him my love and as proof of it, the gift of all gifts, the cherry of my innocence.

He, in turn, gave me plenty of heartaches and a copy of *The Prophet* by Kahlil Gibran. Not a very fair exchange I think in retrospect.

When Marc came on the scene, it looked as though he could be the proverbial "breath of fresh air" I sought. Tall and athletic in build, and while not my personal preference, his red hair suited him as well as his spaniel-like brown eyes.

Marc was open and direct, a young man who knew what he wanted in life and who was determined to get it. And if I didn't quite love him with a passion, well, there were compensations. He was strength, which was something I needed more than anything at that stage of my life. Besides, I'd loved Russell with a passion, and where had that gotten me?

What did Marc see in me? one might ask. Well, for one thing, I'm leggy and I'm tall—at least above-average in height, considering that the women Marc had been exposed to previously had all been well under five feet five inches. I wore my straight hair down to my waist, as was the style, and it was blond . . . well, actually reddish, but fair, which was what counted. My complexion and eyes completed the picture of the typical all-American cheerleader type.

Yet here I was studying journalism, hoping to make a career of it.

In Marc's own words, I represented a Jewish boy's fantasy come true. A Jewish brain in a *shiksa*'s body.

We began seeing one another regularly. At first it was the usual collegiate events. Frat parties, rock concerts, football games. Then pretty soon we advanced to more intimate pastimes.

Marc was delighted with my enthusiasm toward sex. From the start, he stated with democratic zeal, that he was glad I was an "experienced woman," meaning that I was not a virgin.

The fact that I'd been with one man was seen as "experience." Had I been with five men instead, I would have been written off as promiscuous. There was an unspoken law that defined such rules. For while the pill was becoming increasingly popular, people still thought and felt more or less as they always had.

Though my nonvirgin status didn't seem to bother Marc— "Big issue over little tissue," he used to say—I think he was relieved to hear that Russell had transferred to Stony Brook.

Making love to Marc was an experience. Actually he was quite an accomplished lover, though admittedly my own lack of experience didn't give me much of a yardstick with which to make a comparison. All the same, Marc had it down to a science. Knowing all the tricks of foreplay, he eventually calculated how long it usually took for me to become properly aroused.

Seven and a half minutes.

He experimented with different positions and encouraged me to do the same. But his being a natural athlete enabled him to bend in ways only an Olympic contender would dare attempt. Nonetheless, I enjoyed myself thoroughly.

And yet, despite my enthusiasm and Marc's expertise, something was missing. It was that extra-special tenderness two lovers feel for one another. I lacked it because I never really felt it, not toward Marc at any rate. And though Marc, I believe, felt it, he didn't seem to have the capacity to show it. If only he had, then maybe. Maybe.

We took an apartment off campus. And while Marc worked in the school bookstore as he finished up his graduate studies, I completed my last year of journalism. By this time Marc and I had become good friends. I trusted him, knowing he couldn't hurt me.

Neither one of us had any reason to linger in Syracuse, a gray, dismal city in the heart of New York's snow belt, so a few months after graduation we moved back to New York City.

Marc's parents live in Forest Hills, mine in Florida, by way of Brooklyn. Against their wishes, we moved into an apartment together in Greenwich Village, not far from New York University.

Within two weeks, Marc had found himself a position of great potential in the business affairs department at CBS. At that time the network had never been hotter, introducing to the public such memorable programs as *All in the Family*, *The Mary Tyler Moore Show*, and *Maude*. It was during the reign of Freddie Silverman then that Marc was fortunate enough to hook up with the Columbia Broadcasting System.

As for myself, I learned quickly just how little weight is given to a journalism degree. So with Marc's income as security, I sat down and began writing and submitting articles to such magazines as *McCall's*, *Family Circle*, and *Cosmopolitan*. I had my share of rejections at first, but soon began to receive letters of acceptance as well.

The material I wrote fell under the heading of what is

generally termed "light reading." One day while visiting the dentist, I picked up a copy of *Highlights* magazine. Skimming through it, I thought I might try my hand at writing a children's short story. It was a good idea. I was shortly submitting to publications such as *Jack & Jill* and *Humpty Dumpty*. Within a year, I'd found my niche, writing short stories for children's magazines. And I might add, I was getting a reputation as a damn good writer in that particular genre.

One story I had written introduced the character Kelly Cockroach. I was asked by the editor for more Kelly stories. Thus a legend is born.

By the time Marc's transfer to Los Angeles became official, we were pretty much prepared for it. It seemed inevitable that sooner or later Marc's career in the television/film industry would necessitate a move out west.

Though my editor hated to see me go, I assured her that my move to southern California would in no way effect the future of Kelly Cockroach. And it hadn't. Except perhaps to give Kelly a more relaxed, laid-back way of approaching life.

And so here we were, two New Yorkers adjusting to Los Angeles living. It took some getting used to.

I called Bullock's Bloomingdale's, referred to freeways as highways, and had to learn to stop hailing cabs while standing in the middle of Wilshire Boulevard.

I missed New York.

Not so much the museums and the opera, as many New Yorkers profess, but the ethnicity, the change of seasons, the night life, and the sheer vibrancy of the city.

But as time passed, I slowed my pace and acclimated myself as best I could. The transition was of course made easier by Marc's acceptance, and thereby my own, into the social web at the network.

As for our relationship with one another, the kindest thing

to be said is that it had reached an impasse. It was, as Marc put it, comfortable. Too comfortable for either one of us to think about disrupting.

For Marc, I was the perfect executive's mate. I looked good, I knew how to dress and how to entertain. And aside from that, I even had my own work to keep me occupied. The little lady wrote books. Children's books no less, which was nice and, well, sweet—but not to be taken very seriously and therefore not very threatening.

But in the past year, Marc and I had been having what is euphemistically called "difficulties."

I thought he was becoming a regular Sammy Glick, moving up too far too fast; he felt I just wasn't keeping pace. I told him that I thought his "friends" were phonies and users; his response was that one learned to weed out the phonies and use the users.

Something had definitely happened. Either Marc had changed or I had. Maybe we both had or hadn't. In any case, there were other problems, far too many to pinpoint and enumerate. The bottom line was that our relationship had become static and I was stagnating within it.

And yet I still wanted to marry this man. Maybe it was because I had made such an investment of time into our affiliation. Or that I just wanted to get married. Or that I was afraid of being left alone to start again with someone new. Possibly I felt all three.

But it could also have been only my desire to share his name that made me want to marry Marc.

Beaumont is a deceptive name. Marc's paternal grandfather arrived from Pinsk or Minsk or wherever in Russia he was from with the name of Shoenberg. It was Marc's uncle Louie who had had the bright idea of Americanizing it.

Schoen, having been derived from German, is Yiddish for pretty; *berg*, likewise, means mountain. "Beautiful mountain." A lovely thought, which might be even lovelier still in a more melodic language. Some deftly applied French, therefore, permitted the Schoenbergs to carry on the line as Beaumonts or, in some cases, Belmonts. Through further French translations, Greenbergs emerged as Vermonts, Rosenbergs as Rosemonts and Goldbergs as Ormonts. More direct Yiddish to English translations transformed Weisses into Whites, Schwartzes into Blacks and Schlessels into Keys. A simple process really if one knew the nuances.

Obviously Marc's uncle Louie had.

My own relatives hadn't had such foresight. Though in fairness to them, there wasn't much one could do with our name even if one wanted to. A *stein* is a glass. But a *finkel* is a finkel is a finkel. Finkelglass? Not much of an improvement, I'm afraid. Of course, I myself could have changed my name legally, but was reluctant to do so. Family pride and all.

No, the only way I intended to change Finkelstein was by marrying out of it.

Susan Beaumont. Lovely. But was it a good enough reason to marry Marc?

I pondered this question carefully that evening as I looked at him propped up in bed, watching TV while he enjoyed his Mallomars and milk.

✄ 4 ✄

Here today and gone tomorrow.

Anonymous

"Michael's dead."

I'd asked Stephanie to repeat what she had said, since at 9:30 A.M. on a Saturday morning I am far from being my sharpest. Especially after just being awakened.

"That's what I thought you said."

I pulled the long cord of the phone across Marc's body to my side of the bed. We had a phone in just about every room of the house, one of Marc's "idiot-syncrasies." The one into which I now spoke was a French Provincial model.

"Michael who?," I spoke softly so as not to wake him.

"Cole."

"That's impossible," I said stupidly. "He just did my hair yesterday."

"Susan, I'm telling you it's true. Michael Cole slipped in his shower last night and split his skull wide open."

"Oh, how awful!" My hand automatically went to my head where, less than twenty-four hours before, Michael's hand had been. Michael, whose own head was now split in two.

"Stephanie, it's not even ten o'clock in the morning. How in the world did you find all this out?"

"Barbara Keiser had an eight-thirty with him this morning. Jean Paul called her to cancel. The manager found his body."

"Oh."

I marveled at my friend's ability to collect any scraps of

24

news or gossip in this town way before anyone else. So effective was her antenna that frequently she heard, absorbed, filtered, and channeled tidbits of information even before it reached Ms. Rona.

"To tell you the truth, I can't see how it happened," she said.

"What do you mean?" I asked, suddenly aroused by morbid curiosity.

"Just that Michael had a railing on the wall and those rubber pasty things on the floor of his bath. I remember teasing him because they were the shape of snakes, and I thought that was very phallic."

"Stephanie!"

"Well, I did! Look, I just meant that with all those safeguards, I can't imagine how he managed to slip, that's all. Unless, of course, a bar of soap just got the better of him."

A vague and uncomfortable feeling came over me. Suddenly I recalled the conversation I'd overheard the day before, along with Michael's flippant remark about finding his mutilated body floating face down in the ocean.

Now here it was the next day and Michael had died, and an ugly death at that. Was it merely a weird coincidence?

"Listen," Stephanie interrupted my thoughts, "are we still on for brunch at Nate and Al's?"

"Would you mind awfully if we made it another time, Stephanie? I'm not really up to it this morning."

"Sure thing, kiddo. I'll talk to you soon. Go back to sleep."

"Thanks. I'll try."

"You know, I'm thinking of trying out this new hairdresser I've heard about over on Beverly Drive. Supposed to give good shampoos and great head . . . massages."

"Good-bye, Stephanie."

"Good-bye, Susan."

As quietly as I could, I placed the receiver back in its cradle, which sat on Marc's night table.

The weekend passed uneventfully. I took care of the chores I usually leave to Saturday mornings. Shoemaker. Pharmacy. Cleaners.

Marc and I played tennis with friends of his—some honcho at the network Marc was trying to get in good with, and the honcho's wife, a woman at least twenty-five years his junior. As usual Marc told me later that I had played a pitiful game. This time he was right. I was worse than usual.

Somehow I couldn't get my mind off Michael Cole.

Call it my writer's vivid imagination, but I just couldn't get it out of my mind that Michael's death was no accident.

But what should I do about it? What *could* I do about it? I had nothing to go on other than a conversation I'd overheard and my own intuition.

Who could I go to with such vague speculation? I felt Marc out by asking him if he could think of any way Michael's death might have been something other than an accident; he told me to stop trying to play Nancy Drew.

That left Marc out as a confidant.

Who else was there? I couldn't go to the police with something as flimsy as "woman's intuition." They'd laugh me right out of the station.

It was then that I thought of Bucky Johnson. Not even his name had crossed my mind in ages.

Bucky, a nickname that came about due to his pronounced overbite, was actually Roger S. Johnson III. He and I went back to our journalism days together at Syracuse. Though he came from quite an affluent, "old money" Bostonian family, he was unaffected and was much liked and admired by his fellow classmates. Bucky, I'd always imagined, had kind of a crush on me, but knowing that I didn't feel the same, he was content to remain just a good friend.

And that he was. Being an excellent student and having a natural flair for journalism, he was always coming to my assistance on various projects I was involved with.

Upon graduation, I'd heard that Bucky had had a job offer out west, and despite his family's objections—with his talent and family connections, he would have had no difficulty securing a position on any of a number of Boston circulations—flew out here and settled in Los Angeles.

As is often the case, we lost touch after one or two letters, but there always remained a soft spot in my heart for Bucky, a sensitive and truly decent human being.

It was only by accident that I ran into him in a department store a week after I had moved to LA. He took me out to lunch, and we filled each other in on what had and hadn't come to pass in our lives. Bucky told me he was an editor on the *Herald*, a fact that didn't surprise me, and that he had come out of the closet, one that did. He also told me that he was very happy with his life, and that pleased me greatly.

Since that time I had only seen Bucky occasionally. Marc hadn't ever really taken to Bucky before, and Bucky's being gay clinched his dislike. Marc is the sort of man who becomes very defensive around homosexuals. He feels threatened. I saw no point in exposing Bucky to Marc's thinly disguised hostility. Bucky sensed as much and understood. I dropped in on him whenever I happened to be in downtown Los Ángeles, which wasn't often, so I hadn't seen or spoken with him in some time.

But now I thought of Bucky and was sure he would at least hear me out. As a journalist, he was prepared to accept anything. And he certainly would be an unofficial channel.

I looked through my address book and found Bucky's home number. He lived in the Hollywood Hills with a roommate named Gary, who was also his lover. Gary picked up and called Bucky to the phone.

"Hello?" It was nice to hear his voice again after so long a time.

"Buck? It's me. Susan."

"Susan! Well, as I live and breathe. So it is. How've you been?"

"Fine. A little bored lately, but fine otherwise."

"Sorry to hear you've been bored and how *is* Marc these days?"

A nice, subtle segue.

"All right. Getting richer."

"And that bug of yours?"

"Kelly's fine too. Look, Bucky, I was wondering if you're free for lunch tomorrow. There's something I'd like to discuss with you."

"Well, I'll have to check my calender, but I'm fairly sure it's clear, and I'd love to see you. You sound so serious; is anything wrong?"

"No. Not really. Well, I'm not sure."

"You're going to have to clarify all three of those answers when I see you tomorrow."

"I will. But I'm warning you now. You may think I'm crazy."

"I doubt it. Beautiful, yes. But crazy, never. Is twelve o'clock too early for you?"

"Twelve o'clock would be perfect."

"Great. Unless you hear from me, why don't we plan to meet at Joy Fung. It's a little Szechuan place off Hill. Do you know the one I mean?"

"I think I've passed it on my way to your office."

"All right then, noon it is."

"Terrific. And Bucky? Thanks."

"Thank you."

I hung up feeling good. Not only was I going to get to see an old, dear friend, I was beginning to feel motivated, spurred by new energy. Ironically it took someone else's death to make me feel alive once again.

Marc asked me who was on the phone. The phone to which he referred was the one in our kitchen, an old-fashioned Kellogg replica.

"That fag?" Marc responded when I told him I'd been speaking with Bucky.

At that moment I had a terrific urge to take the Mallomar he was holding and shove it in his smug face.

✄ 5 ✄

To fish in troubled waters.

Matthew Henry

I entered Joy Fung and allowed my eyes to adjust to the
darkness. As they did, I noted that the restaurant's shabby
exterior complemented the equally shabby decor inside.

Tacky Chinese lanterns hung low over tables. Set upon
the tables were vases of plastic flowers, each color coor-
dinated to match the crepe paper tablecloths upon which
they'd been placed.

I loved it.

Its seediness reminded me of all the neighborhood Chinese
restaurants I'd frequented growing up in Brooklyn.

Bucky waved to me from a corner booth in the back of
the restaurant. In the darkness I could barely make out the
silhouette of a man's figure across from him, seated with
his back half-turned toward me. I walked to the table somewhat dismayed; I had assumed this was to be a private
luncheon.

"Sue," said Bucky, rising, "I'd like you to meet my good
friend, Nick Comici. Nick, another dear friend, Sue Finkelstein."

Even in the dimness the distinct features of this man's
face were apparent. His black, curly hair grayed at the
temples. And his eyes were catlike and green. But oddly
enough, what I found most appealing was a mole on his
right cheek and the slightly off-center bump on his nose,
which I thought gave his face character.

All in all I'd have to say that my first impression of Nick

Comici was that he was extremely handsome, in an offbeat sort of way.

So mesmerized was I that apparently moments passed in silence before either of us said a word.

"Well, whaddya say we stop all this small talk, Sue?" Nick finally said in his gravelly voice.

Another smart-ass New Yorker I didn't need.

"Please, have a seat. I didn't know Bucky had any really classy friends."

He rose, allowed me to slide in between himself and Bucky, and then looked at me and smiled. I returned the smile, and it was at that moment that I became conscious of my appearance. My mascara felt caky; my skin, Crisco-coated. I was suddenly very thankful for Joy Fung's poor lighting.

I hadn't given much thought to my dress that morning either. Black skirt. Green silk shirt.

Too high-necked perhaps? What was that he said about my being classy? Maybe he'd meant to say prissy. But he did say classy. Was I overdressed? Well, I suppose next to his Hawaiian print shirt, patched faded jeans, and Yankee baseball cap, Bozo the Clown would have appeared classy.

Still, he had something. He definitely had something, no doubt about that. He couldn't be gay. Or could he? My thoughts raced on and on.

What the hell was he doing there? That's what I wanted to know.

Bucky cleared that up soon enough.

"I hope you don't mind my inviting Nick to join us for lunch. He kind of dropped in on me unexpectedly about an hour ago."

Bucky went on to say that he and Nick, whom I learned was a contributing writer for *New York* magazine, had met several years ago during a nationwide journalism seminar and had since established an enduring friendship.

I seemed to recall Nick's name in connection with some excellent investigative articles on New York's slumlords as well as an exposé of kickbacks within the city's elementary school system. So his thorough job of reporting had finally brought him to national attention.

Nick was presently out on the Coast for what he professed to be a well-deserved vacation.

He smiled at me again with an expression of false humility.

"I hope I'm not intruding," he volunteered. "I promise to sit back and quietly merge into the wall."

"Seriously, Sue," said Bucky, "if you really need to speak with me privately, we can tell Nicky here to take a hike. But subtle like, so as not to offend him."

I laughed and told Bucky that I didn't think it necessary for Nick to leave on my account. And truthfully, I didn't. Especially since I was beginning to enjoy being the focal point of attention.

The waiter came and took our orders, all of which were chosen in Chinese, no less by Bucky, who prides himself on being a gourmet of sorts and a *mavin* of various cultures and cuisines. Our waiter thanked him and left.

Bucky hastened to assure us that the decor was very misleading and that Joy Fung boasted some of the finest dishes in town.

"I don't know quite how to begin," I began tritely when asked by Bucky what was on my mind. "It's this friend of mine. Well, maybe friend is too strong a word. I should say acquaintance. Although maybe friend—"

"Someone you know and like?" suggested Bucky helpfully.

"Yes. At least, I knew him before he died. And that's what's so fishy."

"His death?" asked Bucky.

"Exactly. You see, I wouldn't swear to it, but I have this terrible feeling that Michael was killed."

"Michael?" Nick seemed to awaken to the name. "Uh, this guy Michael someone you'd, uh, been involved with?"

Curious his asking that.

"No, that would be Marc. And he's been dead for some time now," answered Bucky, pointing to his head.

"Bucky!" I tried to sound as reproachful as I could.

"Sorry. All right. You say your friend Michael was killed. I assume you don't mean killed like in a car crash, but that there might be a question of foul play surrounding his death. Am I correct?"

"Right. But it may not be anything more than a hunch on my part," I confessed.

"Well, hunches usually have some basis. Suppose you tell us where you're coming from," Bucky said.

I related my story. First, I gave them a kind of thumbnail sketch of Michael Cole. I repeated what I'd overheard at Jean Paul's, including Michael's last remark to me. Finally I told them about Stephanie's phone call the following morning and about the safeguards in Michael's tub.

"How'd you say you knew what kind of a bathtub this guy had?" inquired Nick innocently.

"I told you, I . . . Stephanie's seen it."

"I see," he continued smoothly. "So your information is all hearsay, is that it?"

"You could say that," I snapped back.

His coolness irritated me.

"I'm sorry."

"I'm not."

"I meant that I'm sorry to have offended you."

Bucky whistled, so loudly in fact that half the restaurant's diners turned around.

"Okay, kiddies. Enough! Truce. Suppose we get back to

the main point," he said. "When was it you said your hairdresser died, Sue?"

"Saturday morning or late Friday night. I'm not sure which. But his body was discovered on Saturday morning."

Bucky reached into his attaché case, explaining, "Sometimes Saturday deaths don't make the obits until Monday."

He opened the morning edition to the obituary column and scanned it until he found what he was looking for.

He read aloud. "'Cole, Michael J. Age twenty-eight. Died unexpectedly late Friday evening. He is survived by his sister, Alison, who asks that in lieu of flowers donations be made to Save the Whales. Ecumenical services are to be held Wednesday morning at eight at the H. R. Funeral Home in West Los Angeles.'"

"Save the Whales," repeated Nick. "Spare me."

"'Services to be held on Wednesday,'" Bucky reread these last few words.

This was all beginning to seem anticlimatic. I played with my food, feeling rather foolish.

"Maybe I should apologize for wasting your time," I said.

"First off," said Bucky, "you never waste my time. If you weren't here, I'd have had to entertain Nicky alone."

"A dismal prospect," remarked Nick.

"Besides," Bucky continued, "what makes you certain your instincts are so off base? I mean, you didn't actually expect the obituary to read 'Michael Cole died Friday night of a bashed-in skull, murder speculated. Would all suspects please step forward?' C'mon Sue, if there's anything behind your suspicions, you're going to have to dig for it."

"You mean investigate on my own?" I asked.

"That depends on what you mean by investigate. Plunging in head first and pointing fingers wouldn't be wise, and it wouldn't get you anywhere . . . except maybe to the morgue if you really are onto something."

"What do you suggest?"

"Well, if you'd like, I can poke around, tap some sources, see what I can pick up around the paper. And then maybe we'll know where to start."

Nick had been quiet during my discussion with Bucky. He didn't wait for an answer now.

"I'm going to have a lot of time on my hands these next few weeks. I mean, there's only so much sand and surf a New Yorker can take." He turned to me. "Maybe we can make a deal. If you're willing to do some sight-seeing with me, I'll offer you the expertise of an investigative reporter. Deal?" he asked, extending his hand.

I didn't even take a moment to think about Nick's offer before accepting.

"Deal," I said and shook on it.

"Great," said Bucky, "I'm always happy to have one friend help out another." He winked. "Less work for me."

And raising his teacup, Bucky declared that a toast be made "to friendship."

"To success," I added, raising mine.

Nick joined us in raising his cup and loudly suggested that we "lift our cups to Save the Whales."

Our waiter had just come by with a dessert tray of nutballs, small tea cakes, and fortune cookies. Hearing Nick's words, he dropped the dessert tray on the table and said, "Yessiree, we save 'em. I come back with doggie bag right away."

That just about completed lunch.

✂ 6 ✂

The less we know, the more we suspect.

H. W. Shaw

Bucky had excused himself after lunch to get back to work, and I offered to drive his friend back to his hotel since he hadn't a car. On the way, Nick reminded me of my promise to see the sights with him.

So far I'd shown him the Marina, parts of Venice and Santa Monica. The Santa Monica pier was the last stop on today's sight-seeing agenda. It was a glorious day. The air was unusually clear for June, and the mountains were the perfect backdrop to the inviting waters of the Pacific.

Showing someone the sights of Los Angeles made me feel more appreciative of the city and more like a native. It was a good feeling.

By this time I knew more about Nick Comici than he did of me. For example, I knew that he was born and bred in Manhattan, and that he was thirty-seven. And I knew that he'd graduated from Columbia University's School of Journalism. I found this impressive, considering the school's excellent reputation, but also somewhat surprising, since his streetwise manner belied his education.

I also learned that he was divorced nearly four years, had no children, and owned a hamster named Moriarity.

So unnerving were Nick's looks to me that I found myself staring at him as he spoke.

"What's the matter?" he asked once. "My face dirty or something?"

36

"Uh, no," I replied, embarrassed. "Fact is you have a rather uncommon face . . . interesting."

"Interesting?"

"Yeah. Kind of like your name . . ." Quick save, Susan! "Say, what kind of name is Comici anyway? I don't think I've ever heard it before," I said.

"Probably not. It's pretty unique. *Comici* means "comic" in Italian, you see."

"Oh, really? Were your ancestors comics, do you suppose?"

"In a manner of speaking. Take my uncle Salvatore Comici. He cracked me up when I was a kid. I remember he used to place a real plum into my cousin Irene's bowl of waxed fruit, you know? Then when company came, he'd pop it into his mouth and wait. And it wouldn't be long before someone bit into a waxed apple. Funny, huh?"

"Hilarious."

"He thought so. Continued pulling the same stunt 'til the day he died at the age of eighty-two."

"How'd he die?"

"One day someone stuck a waxed plum into the bowl. Uncle Salvatore popped it into his mouth and choked to death . . . but he died laughing. See, he enjoyed a good joke, even if it was on him."

I couldn't stop giggling. "So comedy runs in your blood, huh?" I asked finally.

"Nope. Comedy's my means of survival. It's music that runs in my blood," he said, and with that he produced a harmonica and began to play.

I soon discovered that Nick carried a harmonica with him at all times and played it whenever he was given to long stretches of thought.

I volunteered very little about myself that afternoon. I told him something of my writing background, but about my relationship with Marc I said nothing, and wisely he hadn't asked.

We were approaching the carousel when Nick had a sudden idea.

"Hey, listen, this beauty parlor or hair salon, whatever you call those places now, where'd you say it was?"

"I didn't. But it's in Beverly Hills, on Rodeo."

"They keep some kind of record of who comes in to see which stylist, don't they?"

"Sure. Each operator keeps his or her own appointment book aside from the one at the front desk," I explained. "Why?"

"From the phone conversation you described, we'll assume your friend was expecting this person he'd just had a falling out with to come to the shop later that day."

"So you think that one of Michael's clients could have had something to do with his death?"

"Let me put it this way, Sue. It wouldn't hurt to see who had appointments with him that day."

"Well, what do you propose we do? Just walk in and ask Jean Paul for Michael's appointment book? I mean, wouldn't that arouse suspicion?"

"I'm sure it would. So between us I think we can come up with a more subtle approach. C'mon."

"Hey, slow down, Nicky."

Not only did he slow down, but he stopped altogether.

"Do me a favor? Call me Nick. I hate Nicky. Always have. Nicky's a hangover from my youth. Where I grew up, there weren't any Nicks, Pauls, or Johns. There were only Nickies, Paulies, and Johnnies. Now I ask you, do I look like a Nicky to you?"

I looked over his six feet two inches frame. Truthfully he was no more a Nicky than I was a Su-Su.

I held out my hand to him.

"Nick Comici? How do you do? Susan Finkelstein here."

He grinned and held my hand.

"Nice to know you, Susan."

The usual hubbub and activity in Jean Paul's was testament to the cliché that life indeed does go on. As a matter of fact, the place was hopping, brimming with talk of Michael Cole's death. I had guessed that Michael's passing would be a great blow to the Beverly Hills community. Overhead snatches of conversation that day convinced me I was right.

"Diane darling, did you hear?"

"I love your Vuitton, dear, yes, I did, isn't it awful?"

"Thinking of Michael's beautiful body lying naked in a pool of blood gives me the chills."

"Thinking of Michael's beautiful body lying naked anywhere gives me the chills."

And so the talk went. To have been a bed partner of Michael Cole at one time seemed to be a mark of great status, although the reason why eludes me. It didn't strike me as a particular distinction, since Michael's appetite for sex was apparently insatiable. As the saying goes, he'd fuck mud.

While I looked around the salon, Nick stood talking with the receptionist at the desk. Though I couldn't make out what he was saying, he appeared to be gesticulating in my direction. I smiled. The receptionist, a young girl with perfectly manicured juliette nails, stared back at me blankly. Finally I heard Nick thank her.

"What was that all about?" I asked him when he approached me.

"I explained that you think you might have left your earrings over at Cole's station on Friday and that you'd like to see if you could find them."

"Where's Jean Paul?"

"I was coming to that. He went out for cigarettes, but he's due back soon so here's what you're going to do."

Nick explained how I was to casually but quickly make my way over to Michael's station and pretend to be looking for earrings. In actuality, Nick wanted me to flip Michael's appointment book to Friday and try to jot down or memorize as best I could the appointments Michael had after mine.

Nick left to wait for me in the car. For a quick getaway, I wondered?

I did as he instructed, feeling inane and very nervous all the while. Nothing had been touched yet. It was a strange sensation, as though Michael were still alive.

Pictures of nudes and seminudes were taped, as always, to his mirror beside postcards from various parts of the world. On his counter were an unopened bottle of Dom Pérignon, ribbon still attached, a heart-shaped porcelain pill box, various combs, scissors, brushes, and his appointment book.

I had to remind myself why I was there; I flipped the book to Friday the twenty-sixth and in my own style of shorthand jotted down as much information as I could onto the back of a gas bill I'd forgotten to mail. When I finished, I threw both the envelope and pen into my purse and turned to leave.

"'ave you found your earrings, my dear?" Jean Paul asked in saccharin tones while dragging on a thin, black Gauloises.

Obviously he had approached Michael's station as quietly as a Parisian mouse. But my back was toward him, so how much would he have seen?

The mirror.

I took a deep breath and tried to convince myself that it was guilt that was causing me to feel so much like a criminal. After all, I could have been jotting down any of a number of things.

"Jean Paul. You startled me. No, no I haven't."

"I'm so sorry. Were zey very valuable?"

"Zey . . . I mean, they were of sentimental value. Not to worry, though." Then in a different tone I added, "I . . . I'm so sorry . . . about Michael I mean."

Jean Paul looked at me closely.

"Yes, eet ees always a great tragedy when one so young dies so suddenly."

Maybe it was his somewhat ominous tone. Or the intensity of his stare. Maybe it was my own paranoia. I don't know. All I do know is that beads of sweat were beginning to merge and to trickle down my silk shirt, and I suddenly wanted very much to make a speedy exit.

I bid a quick farewell to Jean Paul and damn near flew out the door of the salon. Almost immediately I heard strains of "The Daring Young Man on the Flying Trapeze" wheezing out of a harmonica. The incongruity of it, combined with my relief at being out in the fresh air, made me feel almost euphoric.

Nick stood in casual repose, leaning against the window of a boutique next door and looking as collected as Bing Crosby in *Going My Way*. My expression must have given me away.

"I assume that was Jean Paul who walked in. Get anything?"

"A cold stare. And maybe a threat, I'm not sure. Would you mind if we talked in the car?" I asked.

"Did he shake you up that badly?"

"No . . . yes. . . . Can we just talk about it in the car?"

"Want me to drive?" he offered.

"Please. If you don't mind."

I threw the keys across the top of the car and got in on the passenger's side.

We didn't speak for a few moments. I didn't even comment on Nick's driving, which was the sort that gives New Yorkers their reputation. Finally Nick broke the silence.

"I'm going to have to rent a car while I'm out here, I guess."

"Mmmm."

"Maybe a Masarati."

"Mmmm."

"Or a Rolls or a Bentley."

"That's nice."

"Susan."

"I'm sorry, I was thinking of the way Jean Paul looked when he spoke to me."

"Threatening?"

"That's just it. I don't know if there really was something to it or if I'm just letting my imagination run wild. I mean, at this point someone could say 'boo' to me and I'd jump a mile."

"Well, let's just put Jean Paul in our 'maybe' category of suspects and go on to the others. By the way, would you mind telling me where we're headed? It's my nature to be inquisitive. Particularly when I'm in the driver's seat."

"We'll go back to my house, if that's all right with you. We can talk there."

"I've heard that one before," he said, arching his eyebrows Groucho-style.

"Stop that. I'm dead serious."

"Must you use such a morbid adjective? This murder business is killing me as it is."

"Nick, please."

"Okay, but I think we should take our minds off Michael Cole until we reach your home. You know, concentrate on something else for a while."

"Like what, for instance?"

"Like what? Well, like let's see how many personalized license plates we can spot on the road."

"Nick, I hate to be the one to break this to you, but that's all Los Angeles is. Just one big personalized license plate. Very chummy."

He paid no attention to me.

"Now there's a cute one. 'I-M-E-Z-R-U.'"

"Too obvious."

"All right, how about the red Beetle? 'BUG ME.'"

"Coy."

"Check out the guy with the rhinestone-studded cowboy hat."

"In the purple Caddy?"

"You got it. 'NO WIFE.'"

"No wonder."

I was getting back into the swing of things when suddenly we were cut off by a beat-up old convertible. A Buick or a Chevy. Nick had to swerve sharply into the right lane to avoid a collision. Fortunately the traffic was light.

"Son of a bitch!" Nick shouted. "Did you see that?"

"Could I miss it?" I answered breathlessly.

As the car sped away, I made note of its Save the Whales bumper sticker.

"She saves whales too," I added feebly.

"I don't give a shit if she saves Green Stamps. She almost demolished my left fender."

"My left fender," I reminded him.

"Right . . . whew! That was a close one. Where were we? Oh, yeah, the license game."

"I'll pass."

Somehow the impact of a near accident was enough to remind me of my own mortality.

Nick made no further comment. He simply took out his harmonica and, as best he could with one hand, proceeded to play. For the remainder of the ride I sat quietly meditating as I listened to his rather mournful delivery of "The Daring Young Man on the Flying Trapeze."

✂ 7 ✂

Good manners is the art of making those people
easy with whom we converse. Whoever makes the
fewest persons uneasy is the best bred in the
company.

Jonathan Swift

A man's house is his castle. And I'm the king of this castle.
Ralph Kramden to his, wife, Alice
The Honeymooners

"Some layout!" was Nick's comment on my living quarters.

"I like it," I admitted.

"What's not to like? This place is incredible. It must be worth a mint these days."

"Five hundred seventy five thousand. Marc had it appraised a few months ago."

He whistled.

"Your friend must be doing well," he acknowledged. "You both must be."

"Yes. I suppose we are."

"Lucky you."

"Lucky me."

Nick walked over to our piano.

"Baby grand...nice," he remarked, adroitly changing the subject. "Who plays, you or Marc?"

"Neither of us does," I confessed. "Marc just always wanted a baby grand. So as soon as we could afford one, we bought it."

He played a short piece.

"That's beautiful, what is it?"

"Mozart's *Jupiter* in C Major. You know, Mozart was supposed to have been buried in a pauper's grave."

"Supposed to have been?"

"Yeah, his coffin was being carried there when a thunderstorm came up and his pall bearers ran for cover. Now these pall bearers, they return, right? But the coffin's gone! Thereby causing the mortal remains of one of the world's most gifted geniuses to be lost forever. So, Susan, do me a favor. If you happen to be around for my funeral, stay close to the coffin, will you?"

I giggled.

"I'm serious. Even if it rains. Bring an umbrella or something."

He closed the piano and continued to look around.

"Nice, very nice," he said with approval.

He was greatly impressed, and I was beginning to be embarrassed, feeling the color coming to my face.

"You're blushing. Do compliments embarrass you?"

"Sometimes," I admitted.

"You know, human beings are the only animals that can blush. And as Mark Twain pointed out, we seem to be the only animals that need to."

"No kidding. Hey, listen, what do you say we go into the kitchen. That way I can prepare dinner while we talk."

"Great. What's for dinner?"

"Are you staying?"

"I don't know. Am I?"

"If you'd like."

"I'd like. But only if you allow me to do the cooking."

"Are you any good?"

He grinned.

"At cooking I mean."

"Oh. That too. How does Fettuccini Comici sound to you?"

"Wonderful. Anything that I don't have to cook I love to eat."

"I . . ." he began.

"Don't say it."

"I was only going to promise you the best dinner ever."

"Oh. By the way, I should warn you. Marc's preferred cuisine is strictly meat and potatoes so don't be surprised if his reaction to your efforts is less than enthusiastic."

"He'll be a challenge. C'mon, lead the way."

Nick soon made himself entirely at home in my kitchen. And while I assisted him by chopping, peeling, and grating, we went over the list of names I'd obtained from Michael's appointment book.

"What's this first name here?" he asked, peering at my chicken scratches. "Ailing Baboon?"

"Let me see that." I took the envelope from him. "That's Ellen Bethune!"

"Oh!" Nick exclaimed. "Maybe you should read the rest."

"All right. Ellen Bethune, eleven-fifteen A.M. Then there's a cancellation at noon. Lunch at twelve-thirty. Mrs. Estelle Fagelman at two and M. S. Rosenbloom at three. Seems that was the last appointment."

"Let me see?"

I handed him the envelope.

"What's this name at the bottom? Alice?"

"Oh, Alison. Michael's sister. His appointment book indicated he'd be seeing her later. I wasn't certain that could be considered a bona fide appointment, but I thought I'd scribble it down anyway."

"And scribble you did. Is that it?"

"Yep. Jean Paul startled me, but not before I got down all the names."

"Good. Do you know anything about any of these people by any chance?"

"There was an attractive woman who came in for her

appointment when I was leaving. Mid-thirties. Salt-and-pepper hair."

"Ellen Bethune or Estelle Fagelman, you think?"

"Ellen Bethune. I've never met her, but Stephanie knows her, and from her description, I'd say that was her. As I said, I don't know her, or the others for that matter. For some reason, though, the name M. S. Rosenbloom strikes a familiar chord."

"Think your friend Stephanie might be helpful?" Nick asked.

"Could be. She knows a lot of people in this town."

"Dates?"

"Some. Some just acquaintances."

"No. Do you have any dates? I'm making a torte that calls for dates and nuts."

"Oh, sure. I think I've got some dates in the cabinet above the sink. Nuts too."

"Thanks," he said as he reached for them.

He'd made terrific progress in the kitchen all the while we'd been speaking, and if the aroma emanating from the oven was any indication of what to expect, dinner was truly going to be a treat.

"Dinner should be ready in an hour," he announced, as if reading my thoughts. He folded his towel on the bar along the counter and seated himself beside me. "What time's Marc due home?"

"In about forty minutes or so."

"You don't think he'll mind having me as a dinner guest?"

"No. Not at all. Why should he?" But even as I asked the question, I had my doubts.

"Good. I hope he likes my fettucine and my torte."

I didn't want to be the one to tell Nick that Marc would hardly know the difference between a torte and a tortilla.

"What about the names?" I said in an effort to get things back to more comfortable ground.

Nick had taken out his harmonica and begun to play. He stopped to answer me.

"Call Stephanie later. Find out if she knows anything about any of the names on our list." He then continued playing.

"Right. And then what? I mean, where do we go from there? We can't just call these people and ask if they had anything to do with Michael's death?"

Nick shrugged.

"Gotta find a common denominator. You know. Some way to reach them all."

"Michael Cole," I said. "That's what they all had in common, but he's dead. How else can we get to them?"

"You'll think of something. You're a very clever girl, Susan."

"I can't think of anything with you playing that thing. If you must, do you think you could attempt something other than "The Daring Young Man on the Flying Trapeze?"

"Why, of course," he said with sudden enthusiasm. "You should have said so. Something more upbeat, maybe?"

I found Nick's new tune even more distracting. The song was familiar. I'd heard it recently, but I just couldn't place it.

And then it hit me.

"I know that tune!" I shouted.

"Ah, but can you name it in three notes?" Nick asked.

"No, really. I just thought of a way of getting myself right into anyone's home," I said, motioning wildly at the list of names. "At least it's worth a shot."

"I'm listening."

So Nick listened. And continued playing "Happy Days Are Here Again" as I talked to him about the joys of Tupperware.

* * *

Stephanie lives on the eighteenth floor of a high-rise condominium in Century City with her cat, Halvah. On my first visit to her apartment, I asked her whether the threat of an earthquake didn't terrify her as it did me.

"Natural disaster. Nothing to be done about it," she said casually.

I dropped the subject.

As I waited for Stephanie to finish applying her makeup, a process that takes nearly an hour, I thought back to the night before.

Marc's initial reaction to Nick was tempered by the fact that Nick was wearing an apron, had cooked a magnificent dinner, and more to the point, was a friend of Bucky Johnson's. Marc's great insight into people led him to the natural conclusion that Nick was gay.

Nick's opinion of Marc was probably fixed at the point that Marc smothered an avalanche of ketchup on Nick's delicately seasoned fettucine.

The evening was less than auspicious. In fact the only flicker of excitement was Marc's informing me that we'd been invited to a rather splashy affair. One of Hollywood's "A" parties according to Marc, who preceded to rattle off an impressive guest list, which included, to the pleasure of both Nick and myself, Meyer S. Rosenbloom.

It was after Nick had left and Marc had turned in for the night that I phoned Stephanie. Not wanting to take her into my confidence just yet, I merely told her that I'd given serious consideration to her suggestion that I try selling Tupperware and thought I might like to give it a whirl. After all even if I did get to meet Rosenbloom through legitimate means, there were still the others to consider. Stephanie promised to set up a lunch with Mitzi for the next day.

At 11:40 A.M. Stephanie still wasn't ready. We were meeting Mitzi at noon at a nearby cafeteria, so actually we had plenty of time.

It was Mitzi's idea to meet at Clifton's, one of LA's few well-known cafeterias. Clifton's, located in the heart of the Century City shopping mall, is a colorful place, patronized by a motley assortment of people. These included the elderly, many transplanted easterners, and an over flow of Century City business people. The food was basic, and the atmosphere unpretentious, much like Mitzi herself, I'd been told. Stephanie also informed me of Mitzi's insatiable need to be surrounded by people—all sorts of people—twenty-four hours a day. So while Clifton's wouldn't necessarily have been everyone's number-one choice for a restaurant with ambience, I could certainly see why Mitzi would love it.

Clifton's was Horn and Hardarts, west.

My suggestion that we walk the four blocks was nixed by Stephanie, who wheels everywhere regardless of proximity.

Stephanie would truly feel the pea beneath her mattress.

In the elevator I carefully broached the subject of Ellen Bethune.

"I think I saw your friend Ellen at the hairdresser's last week."

"Kurtzman or Bethune?"

"Bethune. She's nice-looking."

"Mmmm, she's originally from Alabama or somewhere around those there parts," Stephanie drawled. "Now she's a typical Encino suburbanite."

The door opened on ten, and an aged woman slowly entered the elevator.

"Then she's a nice looking typical Encino suburbanite," I countered.

"She should be," said Stephanie. "She's paid enough for it. Plastic nose. Rubber boobs. That woman must float in her hot tub."

The old lady chuckled.

"Well, if she's got the money . . ."

"She does. Her husband's Frank Bethune."

"Of Bethune Realty?"

"The one and only."

"Why, he owns half of the Westside."

"Sure does. And I think he's running for something or other this fall, too. Oh, Frank's a powerful guy all right. Though you couldn't tell from looking at him."

"Why's that?"

"I don't know. I guess you'd say he's somewhat of a cross between Don Knotts and Woody Allen."

The elevator stopped again, and the old lady hobbled out, the scent of lilac leaving with her.

"Sounds attractive," I said. "Does Ellen take her business elsewhere?"

"Fool around, you mean? I'm not sure. If she did, she'd have to be very discreet about it. Frank may look like a nerd, but he's shrewd. If he found out she'd been unfaithful, it wouldn't surprise me if he ditched her. No, Ellen's a sharp Southern belle, and I think she's gotten too used to the golden eggs to risk killing the goose."

But would she kill a hairdresser? I wondered.

The elevator stopped at the garage level, and we exited in the direction of Stephanie's car.

"Think she'd be interested in buying some Tupperware?" I asked.

"I doubt it, but one never knows. After all, her food should be at least as well preserved as she is."

"I'll keep that in mind."

"Why?" Stephanie asked. "Are you looking for clients already? You haven't even met with Mitzi."

"I'm making up a roster," I lied.

"Uh-huh, sure you are. All right Susan, stop jerking me around. You're treating me like a complete moron, and that's sure to strain our beautiful friendship. Now what the fuck is with you lately?" she demanded as we got into the car.

Knowing that I couldn't keep up this pretense with Stephanie much longer and anticipating that I might need to enlist her aid at a future time, I decided to take her into my confidence.

I told her about my suspicions concerning Michael, my day spent with Nick, and my confrontation with Jean Paul. I finished by relating what had transpired at my none-too-successful dinner the night before. By the time we'd pulled into a nearby gas station, I'd confessed everything.

"That certainly explains a lot," Stephanie nodded. She turned to the attendant, and before he could ask how much gas she needed, he was off "being a dear" and looking under the hood. "I mean, your deciding to sell Tupperware for one thing and your sudden interest in Ellen Bethune for another. Do I know any of the other suspects?" Stephanie asked with glee.

"They're not suspects, Stephanie," I said, though in truth that's exactly how I had come to think of them. "But frankly I've been sort of hoping you might be familiar with at least a few of the names I copied out of Michael's book."

"Well, for God's sake, who are they? This could be fun." Stephanie winked at two other attendants, and before long windows were being washed and tires were being checked. Did I mention that we were at a self-service pump?

"It's not supposed to be fun. If it turns out there's any basis to this we're talking about murder," I said, self-righteously.

"I find fun in any situation," argued Stephanie. "Besides, I'd like to know what you've been having with that Italian Stallion of yours if it's not fun."

My friend doesn't pull punches.

"Okay, Ellen Bethune we've discussed. Any connection with Micheal?"

"None that I know of," Stephanie admitted. "She appears to be devoted to Frank. But then as I said, with Ellen discretion would have to be the name of the game."

The three attendants all appeared at the window, each toothy-grinned and apparently overjoyed at the prospect of pumping gas for Stephanie.

"I don't think I'll be needing any gas today, but thanks anyway," said Stephanie.

With that and a sweet smile, she pulled out of the station, leaving Moe, Larry, and Curly more than a little dumbfounded.

"Estelle Fagelman," I continued, amused but not surprised by Stephanie's actions.

"Doesn't ring a bell."

I was beginning to lose hope.

"If you're checking out people who might have wanted to see Michael dead," Stephanie pointed out, "what about Tracy Simms?"

"The actress? What was she to him?" I asked.

"Only his ex-wife," she replied.

"No kidding! It didn't occur to me that Michael had ever been married."

"I don't think it occurred to him very much when they were. That's why she left him."

"Tracy Simms. They must have made a handsome couple. But what motive would she have had for killing him? She certainly has enough money in her own right."

"A woman needn't have a plausible motive for doing in her ex, honey. She was married to him once. Isn't that reason enough?"

"Could be. I'll make a point of checking her out too. Where were we? Oh, yes. All right, now the next guy I'm going to be meeting very shortly, thanks to a freaky coincidence."

"Who's that?"

"Meyer S. Rosenbloom. Ever hear of him?"

"Susan, as an actress I've made it my business to know about every powerful man in this industry," Stephanie stated seriously, "and Rosenbloom is right up there at the top."

"So Marc tells me."

"Of course Marc would know, being right up there himself. Almost."

"I'll be meeting him at a party in a few weeks. Think a man like Rosenbloom is capable of murder?"

"He's an agent, he's capable of worse," Stephanie assured me as we pulled into the underground parking structure.

"To tell you the truth, I can't picture any of these people murdering Michael."

"Go on," Stephanie prompted. "Who else is on your list?"

"That's about it. Oh, I almost forgot. What do you know about Michael's sister?"

"Alison? Not much. Why?"

"Her name was in Michael's appointment book that Friday too."

"Surely you don't suspect fragile little Alison of having murdered her very own brother? Why, she's a butterfly."

"Even butterflies flutter their wings now and then," I reminded her on the escalator. "Nick says everyone has to be considered guilty until proven innocent."

"This Nick sounds like a cynic. Charming. I think I'm going to enjoy meeting him. So let's see, we have four suspects. Five, including Alison," Stephanie figured.

"Six if you count Jean Paul."

"Jean Paul?"

"Sure. Think about it. He wasn't in the shop when I was there at ten-twenty. Nothing says it had to be someone in his appointment book Michael was arguing with on the phone that morning."

"Good point. My, my, my, Susan. I'm impressed. Really.

You've been thinking this thing through very carefully, haven't you?"

"It's a diversion," I said and then regretted my own callousness.

As if to echo my feelings, Stephanie said, "Watch it there, kiddo. That sounded like something I'd have said."

"You're right," I agreed. "I'll watch it."

"C'mon then," she said as we approached the entrance to Clifton's, "let's talk Tupperware."

✂ ❮ 8 ❯ ✂

Let's talk of graves, of worms, of epitaphs.

William Shakespeare, *Richard II*

I hadn't attended many funerals in my lifetime, three to be specific. My grandfather, uncle Arthur, and Marc's cousin once removed . . . permanently so, I'm afraid.

As a matter of fact, all things being equal, I have attended more weddings and baby showers than I have funerals. I don't know that that's significant in itself, but it is somewhat of a positive statement in favor of life.

Michael's funeral resulted in a surprisingly meager turn-out. There could not have been more than a dozen people in the chapel of the funeral home that Wednesday morning, myself and Nick included. I wondered whether some of Michael's "friends" hadn't thought it strategically wiser to abstain from attending his service.

The funeral director was a congenial man whose gleeful eyes indicated that he enjoyed his work zealously. Appropriately, his name was Horatio Reeper. It was by speaking with him that we had gained admittance to what was pretty much a private affair. Nick told him that he was a New York reporter on assignment, and that he was here in Los Angeles to research how southern Californian funerals differed from those in the Big Apple.

Mr. Reeper was only too delighted to accommodate someone wanting to know more about the profession he loved so much.

"I'm just sorry you chose this particular service to observe," he apologized.

56

"Why do you say that?" asked Nick.

"Oh, these Ecumenical types have such terrible turnouts, as you can see. Give me a good Catholic Mass any day," he chuckled, elbowing Nick's ribs.

Before he would allow us to be seated, we had to promise that we would return in the future for a more upbeat service.

Nick and I were escorted to our seats by a hunchbacked usher who seemed to scowl at Nick for no reason.

"Maybe he's got the hots for you, Esmerelda," Nick suggested.

"Thanks, but no thanks. I take my men straight," I assured him.

"So I've noticed."

"Shh," I shushed him, "the service is about to begin."

Michael's closed coffin was set out before us, and despite Alison's request, it was encased in bouquets of white orchids.

I blanched in spite of myself as I watched a female minister approach the pulpit.

"We are gathered here to pay tribute," she began, "to one Michael Cole, who was so suddenly and tragically taken from us. To Michael, who lived his life to the fullest, and who in his lifetime gave service to so many . . ."

And how, lady!

"Who upon the death of his mother nearly ten years ago," she continued, "took on the spiritual responsibility of caring for his younger sister, Alison."

At the mention of her name, the minister looked up and smiled with empathy at a thin girl with auburn hair.

It was then that I first noticed Alison. She sat in the first pew, dressed in a short-sleeved, navy-blue suit that revealed her spindlelike arms. She looked so pale I thought she would collapse at any moment. And I've no doubt she would have had it not been for a supportive friend who sat beside her, patting her back and furnishing her with Kleenex.

"To Alison, her brother Michael was everything. Father. Brother. Friend. She adored him, and it is to her that our hearts go out this morning."

Nick was obviously bored to tears and occupied himself as I did, sizing up our fellow mourners.

I followed his gaze as it strayed to the woman seated four pews in front of us. I couldn't blame him for staring.

Beneath the black veiled hat, one could not mistake the impeccable beauty of Tracy Simms. Her coal-black hair was pulled back away from her face, her sultry mouth quivered slightly at the mention of her former husband, and her violet eyes filled with tears. She clutched a handkerchief fiercely. Could this have been an act? If so, her performance was brilliant. But for whose benefit was it being staged, I wondered.

"Not bad," Nick whispered.

"His ex," I informed him.

"Why was he fooling with hamburger when he had steak like that around?"

Nick has an eloquent way with words.

"He cared so much about so many things," the minister droned on.

Yes, Michael cared. But mostly about himself, from what I could surmise.

The pew I sat in shook slightly as someone sat down nearby. I let my eyes wander. To Tracy . . . to Alison . . . and out the window where I noticed a charcoal-gray Cadillac pulling away from the funeral home.

Just then the sensation of being watched came over me. Feeling the warmth of heavy breathing upon my neck, I turned slightly to see who had seated himself behind me.

I found myself face to face with Jean Paul, who was serenely inhaling a Gauloises.

Though no words were spoken, the eye contact between us was intense. I held my breath.

Finally Jean Paul murmured a polite "Mademoiselle" in recognition and turned to face the pulpit once more.

I recalled my last meeting with Jean Paul, and I moved closer to Nick. Misinterpreting my intentions, Nick placed an affectionate arm around my shoulder and pulled me closer to him. And though his motives were questionable, I felt good, protected.

I had seen Nick only the previous afternoon. He called me soon after I returned home from my lunch with Stephanie and Mitzi to ask if I would resume my duties as tour guide.

We crammed as much as we could into three hours, which included a visit to the Griffith Observatory and a roller-skating tour of the Los Angeles Zoo. Wearily we ended up in downtown LA, in the Mexican section known as Olvera Street, where we marketed for the remainder of the day.

I found myself speaking with Nick about things I'd never discussed with anyone before.

I confided in him my childhood dreams of becoming a jazz singer after I'd heard my father's Billie Holiday records and then of wanting to be a scientist after reading *Madame Curie*. I admitted my fear of lightning storms and described to him the devastation and loss I'd felt at my grandfather's passing. And the exuberance of seeing my name in print for the first time.

I told him about Russell. And then about Marc.

He told me about his marriage, why it had failed.

"We were high-school sweethearts," he explained. "Everyone always assumed we'd get married. So when Donna was three months pregnant, that's exactly what we did."

"I thought you said you didn't have any children?"

"I don't. She miscarried in her fifth month. Took it real bad. All she ever wanted was to have kids. Three years later she got pregnant again. And missed again. She just couldn't seem to carry to full term."

"How awful for her, and for you," I said.

"But more so for her," Nick admitted. "I was willing to adopt, but Donna wouldn't hear of it. Worst part was she blamed herself. I don't know how or why we did it, but we stayed together nine years. And then things started going downhill so fast, we had no choice but to get divorced. And let me tell you, divorce in a Catholic family's still a big thing. But we did it. And that was that," he said.

"You two still, well, you know, on good terms?" I asked.

"We exchange Christmas cards if that's what you mean. She got married last year. To a widower . . . with three kids. Best thing that could've happened to her. So everything turned out for the best, I guess," he said quietly.

We were both quiet for a while. And then we talked some more.

We talked about everything. Everything, that is, except the chemistry that was obviously drawing us nearer and dearer to one another.

The fact was I hadn't felt as close to another human being in a long time, if ever. My feelings, however, were divided, encompassing both guilt about Marc and exhilaration for myself.

The funeral-home minister was just winding up her praise of Michael's virtues when I looked up. She actually sounded as though she believed what she was saying. The thought fleetingly occurred to me that perhaps Michael had made his mark upon her life at some point. Not so highly improbable. I mean, this being Hollywood, why should Michael's sexual escapades have excluded the clergy?

"And so let me conclude my sermon by asking that we join together in praying for Michael Cole, and also that we find solace in the knowledge that at last Michael's soul can rest in peace. Amen."

Her last words struck me as being just a little ironic. For while in death it may very well have been his soul that rested in peace, in life it was Michael's cock that had rested in peace and pieces all over town.

As soon as the minister had finished, Nick went off to speak with Horatio Reeper, but he reappeared in a jiffy.

"Did you and Boris have an engrossing chat?" I asked.

"Horatio. Very. Do you know who's responsible for all those lily-white orchids?" Nick asked me.

"The Southern Chapter of the Cosa Nostra?" I ventured.

"Tracy Simms," he said, ignoring my comment.

"Well, that was certainly decent of her."

"Mr. Reeper agrees with you. He thinks it's added a very classy touch to his simple but elegant maple coffin. Unfortunately Reeper says that the sister was not as pleased. Come on, I think it's time we offered our sympathies."

Alison's supportive companion was walking some of the mourners to the door as we approached. Tracy Simms, however, had beaten us to the proverbial punch. The scent of her Joy perfume filled the air.

Nick pressed my hand, and I stopped as he slowly removed a pack of Lucky Strikes from his pocket and deliberately took his time in lighting a cigarette.

Though it wasn't easy to make out all of what was passing back and forth between Alison and Tracy, it was apparent by the tone in which they spoke that they were behaving less than civilly.

"I specifically requested . . ." cried Alison, undoubtedly referring to the orchids.

Tracy's deeper, more composed voice made her words difficult to follow but I picked up phrases here and there.

". . . A child . . . you always will be . . ."

". . . Never loved him . . . never understood him as I did . . ."

". . . I knew him better . . . desired . . ."

". . . Filthy . . . you had no right to come here . . . if . . . any decency . . ." Alison's voice was becoming shrill.

". . . Don't talk . . . decency . . . the truth . . . angelic . . . really killed Michael . . ."

Jesus! What I would have given to have heard it all.

"Get out!" Alison screamed. "Get out!"

Then Tracy smiled viciously and said something inaudible.

Whatever she said was effective. In fact, one might say that it was the straw that broke the butterfly's wings. For with one quick sweep of the hand, Alison smacked Tracy's face so hard it knocked her hat and veil off her head, causing her long black hair to tumble to her shoulders.

Tracy lunged forward, grabbed Alison's frail arm, and dug her carefully manicured nails into it, drawing blood.

Alison's wail pierced the air. She was like a wounded animal, injured by both word and deed.

At this point, Nick jumped in and attempted to separate the two.

Alison's friend was charging down the aisle, coming to her aid.

Tracy had by this time retrieved her hat and was trying to regain her composure, remembering her stature as a renowned film star, I suppose.

Without so much as a word to anyone, she turned abruptly and stormed out of the chapel.

I started to follow her, but Nick advised against it.

He helped Alison recover the beads of her purse, which had fallen off and onto the floor in the struggle.

As he did so, I continued to watch Tracy out of the corner of my eye. She entered the reception area, hesitated, and then walked over to Mr. Reeper, who stood in the doorway with arms crossed. He had obviously witnessed the scene that had taken place and seemed to have enjoyed it.

Speaking with Tracy Simms, Horatio Reeper took on a completely different personality. His cheerful, almost obsequious demeanor had been replaced by an air of authority, as if he somehow had the upper hand.

His smile, which had only been pathetic previously, was now that of a barracuda. In some ineffable way this seemingly laughable creature had been transformed into a horrendous, even sinister human being.

I hadn't the vaguest notion of how or why it was happening.

My curiosity increased when I saw Tracy look about her before taking out a substantial roll of bills and handing it to Reeper.

Of course I couldn't see their exact denomination, but from the way Reeper counted the bills, I'd say it was a sizable amount.

It couldn't possibly have been payment due for the flowers. The orchids would have to have been gilded to cost so much.

Payment for what then?

Morbid thoughts flashed through my mind.

Had Tracy paid the funeral owner to include something kinky beside her beloved ex-husband's body? A lace garter maybe? No, not for that amount of money.

Or was he being paid to overlook something that might arouse suspicions as to the true manner in which Michael Cole had met his death?

Was it hush money I saw being passed from one to the other?

I was baffled.

Tracy then slipped out the front door, leaving Mr. Reeper to assume once again his congenial ways. He was, I thought, unaware of my having witnessed the transaction.

All this had taken place in moments while Nick, assisted by Alison's friend, had been trying to restore Alison's calm.

"Are you all right?" I asked Alison.

"Yes, I'm fine now." She looked absolutely drained.

"I'd like to thank you," she said to Nick, "for stepping in, I mean, Mr. . . . ?"

"Comici. Nick Comici. This is my friend Susan."

"Well, thank you again, Nick. I'm Alison," she said, extending her hand to him.

"What happened?" her friend asked breathlessly.

"Nothing. I . . . I'd rather not go into it now if you don't mind, Cinnamon."

As if suddenly remembering her manners, she made introductions.

"Excuse me, Cinnamon Blake . . . Nick Comici and . . . and his friend Susan."

I can't say I cared much for the sound of that. I felt a little like Flicka of *My Friend*——.

"How do you do?" I said.

"Were you . . . um . . . close friends of . . . Michael's?"

I felt sorry for her; it was obviously a strain for Alison to say her brother's name.

Before I could respond, Nick answered for us.

"I'm writing an article on funerals. You know, comparative services, prices, that sort of thing," he explained.

"Oh, really? How fascinating," said Alison, sounding anything but fascinated.

"I'm sorry, about your brother, I mean. And that you had to be put through such an ugly scene," said Nick.

"Thank you."

"You know what ex-wives are like, Mr. Comici," said Cinnamon.

"Yeah, well," Nick replied, "guess everyone's . . ." he searched for a word, ". . . distraught, at times like this. After all, she was once married to the guy. I'm sorry, to your brother, that is."

"I suppose," Alison conceded softly.

"Alison," I said, cautiously changing the subject, "you're satisfied that Michael's death was an accident, aren't you?"

A puzzled look passed between the two young women.

"I mean," I added hastily, "it couldn't have been suicide or anything."

"It wasn't suicide," Alison said with conviction as tears began to fill her eyes. "Michael loved life, he'd never have committed suicide."

Cinnamon placed her hand on her friend's shoulder, and I regretted having asked the question.

"Say, if you're, like, looking for a really good story . . ."

"Yes?" Nick encouraged her anxiously.

"How about covering Save the Whales? We could always use the publicity," Cinnamon said.

"Cinnamon's our chapter chairperson," Alison added quietly as she dried her eyes.

"Well, of course, that's a possibility," Nick said, trying to be diplomatic, "*definitely* a possibility. Why don't I sleep on it and get back to you?"

Cinnamon agreed to this and handed him her card.

Unlike Alison, Cinnamon was not a very pretty girl. She did, however, have a sweet smile. If the expression "pleasingly plump" could be applied to anyone, it was certainly right for Cinnamon, whose ample breasts and short stature reminded me of my aunt Bea.

Cinnamon looked as though she were twenty-four going on fifty-four.

"I'm sorry we had to meet under these circumstances," Alison was saying. "Death is such a personal affair, don't you agree?"

"I know what she means," Alison's friend interjected. "The last funeral that touched me personally was Kennedy's. John Kennedy's that is. . . ."

Cinnamon was now chattering away incessantly. I might have strangled her if I thought it would help put a stop to her talking.

"... And after all, it would, of course, make, like, an incredible impression on a girl of eight. ..."

I was only half-listening to Cinnamon's babblings by this time as I watched Alison. She looked more like a butterfly than ever. A frightened, trapped butterfly at that.

"... I'll never forget it ... the teachers broke the news to us in class and let us all go home ... well, actually it was only, like, a half-hour or so before school would have let out anyway, but it's funny the things you remember from when you were a child ... like when Marilyn Monroe died, for example ... still, if you want to talk total devastation, I'd have to say it was the day John Lennon was shot. ..."

Christ Almighty! This kid was a memory bank with a fixation for funerals.

"Marilyn Monroe!" Nick exclaimed, snapping his fingers. "I almost forgot! I promised my editor I'd take a few pictures of her grave as part of my assignment. He goes for schmaltz, and you know, with the roses and all. ..."

I could have kissed him.

"Well, we've got to be going ourselves," Cinnamon replied defensively. I suppose she was miffed at having had her death saga curtailed.

Alison looked so much younger than her twenty years as she smiled and shyly extended her small hand to me. On her other hand, she wore a small but exquisite sapphire-and-diamond ring.

"It's lovely," I commented.

"Thank you. It was the last present my brother ever gave me," she explained softly.

As Nick and I left the funeral parlor, Reeper took Nick aside. This is it, I thought. He planned to doublecross Tracy by tipping off the press and really putting his funeral home on the map.

Instead he merely said with a wink, "There'll be an all-black service at two o'clock today. Thought you might like to stick around for all that gospel stuff. Lots of wailing and foot-stomping, you know."

Nick declined, promising again to take a raincheck.

"At least sign our guest book," Reeper insisted.

As Nick went off to sign the register, I felt a piece of paper being pressed into my hand.

"We're often mistaken in what we believe we have seen," Reeper whispered cryptically. "Isn't that so, Miss Finkelstein?"

It sounded so much like a line from a grade-B film that my first impulse was to laugh. But I knew he was serious.

I was speechless. Fortunately Nick came back before I could say anything, assuming, that is, that I had anything to say.

Upon leaving the funeral parlor, I looked into my hand and was shocked to discover a one-hundred-dollar bill.

Here I was being given hush money for something I knew too little about to hush up. It was absurd. All of it.

As we walked away, I noticed Reeper peering out the front window, the "hunch" at his side.

Involuntarily my body trembled as another chill ran through it, the second that day.

"What's the matter, Susan?" Nick asked. "Think someone's walking over your grave?"

I hoped not.

I didn't expect Nick to be cashing in his raincheck with Horatio Reeper on my account.

We discussed Tracy and Alison on the way home and the explosion that had taken place between them.

"It's a good thing Alison's friend was there. You know, the girl with a flavor for a name?" Nick remarked.

"Cinnamon."

"Right. 'Cause I don't think she'd have been able to hold

her own against that Tracy Simms. Wow! Now there's someone who wouldn't intimidate easily."

"Think so?" I asked, feeling a slight twinge of jealousy.

I relayed the scene I had witnessed between Tracy and Reeper, concluding with the hundred-dollar bribe Reeper had slipped me. That I'd made an impression on Nick was apparent and for the remainder of the ride we speculated as to the nature of such an unlikely relationship as Tracy and Reeper's.

We ended up at the public library, where Nick claimed he wanted to "look into a few things." Slipping into the driver's seat, I waved as I drove away.

I walked into the house, kicked off my shoes, and tried to make a quick decision as to whether I should go to the bathroom or play back my answer machine. I decided to listen from the bathroom as the machine played back my messages.

"Hi, Sue. This is Sharon Campbell. I received your message from our answering service, and Jeff and I are delighted you and Marc can make our shindig. Talk to you soon."

Not likely, I thought. This is the age of service-to-service communication.

The next voice was Marc's.

"I wanted to remind you that I'll be working late tonight, so don't hold dinner for me."

There were two beeps after Marc's message, indicating hang-ups. Person or persons who, for some reason or another, thought better of leaving messages.

"Sweetie!" It was Stephanie. "I hope Michael's funeral was a blast. Just phoning to let you know that we're on for tonight at Ellen's. So put on your best Tupper smile, and call me as soon as you can."

Our lunch with Mitzi had been a thorough success, with Stephanie having built me up as the best salesperson since

Willie Loman. Stephanie assured me we'd "work" a Tupperware party together as soon as possible.

But tonight? She certainly got those wheels turning
quickly. Well, that was good. My momentum was high.

"Hi, honey, it's just me."

The sound of my mother's voice, as usual, made me
homesick.

"We haven't heard from you in a while," she continued.
"Is everything okay with you and Marc?"

No, not really Mother. But how do I explain this to you,
a woman who has been happily married for nearly thirty
years. You wed during the Era of Simplicity and Commit-
ment, you lucky duck.

✂ < 9 > ✂

The universe is merely a fleeting idea in God's mind—a pretty uncomfortable thought, particularly if you've just made a down-payment on a house.

Woody Allen

Stephanie and I arrived at the Bethune's at 8:45 P.M. Though it was already near dark when we got there, the house lights were on, and I could see that their home had a certain air of distinction, set back among rows of willow trees.

Expensive but in good taste, I thought to myself as I pulled my Toyota up behind the Seville in the driveway.

We grabbed hold of cartons containing Tupperware and waddled over to the door. It was several moments before a tiny, dark woman responded to our ring, and we were admitted.

We were shown into a small hallway, where we placed the boxes on the floor.

"Una momenta," the woman said, flashing us a gold-toothed smile as she left the room.

Ellen appeared almost immediately, wearing a lavender lounging gown. She looked lovely but washed out.

Ellen and Stephanie exchanged kisses, and then Stephanie introduced me. Ellen showed no signs of recognizing me from Jean Paul's.

"It was nice of you all to come," she said to us graciously, holding out an emerald-and-diamond-studded hand. I detected a very slight southern accent.

"No, please. It was wonderful of you to have us," I

70

protested. "And at such short notice. I hope we're not inconveniencing you."

"Not at all," Ellen replied.

Was I imagining things, or did she hesitate before responding? Stephanie told me that in proposing the idea of a Tupperware party to Ellen, she had purposely introduced the name Andrew Willis into the conversation.

Apparently this Willis fellow is on the Board of Directors of a very exclusive eastern girls' school, a school that Ellen was most anxious to have her daughter, Roslyn, attend. Stephanie casually mentioned the fact that Andrew Willis was a close acquaintance of her father.

Needless to say, the transition from girls' schools to Tupperware was as smooth as silk.

"Well, just show us where you'd like for us to set up, and we'll get started," Stephanie was saying.

"Of course. Right this way. I thought the den would be most appropriate, don't you agree, Sue?"

"What? Oh, yes . . . the den . . . perfect."

I was fascinated with the manner in which this house was decorated. I observed, as we passed the living and dining rooms as well as the kitchen, that the rooms, while spacious and certainly expensive in their furnishings, emitted no real warmth.

This was partially due to the predominance of Oriental design, of which I admit I am not fond.

Wherever I looked, I saw porcelain, porcelain, and more porcelain. I was surprised to see that a crack ran down the center of one particular statuette, a small court jester. It looked as though it had been broken and put back together. The fact that it was marred distinguished it from what was an otherwise flawless collection of vases, music boxes, and dolls. All priceless, I'm certain.

So preoccupied was I with these curios that I apparently neglected to watch where I was walking and consequently went sprawling over a Tiny-Totter Scooter. The carton I held fell out of my grasp, causing various pieces of Tupperware to fly in all directions.

"Oh, my goodness," said Ellen, seemingly appalled that anything so unladylike could occur in her home. "Are you all right?"

"Sure," I said as I picked myself up, feeling exceedingly foolish. "I just hope the Tupperware is," I joked.

"Aha! But Tupperware's unbreakable," Stephanie reminded me. She then turned to Ellen assuringly. "That's one of its most remarkable features—durability."

Stephanie's a born salesperson, not one to let an opportunity pass.

"I'm very sorry, my four-year-old can be a little careless with his belongings," Ellen explained. "Juanine isn't the best housekeeper but she needs the job to support her family in Caracas and she's great with Stephen; I'd be a meanie to fire her."

And a fool as well since you undoubtedly pay her no more than one hundred dollars a month.

Guests began to arrive just as Stephanie and I had finished setting up. Ellen was right about the den; it was the least formal of all the rooms I'd seen.

We placed the Tupperware on two bridge tables situated in front of the window.

When Ellen asked about refreshments, Stephanie had suggested that she keep it simple.

Laid out on a cocktail table were platters of cheese, iced shrimp, caviar, and imported biscuits. On the sideboard was a pewter coffee urn with two cheesecakes beside it, one pineapple, one chocolate.

Simple is a relative word.

Five of Ellen's friends showed up. In behavior and style, all of the women were clones of Ellen. Still they were friendly enough, and they seemed to be amused at the idea of a Tupperware party.

I sat to the side as Stephanie took the spotlight.

To get the group into the spirit of things, we played various games, with Tupperware for prizes. This warm-up technique, I discovered, is employed at all Tupperware parties.

I'd forgotten how much fun getting together with "the girls" for an evening of silliness could be. I wondered for a moment what Nick was up to. I looked up to see the hour and noticed for the first time the family pictures on the wall. It was the only indication of life I had seen anywhere in the house. True, the frames were of porcelain too, but all the same . . .

The one that especially caught my eye was Frank and Ellen's wedding picture. I'd say the photo was taken about ten years ago, judging from Ellen's dated hairstyle.

The next was a family portrait of Frank and Ellen standing beside a pudgy girl of about fourteen years and a boy of about three or four. Roslyn, whom I later learned was Ellen's daughter from a former, disastrous marriage, was not a pretty child. On the contrary, she was quite homely. Mousy hair hung loosely to her shoulders, and her brown eyes had a vacant look. I would have bet that her personality was just as dull. Nevertheless, I was certain that a diet, a nose job, and a father with money would improve her looks considerably and assure her of a successful future.

The boy, whom I assumed to be Stephen, was another story. His smile was captivating, and his brilliant blue eyes illuminated the photograph. Indeed, he was a four-year-old charmer and probably spoiled rotten because of it.

That this photo was taken recently was apparent from Frank's lack of hair. Otherwise Frank was not a bad-looking man. Not that he was handsome, mind you. Just that he looked like half the boys in my senior class of high school, a face in the crowd.

The other pictures, I imagined, were of parents, grandparents, and other assorted relatives. Nothing further to interest me.

As the evening progressed, it took on a partylike atmosphere, reminiscent of a sorority bull session. The jokes became cruder and were tossed about as only women can toss them.

Only the hostess appeared removed from the festivities. Though she managed an occasional smile, it was obvious, to me at any rate, that she was distracted.

I took advantage of the hilarity that surrounded us to approach Ellen privately.

"Silly, huh?" I said to her.

"Excuse me?" she replied.

I knew from whom Roslyn had inherited that vacant stare.

"The games. They're kind of silly," I repeated.

"Oh. Yes. But everyone seems to be havin' fun."

The slight southern drawl again, somewhat more pronounced.

"Yes, they do," I agreed, wondering how best to bring up Michael's name. I decided on the direct approach.

"You know, we've met before," I began.

"Have we?" She was genuinely surprised.

"Well, we never spoke, but I do remember seeing you." I looked straight at her and said, "At Jean Paul's Hair Salon? I believe we used the same stylist."

Whatever vacancy was in her eyes before was replaced now by something else. Fear? Anger? Possibly a mixture of both.

"Of course, you've heard about Michael's death," I continued innocently. "I didn't know him well, did you?"

"No. I barely knew him," she responded too quickly. "Why do you ask?"

"No reason. As I said, I didn't know him well myself," I admitted conspiratorially, "but I understand he was quite a man."

I guess I overstepped the bounds when I facetiously suggested that Michael was the type of character whose death would be welcomed by some. This was obviously too much for Ellen to withstand. Her body tensed, and she tightened her grip on the wineglass she held, causing it to crack in her hand.

As the rest of us rushed about for bandages to absorb the blood that gushed from her palm, I observed that Ellen seemed almost oblivious to the pain. In fact, she made light of it, calling herself clumsy and insisting that we go on as before while she excused herself momentarily.

I shrugged in response to Stephanie's inquisitive stare, and soon the party was in full swing once more as though nothing had happened.

I was surprised to learn from Stephanie at the end of the evening that we, or rather she, had sold nearly $250 worth of Tupperware. In three hours? That's over $80 an hour. I'd have to start giving more serious thought to the Tupperware business.

And yet aside from a night out, what had I actually gained from all this?

Nothing. Zilch. A total washout.

But that's not fair, I argued with myself. I did get to meet Ellen, though admittedly it was too soon to size her up. Mrs. Bethune was more complex than she let on, of that much I was certain. I was still unsure of what to make of her reaction to the mention of Michael's death.

I tried to place her as a murderess. She'd probably have the resolve to "do something in," but as for technique, I was inclined to type Ellen as a woman who would use poison rather than physical violence to accomplish the deed.

* * *

It was a little past midnight when I dropped Stephanie off in Century City and headed back to my own home. I pulled into my garage at twelve-thirty. Marc was not home. I remembered his saying that he would be home late that night. Apparently he was working on a project that was causing him to keep long hours these past few weeks. Ordinarily I wouldn't have minded. In fact, though I hated to admit it, I had found myself enjoying the solitude.

But on this evening as I put my key in the door, I wished that I weren't coming home to an empty house. I even welcomed an argument with Marc.

I took a cup of hot cocoa up to bed with me and crawled under the covers with an Agatha Christie. Trying to match wits with Hercule Poirot frequently takes my mind off my own worries.

This time, however, it didn't work. I was too wound up to concentrate. Perhaps this was all a wild-goose chase I was on. After all, so far there was little to prove that Michael's death was anything but accidental. Why then was I pursuing the matter?

The answer came to me more quickly than I'd have liked. It was Nick.

This supposed "murder" was my excuse to see him. But why did one need an excuse to see one's friends?

Come off it, Susan, that was the point, wasn't it? If Nick were only a friend, you wouldn't need an excuse to see him. Guiltily I thought of Marc. I tried to recall the good times we had had together. And there were many. Unfortunately, each time I conjured up an image of Marc, he would be transfigured almost immediately into Nick. And my fantasies of Nick were embarrassingly explicit.

I suddenly remembered that I hadn't heard from Nick all evening and thought it possible that he had called and left a message for me.

I flipped the rewind switch on my machine and waited

for it to play back what I felt sure was going to be Nick's voice.

Even now the recollection of what I heard next nauseates me. In what sounded like a 45 rpm record being played at 33, a horrid voice was moaning incomprehensible words at me.

My mouth was dry, the residue of cocoa having left a chalky aftertaste.

I switched the recorder on once more, turned up the volume, and sat attentively, waiting. Once again I heard the voice, so distorted that I couldn't even guess its sex.

Though the words were barely discernible, after one or two playbacks I finally understood what was being said. There were only four words, but the message "Let sleeping dogs lie" came across loud and clear.

Helplessly, I did little more than stare at the phone, feeling as though some important part of me had been violated.

I began to walk about the house, carefully securing windows. I even double-locked the door, something I rarely did. I don't think that I actually expected an intruder, but it was my only means of feeling that I was in control.

I didn't want to think about the phone call or about Michael or about the strong possibility of there being a link between the two. Instead I decided on a hot, tension-easing shower.

I stayed in there for nearly a half-hour. The prickle of water hit like needles against my skin; it felt terrific, and I was able to lose myself completely.

My sense of well-being was, however, short-lived. For as I grabbed hold of a bath towel, I heard the distinct tinkle of shattering glass. At first I ignored it, assuming a bottle had dropped somewhere in the house, perhaps off a shelf.

Then I heard it again.

The sound came from the kitchen.

My heart nearly stopped as I stood paralyzed with fear. Scenes from *Psycho* flashed through my mind.

And at that moment I began to sneeze repeatedly, a nervous habit I've had since childhood whenever I find myself in a threatening situation. I clutched a washcloth and held it over my nose.

Then I threw my robe on quickly and forced myself to leave the bathroom and walked through the bedroom, picking up the only weapon available to me, the walking stick Marc had purchased on our trip to London two years ago.

Breathing deeply, I carefully made my way into the corridor. I stopped short and listened to footsteps crunching over glass.

It was as though I were watching myself in a dream. Could this be a dream? No, that glass was for real.

Oh, God, help me, I thought.

I am not courageous by nature, but if there were to be a confrontation, I would prefer to get it over with quickly.

I waited and watched helplessly as the doors to the kitchen seemed to open in slow motion.

I raised my stick, prepared to attack.

"Do you mind telling me why the hell you double-locked the door?"

"Marc!" My body relaxed at the sight of him.

"I told you I was going to be late," he said defensively.

"Yes, I know you did. It's just that . . . tonight I was a little frightened staying here all by myself," I explained.

"A little? Sue, you bolted the goddamned windows. I don't believe I had to break into my own home!" he said, turning off the alarm that had gone off.

"Why didn't you ring?" I asked.

"I did, but I gave up after ten minutes."

"I'm sorry, I was in the shower. I guess I didn't hear you."

"That's obvious."

"I said I was sorry."

"Forget it. Let's just go to bed. I've had a rough day."

"So have I, Marc, as a matter of fact . . ."

"Please, Sue, can it wait? I'm bushed."

"Sure."

As we walked up to the bedroom together, Marc noticed the walking stick for the first time.

"What's with the cane?" he asked.

"This? Oh, well, you see I had a cramp in my leg and . . ."

✂ ❮ 10 ❯ ✂

*Hollywood is the place where inferior people have
a way of making superior people feel inferior.*

Dudley Field Malone

Nick phoned the following morning to tell me he had hopped
a Greyhound for San Diego, where he planned on visiting
with relatives for a while.

When he asked how the Tupperware party turned out, I
said it was fine, but that the details could wait until his
return. Not wanting to ruin his trip, I didn't mention the
memorable phone message. Instead I told him to have a
terrific time and that I'd speak with him when he got back.

The next week passed uneventfully. I was reluctant to
go on with my investigation of Michael's death for I suspected there was a connection between it and the call I'd
received. Besides, without Nick as a coconspirator, my
incentive had waned.

I had erased the call the next day just as one would shower
after a rape. The voice, however, was imprinted on my
brain. Much as I tried, I couldn't conceive of who would
have done such a thing. I briefly considered the possibility
that it was Marc, trying to drive me insane. But on second
thought I knew I was thinking irrationally; Marc's everyday
habits would bring me to the edge of insanity just as effec-
tively in the long run.

No. 'Let sleeping dogs lie' referred to this Michael Cole
business or my name wasn't Susan, Sue, or Susie-Q. But
what could I do about it?

I decided to let the entire incident drop and concentrate instead on my latest book project.

It was the story of Kelly's family tree. Considering the smash success of *Roots*, I thought, it might be a good idea to put Kelly's great-grandaddy on a plantation, making him a boll weevil or something. Kelly's great-grandmama might have been the Scarlett O'Hara of bugs — a ladybug. Whether this is biologically feasible is doubtful, nevertheless I made liberal use of literary license.

The ladybug would be elegant and regal; the epitome of femininity. Something like Ellen Bethune. Only she would ride in a tomato coach instead of a Seville.

I stopped typing and thought of the Seville I had seen parked in Ellen's driveway. On a hunch I reached for the phone and dialed Stephanie's number. I let it ring several times.

"Yes?" Stephanie finally snapped.

"Steph? Am I disturbing you?" I asked.

"Why of course not," she answered icily. Covering the mouthpiece slightly she said, "David darling, would you mind passing me my cigarettes?"

Oh boy, had I disturbed her.

I said quickly, "I won't keep you. I just have one question. What color is Ellen Bethune's car?"

I felt Stephanie's killing stare.

"Gray!"

"Now, Stephanie, this is kind of important. See, it was getting too dark for me to notice. Are you sure it's gray?"

"As sure as I am that I'll get you for this," she hissed and hung up.

A gray Seville. A wave of satisfaction came over me. I knew in that instant that the Cadillac I saw driving away from Reeper's funeral home the week before was Ellen's. I was sure of it.

I put Kelly away, unable to focus any longer, and fixed myself a tuna sandwich.

If Ellen were not a close friend of Michael's, why did she attend his funeral? Better still, why had she left so abruptly?

Admittedly, I was becoming increasingly absorbed in the mysterious circumstances surrounding Michael's demise. In fact, what had begun as a puzzling distraction had blossomed into full-fledged obsession on my part.

Would my fascination have abated had I an inkling of how much deeper I would be pulled into the undercurrent of what lay ahead?

I dressed with care the evening of the Campbell's party. Aware that these extravaganzas were generally attended by sophisticate and funky alike, I tried my best to combine both looks.

It was a tossup between a black floor-length Halston, slit to the waist and a violet sequined cocktail dress, the neckline of which was incredibly revealing.

The Halston would require more accessorization than I had patience for. Still, the cocktail dress was possibly too daring for me to carry off. I had bought it on sale on a whim, but had not yet found neither the nerve nor the occasion to wear it.

I tried them each on a half-dozen times. Marc walked into the bedroom as I zipped up the cocktail dress.

"Don't you think that's a bit slutty looking? Your boobs are hanging down to your *pupik*."

"Thank you for the compliment."

"I'm sorry, honey, I just don't want you to feel uncomfortable, you know what I mean."

What Marc meant was that he wanted the woman clinging to his arm to look like the proper executive's wife.

I tossed a shocking pink ostrich boa about my neck and stalked defiantly out of the room.

Violet is a great color for me. It's becoming to my hair, which, on that night, was pulled back softly off the nape of my neck.

The amethyst drop earrings I wore, a gift from my nana Jenny, accentuated my eyes.

I looked sensational. Dazzling in fact. And I was feeling more youthful than I had in quite some time, my only regret being that Nick wasn't there to see me.

At the party I drank very little, intoxicated sufficiently by the razzmatazz that surrounded me.

As I had predicted, all types were represented. Women bedecked in designer gowns, feathers, and jewels conversed amicably with blue-jeaned young men in loose-fitting shirts. Brooks Brother tweeds mixed with purple-haired punks.

A beautiful Oriental girl wore her coal black hair below her derrière and looked at ease in her harem garb.

This intimate gathering of two hundred people flowed into every conceivable nook and cranny—upstairs, downstairs, living room, den, game room and dining room, which led to the patio and the landscaped Japanese garden beyond. Even in the bathroom a quorum was formed.

A staggering array of food and drink was offered relentlessly throughout the evening.

Pastries were served upon huge, antique bakers' racks that had been mobilized for the occasion. Just looking at the rich, cream-filled eclairs, tarts, and baklava could have put a diabetic into convulsions.

The entire shindig was catered by Rosie O'Grady's, the newest "find" in catering houses. Its theme was turn-of-the-century New York. Waitresses wearing red and white bloomered skirts with bustles, served beer on tap poured by bartenders sporting handlebar moustaches and derbies.

Gaslit lampposts were set up near doorways and everyday

furniture had been replaced by brightly colored park benches and small wooden tables.

In the living room an old player piano tinkled as guests joined in on old favorites. Four men, completely stoned, leaned against an authentic barbers' pole that stood in the den; they entertained listeners with off-key, four-part harmony.

The classiest touch by far was the organ grinder who went from room to room playing songs upon request, as his neurotic monkey jumped about his shoulders smoking a joint.

Only in the game room was one reminded of the times we live in. It had been turned into a wild discotheque, where dancers gyrated madly beneath dazzling, frenzied lights to the provocative sighings of Michael Jackson.

The smell of marijuana permeated the air and in various circles guests could be seen snorting cocaine. When it rained in this town, it snowed, and by the abundance of it available that night, one would not have guessed that the cost of coke was prohibitive or that it was even a luxury. Fact of the matter is, many of those present had been born with silver spoons up their noses.

I wove in and out of clusters, intermittently smiling and sipping my bourbon and water.

There was a fair share of celebrities and psuedocelebrities present. Among the more recognizable were Diana Ross, Liza Minelli, Lorne Greene, and James Earl Jones.

Though many of the faces looked familiar, I didn't know anyone well enough to shoot the breeze with, so to speak.

Marc was standing by the bar with a chalk-faced brunette and a man over whom she towered. Her amazon stature next to his shrimpiness made for a somewhat ludicrous sight. She could have eaten peanuts off his head.

"C'mere Sue, there are some people I'd like you to meet.

Meyer Rosenbloom, Felicia Stakaris, I'd like to introduce you to my a . . . to Sue Finkelstein."

If perchance my photo were to appear in George Christy's column, the caption beneath it would read, "CBS exec. Marc Beaumont and best friend, Sue Finkelstein."

Eight years out of my life, only to be rated "best friend" by the *Hollywood Reporter*.

"Charmed," said Felicia extending a cold, limp hand.

Unlike his low-keyed companion, Rosenbloom himself was hyped to the point of jumping out of his skin at any moment.

"Hiya, sweetheart, where've you been hiding yourself all night?" He chomped on a wad of gum as he asked the question.

"I haven't been . . ." I began.

"Beaumont and I were just saying that live theater in this town sucks . . . I mean it's really *el drecko*, you know what I'm talkin' about?"

"Well, that's not necessarily . . ."

"Now you take New York—I'm from New York originally, you know, Flushing—you take New York, they'd appreciate a talent like Felicia's in New York, but then New York's a dark town, if you know what I mean. Schvartzes and kikes, spics and guineas. Here all they know from are blonds. Blonds selling toothpaste, blonds selling Tampax. Say, you're a good type yourself Susie, ever give any thought to acting?"

I didn't even attempt to reply.

"What's the matter, honey?" he asked. "Cat got your tongue?"

Sensing a confrontation, Marc interrupted.

"Excuse me, I'm hearing some terrific music, I think I'd like to dance."

"Fabulous idea, Beaumont," said Rosenbloom, as he placed Felicia's hand in Marc's. "Why don't you take Felicia here for a spin and let Susie and me get better acquainted, hah?"

Marc was at an awkward loss for words, but not wishing to create a scene, he chivalrously led Felicia off to the dance floor.

"Pretty girl, Felicia," Rosenbloom said when they were out of hearing range. "Pretty, but not very big in the talent department I'm afraid, you know what I'm talkin' about?"

"But you just said . . ."

"I know what I said. But after all, even in this day and age some shuck and jiving are prerequisites to hopping into the sack. Face it kid, in this business sooner or later everyone *schtups* everyone, professionally and otherwise."

"Kind of a hypocritical outlook, don't you think?"

"But a practical one." He spoke more slowly. "Look, babe, let me lay it on the line for you. First and foremost an agent's business is to sell. Same as a realtor, a grocer, or a butcher. A good agent would be a good used-car or refrigerator salesman. A great agent can sell cow shit. I should know. I'm one of the best there is."

Meyer Rosenbloom was the type that gave the entire race of agents a bad name.

"A good agent," he continued, "is worth his weight in gold."

"As is a good actress!"

I turned to see who had made this statement; the voice was not unfamiliar to me.

Tracy Simms stood regally behind me. She looked breathtaking in a sheer white gown. The dress itself was simply styled and trimmed in tiny crystal beads. Every curve and nuance of her voluptuous body was exposed, since she wore a minimum of undergarments.

With her hair piled high on her head, Tracy was a vision; beside her, every woman in the room suffered by comparison.

"Ah, Tracy. You are indeed worth your weight in gold. Trace, I'd like you to meet Susie Finestein."

"Finkelstein," I corrected.

"Finkelstein," he repeated. "And this is my jewel of a client, Miss Tracy Simms."

Tracy's deep violet eyes pierced my own.

"We've met," I said.

"Have we?" she asked, unconvincingly.

"At Michael Cole's funeral?" I reminded her.

"Oh, yes, of course. I believe you were privy to my knock-down-drag-out fight." Turning to Rosenbloom she explained, "My ex-sister-in-law was less than delighted at my presence."

"Michael. Michael. Michael," sighed Rosenbloom, shaking his head. "Even from the grave he's at the core of things. Michael! Michael was a driving force."

"Michael was a bastard," Tracy said, "but he was a hell of a lay."

There was something incongruous about these words falling from the lips of a goddess.

"Yes, I'm sure his talents are being sorely missed all over town," Rosenbloom agreed. "How unfortunate for everyone that he was taken in his prime."

"For everyone?" I ventured.

I now had two sets of eyes piercing my own. I found myself blushing.

"I'm sorry," I said to Tracy. "I just meant that usually someone as popular as your ex-husband was manages to accumulate an equal number of friends and enemies in a lifetime."

"I see what Susie means," said Rosenbloom, thoughtfully, "and you're right, babe, there are probably just as many people out there thankful for his death as there are mourning it."

"Oh, c'mon, Meyer," Tracy said. "You can't be serious.

I mean, all right, granted, Michael was by no means a saint. But I doubt anyone was pleased by his having died."

"And why do you doubt it, love?" Rosenbloom asked. "Michael was amoral, and therefore oblivious to the pain he inflicted on others. He screwed those who interfered with the flow of his life without giving it a second thought," he said venomously. "Quite frankly, Michael Cole just didn't give a flying fuck about anything but himself."

As if suddenly aware of having inadvertently included me in a private discourse, Rosenbloom laughed nervously.

"We must be boring you," he said to me. "Did you know Michael well?"

"Well enough to attend his funeral," Tracy observed.

Careful, Susan.

"As a matter of fact," I explained, "I was actually accompanying my friend. He's writing a series of articles on comparative funeral services. I only knew Michael slightly, but when I heard his service was Ecumenical . . ."

"You thought your writer friend might like to attend," Rosenbloom concluded.

"I know it sounds callous."

"Not callous, babe, merely enterprising," Rosenbloom hissed in a tone that showed new-found respect. He placed his small, clawlike hand on my shoulder and sneered. Whether he swallowed my explanation I don't know. His face was not one that reveals the innermost thoughts. Tracy, however, continued to stare at me, unconvinced.

I was grateful for Marc and Felicia's return. Introductions were made once more, and the topic of Michael Cole was dropped. Tracy seemed amused at the fact that Marc couldn't take his eyes off her.

In fact, for the remainder of the evening, Marc's fascination with Tracy Simms's body was as transparent as Tracy's dress.

Bored with the turn the conversation had taken, I excused

myself and strolled into the garden, where I soon became mesmerized by a garter snake that crawled along the edge of a nearby pond.

I was intrigued not by its surreptitious movements, nor even by its beautiful, iridescent sleekness, but rather by the incredible resemblance it bore to one Meyer S. Rosenbloom.

✂ ‹ 11 › ✂

Tsoris, tsoris, tsoris. *(Translation from Yiddish: "trouble, trouble, trouble.")*

My aunt Bea

Have you ever had a morning when the phone doesn't stop ringing?

The Monday morning following the Campbell's bash was one such morning.

Marc had already left for work, and the first call came at five minutes past eight.

"Sue Finkelstein?"

The feline quality of Tracy Simms's voice was unmistakable.

"Yes. To whom am I speaking?" I thought I'd play her game.

"This is Tracy Simms," she purred. "I wanted to know if we could get together to talk, possibly this afternoon, if you're free?"

I'll say this for her, she was direct.

"To talk?" I repeated.

"Yes, I think I could enlighten you somewhat on the subject of my late ex-husband and his death, about which you appear to be so interested."

"And why would you want to do that?" I asked, cautiously.

"Satisfaction. After all, I was the man's wife."

"What makes you think confiding in me would satisfy you, I'm only..."

"Look," she cut me off, her voice no longer a purr, "can you make it or not?"

I decided I'd better take advantage of the opportunity and save my questions until later, and agreed to drive to her home in Laurel Canyon.

"Why don't you plan on dropping by around teatime. For cocktails," she suggested. "Incidentally, you were right, you know. About a person's being too popular for their own good. I think Michael overstepped himself once too often. And you know what they say, love kills."

I was to puzzle over those words frequently in the days that followed.

By the time the phone rang again at 8:45, I was fully awake. The sound of Nick's voice warmed my body, and as we spoke I instinctively snuggled under my down comforter.

"Hey kid, how y'doin'?"

"Not too badly, how about you?"

"I'm exhausted, I got back late last night."

"How was your visit with your family?"

"Loved it. I hadn't seen Uncle Mario and Aunt Camillia since, oh, since my brother's wedding, I guess. They're priceless. I guess Uncle Mario's a romantic. He kept asking if there was a chance of Donna and me patching things up, even after all this time. Incredible." He laughed.

"Incredible." I didn't laugh.

"Well, now that I'm back, I'd like to see you. Today, if you're free. Tell you what, I'm conducting a little interview for an article I'm thinking of writing. Like to come along?"

"What time's the interview?"

"Eleven-thirty."

"Sure. Why not?"

"Great, I'll pick you up in an hour; we'll have breakfast."

"Pick me up?"

"I borrowed my cousin Freddie's car."

"Wonderful. I'll see you in a little while then. Oh, by the way, what's this article about, the one you're working on I mean?"

"The near-extinction of the modern-day whale."

As it turned out, Nick arrived at my house later than expected. Much later. So we had no time for breakfast.

"We're going to be near the water, better take a sweater or something," Nick advised.

Cousin Freddie's mint '65 fire-engine-red Mustang convertible, with its revved-up radial tires, left me feeling as though I had never left high school.

It also had better pick-up than my Toyota.

"So you're keeping your promise to the whale lady after all," I observed.

"It's the least I could do after interrupting Cinnamon's death narrative. Besides, Alison'll be there. Between the two of them maybe we can piece together another part of the puzzle. Speaking of puzzles, what's been happening around here, anything?"

I tried to organize my thoughts so that I could describe events in sequential order.

First, I conveyed my impressions of Ellen Bethune and her odd reaction at the mention of Michael Cole's name. But it wasn't until after I told him of spotting her Seville leaving the funeral home, that Nick agreed that Ellen was indeed hiding something. When I told him about the odd message left on my phone machine, Nick began to wonder as to whom it was exactly we had rubbed the wrong way. It could be anyone, even someone we had yet to meet; news travels fast in this town.

For the rest of the drive, I described in minute detail, the party, Felicia, and my conversation with Rosenbloom and Tracy. I finished by telling him of my appointment with Tracy, later that day.

"I wouldn't mind going along," Nick said, "for the experience, if you know what I mean."

I knew what he meant. I think.

I was surprised when Nick pulled up in front of Marineland and turned off the ignition.

"Save the Whales headquarters is about a quarter of a mile from here," Nick explained. "It's a nice walk."

"Ah, and I thought you brought me here to watch the seals balance their balls," I said.

Nick took my arm and we walked down the road.

"You're a very perverted young lady, Susan."

"Every one of the eight species of great whales is on the United States endangered species list. Every goddamned one of them," Cinnamon repeated emphatically, "and very little is being done to secure their preservation."

"But isn't that the very purpose of the IWC? To set quotas to allow for their population increase?" Nick asked.

Having listened to Nick ask intelligent, informed questions about whales for close to a half hour, I recalled his visit to the library and realized he'd been doing his homework.

"Theoretically that's true," agreed Cinnamon.

"But in reality the International Whale Commission is a travesty," Alison piped up.

"Let me give you an example, Nick," said Cinnamon. "The oil of the sperm whale is used for lubricating machines for space, computer, and medical technologies. Now I ask you, when you stack small pressure groups such as us against Du Pont, NASA, and the AMA, whom do you think the IWC is likely to favor?"

"I understand what you're saying, but if you'll let me play devil's advocate for just a moment, isn't it true that in

1977 the IWC agreed on a sperm whale quota of seven hundred fifty?" Nick inquired.

"Seven hundred sixty-four," Cinnamon corrected, "and three months later, they changed their minds and raised their quota to 6,444. Each year it gets progressively worse."

For nearly an hour Nick, Cinnamon, and occasionally Alison spoke of whales. Cinnamon complained of harpooning, Nick asked about mammal IQs, and Alison talked of whales as victims, a subject with which she seemed able to identify.

I sat mutely, staring out the window at Marineland in the distance.

"Well, I think I've got enough," Nick said, closing his notebook.

"Super," said Cinnamon. "When will it be published?"

"All depends," Nick answered, ambiguously, "but I'll be sure to let you know."

"Will I be quoted?" Alison asked with childish glee. "My godmother would be so pleased, to see my name associated with such a good cause, I mean."

Cinnamon laughed.

"Honey, Estelle Fagelman is pleased to see your name appear in the telephone book. In fact, she's pleased about anything having to do with you."

I looked at Nick at the mention of Estelle Fagelman's name. His expression hadn't changed.

"She's been terrif through all this," Alison said, alluding to Michael's death. "She would've been at the funeral with the flu if I hadn't insisted she stay home."

"It was, like, terrible," Cinnamon added, "Alison was all alone when it happened. I still feel guilty about having been in New York, but how was I to know that, well, you know. You see, I'd never been east of West Covina in my life and I had no idea how, like, wonderful New York could be . . . the theaters, the restaurants . . . even the Statue of Liberty."

"Of course," Nick attempted to stop her at the pass.

"Anyway, I'm just glad I was able to make it in, the morning of the funeral," she finished.

"I'd have collapsed totally if it weren't for Cinnamon and Aunt Estelle," Alison said, adjusting the comb in her hair. It was decorated with sea shells and coral; I told her how much I admired it.

"Thanks, but it's not mine," she said sadly, as though everything in the world was only on loan to her. "I just borrowed it from Cinnamon and forgot to return it. Here Cin," she said, removing it from her hair.

"Keep it, sweetie, it looks better on you than on me anyway," Cinnamon laughed, excusing herself to check on the tea she was brewing.

"Say, why don't you guys come to our place for dinner? Nothing fancy, stir-fried veggies and rice probably," Alison suggested when Cinnamon had left the room.

I thought I saw Nick turn green.

"Uh, no thanks, it sounds delish, but we've made plans," I said diplomatically.

"That's too bad." Alison sounded genuinely disappointed.

"Yes, it is," I agreed, "but I did promise to see Tracy later this afternoon."

She blanched somewhat, as I'd hoped she would.

"You're going to see Tracy?"

"Yes, well, Tracy's expressed an interest in reading a screenplay Nick's written."

I watched Nick swallow his Trident sugarless.

"I didn't know you were a screenwriter," Alison said to Nick.

"Yeah, well diversification . . . it's the name of the game."

"Well, Tracy's a great actress, all right," Alison admitted. "She can do wonders for mediocre material. Oh, excuse me, that's not a reflection on your writing, of course."

"Sure thing," Nick said.

"Well, good luck with it." She shrugged.

We thanked her as Cinnamon entered with two teapots and four cups.

"Good news," she announced happily, "we've a choice of Chamomile Mint or Poppy Herb."

One would have thought people nowadays had never heard of Lipton.

Nick and I left Palos Verdes at one-thirty and drove into LA for lunch. We hadn't counted on the fact that many restaurants are closed on Mondays.

With limited options we drove through a Jack-in-the-Box, where Nick threatened to knock the block off of an arrogant clown.

Before heading out to Tracy's we stopped at the Holiday Inn where Nick was staying, so that he could check for messages, of which there were none.

I assumed Nick was going to invite me up to his room. I'm glad to say I was wrong; I wasn't prepared for that, yet.

Laurel Canyon is an area heavily populated by show-biz folk. Actresses and actors in particular. Its real-estate value is at a peak despite the threat of mudslides, floods, and brush fires, which just goes to prove that status is a stronger motivation than survival.

We arrived at Tracy's just a little before four.

That the door was slightly ajar didn't arouse my suspicions. Tracy was a free spirit, her life-style informal. She moved with the flow.

The stench of Joy when we entered, overwhelmed us.

"Smells like a whorehouse," Nick commented.

"Tracy?" I called out. "Tracy, it's Susan. Your door was open so I . . ." I began to explain, before I realized the house was empty.

"I'll check the bedroom," I told Nick.

The bedroom was a collage of silk and satin in shades of dusty rose. Tracy's bed was unmade and a lounge dress was lying on the floor.

Her vanity, with its light-bulb-bordered mirror, was out of a '30's movie; indeed it had very likely been a prop in one. The table was neatly set, with the exception of a broken bottle of Joy, whose contents had dripped onto and had been absorbed by the carpet below.

"Susan, Susan c'mon down!"

The tone of Nick's voice prepared me somewhat for what was to come.

I ran down the stairs and followed him to the backyard. A wave of nausea overcame me as I approached the large heart-shaped pool.

Floating atop was the nude body of Tracy Simms, exquisite under the glimmering sun. I knew in an instant she was dead, and two words reverberated through my head. Love kills.

✂ 12 ✂

*Life is a jigsaw puzzle with most of the pieces
missing.*

Anonymous

TRACY SIMMS DEAD AT THIRTY-TWO. ACTRESS'S NUDE BODY
FOUND AFLOAT IN POOL! SEX-SYMBOL TAKES HER OWN LIFE.

The newspaper headlines screamed, while the eleven
o'clock news noted the death with promises of further details
as they came in.

And just what were the details?

That all depended on one's perspective.

Almost immediately after discovering her body, Nick
phoned Bucky and quickly explained our predicament.

Though Bucky favored going to the authorities with our
suppositions, he understood our desire to keep a low profile
for the time being.

Bucky met us at Tracy's house and agreed to phone the
police once we'd left, telling them it was he who had discovered the body when he arrived to interview Tracy Simms
for a series of articles he was writing.

I'm not certain that what we did was legal, much less
ethical; we didn't give it much thought at the time.

And so it happened that Bucky, basking in his glory,
came to write his exclusive—if somewhat fabricated—piece
entitled, "I Walked in on Death."

The article purposefully was more fluff than substance.
Rather than dwell on the curious details of the death itself,
Bucky approached the story from the standpoint of a beau-

tiful actress's swan song. He left out Nick's speculations, and dealt with Tracy's demise exactly as did the police. Traces of vodka and Quāāludes were found in a goblet by the pool alongside of the empty bottle, which was still where we had left it.

On the basis of Tracy's psychiatric history and her recent signs of instability brought on by grief over her ex-husband's sudden death, it was assumed that Tracy had taken her own life.

And while the coroner went through perfunctory procedures, any other cause of death was either not considered or immediately dismissed.

As for Nick and myself, we waited until Bucky arrived, then got into cousin Freddie's "baby" and sped down Laurel Canyon, headed for the seclusion of Mulholland Drive. We needed time to collect ourselves. To sort our thoughts.

"You know when this rigmarole began, I didn't really believe it," Nick confessed.

"What didn't you believe? That Michael was murdered?"

"I didn't believe any of it. The shower, the suspects. Well, let's just say I only half believed it, okay?"

"You . . . ? But then why . . . ?"

"To get to know a beautiful, vulnerable young lady."

"I see. And now? Now, what makes you so sure it's all real? Tracy's death?"

"Oh that, and Reeper's subterfuge, Jean Paul's threat, the ominous message on your phone machine, and the fact that at this very moment our car is out of control."

"What?" I'd realized Nick was taking the canyon very fast, but I'd put that down to impatience, nerves, or just habit.

I looked at the speedometer. We were doing 45 on a 25-mph road.

"Well slow down!" I ordered.

"I'd love to, but my emergency brakes are gone. What

do you want me to do? Throw my foot out the door like an anchor?" he shouted.

I watched the speedometer climb from 45 to 55 . . .

To 70 mph!

Nick shifted the car into neutral. The stick shift rolled around in his hand like a Popsicle.

"Beautiful! They screwed around with the clutch too, son of a bitch!"

Evidentally, this ambiguous "they" to whom he referred were eager to have Nick and me reduced to blood and bones.

As the speedometer tipped 95, I heard Nick mumbling what sounded like the rote incantations of a long-forgotten rosary. Funny, the crutches one reverts to in times of crisis.

For myself, "mommy" was sufficient.

"Nick, do something!" I screamed, covering his eyes with my hands.

"Keep that up, Susan, and I'll do something all right. I'll crash!"

Papers and leaves smacked the windshield as houses, trees, and people whizzed by in a kaleidoscopic blur. A squirrel made a beeline for the nearest tree.

Nick kept his hand on the horn all the while. Fortunately, there were no cars in front of us.

We were quickly approaching the point at which Mulholland and Laurel meet. At a cliff!

"Hang on, baby," Nick said, throwing an arm across my body.

In one sharp turn he steered the car up onto an embankment of pussy willows and dandelions.

Everything stopped.

"You all right?" Nick asked, breathless, as he helped me from the car.

"I guess. I think I bumped my forehead but otherwise I'm okay. How about you?"

"I'm fine."

"Ah . . . ah . . . ah . . . choo!" I sneezed.

"*Gesundheit*," Nick said.

"Thank you."

For a moment, neither of us spoke.

"So?" Nick finally asked. "Did you see your life pass before you?"

"No, did you?"

"No. Only the estimated damage to Freddie's car," Nick replied.

I could tell his nerves were frayed.

"Are you sure someone tampered with it? I mean, couldn't something have snapped or burnt out? Like a fan belt or a valve?" I suggested, flaunting my automotive ignorance.

Nick gave me a patronizing look.

"Freddie's car was in A-1 shape when we got to Tracy's. No, someone cut the brake-fluid line and then jammed the clutch. Must've done it between the time we arrived and the time we left."

I rolled up my jeans and sat down on a huge rock.

"So, Tracy's "visitor" was still somewhere on the premises when we arrived, is that what you're saying?"

"Sure looks that way," Nick said, sitting down next to me. "Seems like someone's a little pissed off at us, wouldn't you say?"

"Does this mean we bring the whole business to the nearest police station or do we continue making like Bogie and Bacall?"

"Honey, believe it or not, we don't have anything tangible to bring to anyone. No, let's go on as planned, that is, if you still want to?"

He looked at me questioningly.

"I still want to," I assured him, as I closed my eyes and blew at a dandelion until it was naked in my hand.

"I'm glad. Because . . . what are you doing, Susan?"

"Making a wish on a dandelion."

"What'd you wish for?"

"Another ten years, at least."

❈ ⟨ 13 ⟩ ❈

The greatest love is a mother's; then comes a dog's; then comes a sweetheart's.

A Polish proverb

"A *micheya*!!" Mrs. Fagelman declared as she smacked her lips over the herring in cream sauce. "Det means . . . ," she began to explain to me.

"I know what that means, it means it's too wonderful for words. I'm Jewish, Mrs. Fagelman."

"You don't say! Call me Estelle. I vas sure you vas a *shiksa*."

Mrs. Fagelman's pronunciation of certain vowels and consonents would have reduced Henry Higgins to tears.

"With a name like Finkelstein?" I proposed.

"Name, shmame, I tought it vas your husband's name anyvays. Nice lookin' fella, your husband."

Estelle Fagelman and I were standing in the kitchen of her apartment, which was in Fairfax, a predominantly Jewish section of Los Angeles. I was helping her prepare the food that was to be served to guests attending her Tupperware party.

Meanwhile, Nick sat in the living room, passing the time with a half-dozen ladies and one gentleman whose cumulative ages must have added up to over four hundred.

"He's not Jewish, he's Italian," I responded. "And, uh, he's not my husband."

"No? Vell vot are you vaiting for dollink? Snow in July? Vot's a metter? He's merried?"

She didn't wait for an answer.

103

" 'Cause I'll tell you straight off d'bet, det kind of henky-penky I don't go for. End I know from vhere I speak."

She put down a platter of cold cuts, and taking my hand, sighed.

With a certain degree of relish, Mrs. Fagelman took me into her confidence, describing her forty-two year marriage to Ben Fagelman. According to Estelle, Ben was a charming and handsome jeweler whose roving eye was attracted to more than mere diamonds. He ultimately bought himself a toupee and shortly thereafter took up with a forty-year-old divorcee, a "bleached-blond-who-hah" were Estelle's exact words. After snipping Ben's face out of every photograph in the house, Estelle went on with her life and eventually met Harry Singer, a retired merchant marine who worshipped the very ground on which she walked. It seemed they were now companions for life.

"So! Enough about me. Tell me about yourself. How did you say you met my Elison? You'll excuse me if I forget tings. I'm older den I look. Vould you believe det when I vas your age I vas a regular beauty?" she asked.

I looked at the small woman before me dressed in a bright crimson dress. Chains of American Indian silver and turquoise hung from her neck and around her tiny wrist she wore a copper bracelet, presumably to ease her arthritis.

Her complexion brought to mind rose petals and ivory; it was remarkably free of wrinkles for a woman her age. Soft emerald eye shadow highlighted her deeply set, pale, blue eyes. Her carefully applied red lipstick and styled silver-blue hair convinced me that Estelle Fagelman was still proud of her good looks. And beyond her looks was a homey earthiness, a "*haimishness*" if you will.

No, it wasn't at all difficult to imagine her the heartthrob she claimed to be so many years ago.

"So anyvays, ve were talkin' about Elison," she reminded me.

"Actually, I haven't known Alison all that long a time," I admitted, quickly adding, "but I do know she's a very sweet girl."

"Elison." Mrs. Fagelman's face lit up at the mere mention of her goddaughter's name. "A little bird, det's my Elison."

The door opened, and Harry poked his head inside. He was a huge man, with a round, full face.

"Nu, Essie? What's taking so long?"

Handing him a bowl of onion dip and a plate of miniature knishes, she said, "Hold on to your horse, Herry. Ve'll be right out. Meanvhile, take this nosh, nobody should starve."

Harry smiled at her and pinched her cheek lovingly before walking out. It was obvious to me that to Harry Singer, the sun rose and set by Estelle.

"Vhere vas I?" Estelle asked when Harry had left the room. "Oh, yes, Elison. She's delicate like a feather, my Elison, same as her mother. End almost as gorgeous, in a different vay, of course."

That Alison's mother was a beauty didn't surprise me. That she was an actress did.

"Mind you," Estelle went on, "she vas no star like Carole Lombard or Hedy Lamarr, but like I say, she vas gorgeous. Unfortunately, she couldn't ect for baked beans.

"I remember she lived upstairs from us vhen Ben end me vas yet in Hollywood. She'd left her husband in New Mexico end came vit her little boy to make a movie star out of herself. Said she studied et some big ecting school, but I knew vhat a *bubbamysa* det vas!"

At this, Estelle shook her head and clucked knowingly.

"So, Charlene vould go trotting out to d'agents, end to d'drectors, end to any *schmegeggi* who'd look, she'd lift her skoits end God knows vhat for a chance to be seen two seconds in a movie. Disgustink!"

Then she softened.

"But who's to judge, I esk you. Should I keep my brother?"

"Who watched her son while Mrs. Cole was being, uh, interviewed?" I asked.

"Who?!" Estelle admonished. "Who else? Me. I vas home most of d'time, so naturally I felt it vas only right to help out vit d'child if I could. No?"

"Yes."

"Sure. So I looked after Mickey, det's Alison's brother. You knew him?"

"A little."

"Terrible."

"I know," I agreed. "It was a terrible way to die."

"No. I meant he vas a terrible person. He vasn't a *mench*, if you cetch my meaning. Even vhen he vas a small boy he did such horrible tings, I'm tellin' you! He'd take a metch, make a fire, end burn d'vings off d'flies vhen I didn't vatch. Vonce, he took a rock end crushed d'head of a sparrow. I said, 'Mickey, Mickey, vhy vould you vant to do such a ting?' End you know vhat he said? He said, 'Because, Mrs. Fagelman. Because I got tired of listening to it sing.' Did you ever?

"Mickey vas no good 'til d'day he died." She shook her head, bitterly. "He and Elison vas like night end day.

"I cen still recall vhen his mother came beck von day end announced out of d'blue skies, she's going to heve a baby. Just like det. A nice how-do-you-do det vas. No husband, not even so much as a vedding bend. Only in Hollywood vould you be so bold at det time."

"So Michael was actually Alison's half brother," I remarked.

"Vhat? Oh yeah, sure, I suppose. A regular doll she vas in d'hospital. You never seen such a baby. Everyone who saw her loved her. Doctors . . . noyces . . ."

"And Michael, what about him? Did he love Alison too?" I asked.

Estelle looked out of the window. She was lightyears away.

"Love. Dere's a good von. A no-goodnik like him knew from love? You should excuse me, but dis man's love vas betveen his legs, if you cetch my meaning.

"Look who he married, a *tzozkalah* like his mother; dey desoived von anotter. End den ven even she valked avay from him, he had d'noive to esk my Elison to move in vit him."

"Why hadn't he asked her before?" I asked.

"Hah, because d'*tzozkalah* didn't vant it. But now he vanted Elison should move in, 'so I can take care of her' he said. End Elison believed him, like she vas under his spell.

"Imagine! Vit d'orgies end d'*mishagas* in his life! I svear to God he had vallpaper pasted up all over d'kitchen of naked people doing, vell, you can imagine vhat dey vere doing! He vanted en angel like my Elison to move in end live d'life her mother, she should rest in peace, lived? God forbid!" she exclaimed, spitting three times.

"Did you tell Michael how you felt?"

I thought she looked at me differently, carefully as she responded.

"On det very day of d'eccident I told him. I vent to him in his shop. It vas d'foist time ve saw von anotter in years, so I made an appointment, anyvays I needed a touch-up," she said matter-of-factly, fluffing her hair.

"To tell you d'true, I vas even surprised he vas villing to take me, but I guess he did it for Elison's sake, he knew how much she loves me. So, ve didn't talk much at foist, end den, during my comb-out I pleaded vit him. I said, 'Please. For vonce in your life, Mickey, be a *mench*. If you love her, really love her, don't ask her to move in vit you.' But he just laughed. Det's vhen I spit in his face and valked out; I didn't even leave a tip. I'm tellin' you, I vas sick vit eggrivation."

"But she never did move in," I pointed out.

Estelle's face relaxed noticably.

"No, she never did. Mickey ... Michael, he vas dead. It vas all over ... all over." Her voice trailed off. I noticed that her eyes teared up as she spoke. "The spell of det Svengali, it vas broken."

"Well it was good you were there for Alison when it happened," I said.

"Yeah, vell, look at me," she said, suddenly cheerful. "D'company is vaitink to eat, and I'm standing around biting your ears off."

I picked up a plate of pickled tomatoes and followed her through the louver doors. I must say, I regarded Estelle Fagelman in an entirely new light.

✂ 14 ✂

*There is not much harm in a lion; he has no ideals,
no religion, no politics, no chivalry, no gentility.*

George Bernard Shaw

It was overcast the following morning, as Nick and I sat in
the The Bistro Gardens awaiting the arrival of Jean Paul,
with whom we'd arranged a lunchtime rendezvous.

"Will you be ordering drinks just yet?" asked a cute little
ashen-haired waitress.

"Just Perrier with a lime twist will be fine for me," I
answered.

Nick ordered a Scotch rocks and turned to watch our
waitress walk toward the bar to place our order.

"If you're not careful," I advised, "you'll get whiplash."

"Just looking," he said. "I guess I inherited my uncle
Mario's taste for good-looking women."

"Your uncle Mario? The proponent of matrimonial bliss?"

"Ahh, but uncle Mario only became so in his later years,
when he had time to reflect. Judging from all the stories
I'd heard about him when I was growing up, he was quite
a blade in his youth. In fact, I remember there was one
thing he used to say in his defense all the time."

"And pray, what would that be?"

"He used to say—and he believed this sincerely—he
used to say, 'I don't like to cheat as a habit; then again, I
don't like to chew gum as a habit neither, but every now
and then I get the urge for a little piece!'"

"Your uncle's a real Will Rogers, huh? Phenomenal insight and profundity." I laughed.

109

"Something which you'll notice I, too, inherited. And if you're thinking that my thinking's like my uncle's, let me assure you, I know a good thing when I find it."

He took my hand and smiled. "Have I found it, Susan?"

"You forget, for all practical purposes, I'm married. Or at least committed, more or less," I dodged.

"More less than more."

"Please, Nick. Can we drop it for now? We've had an unbelievable time together and you've been terrific about not pushing me, emotionally or otherwise. Don't push me now. I need time to think. I owe Marc that much, don't I?"

"Yeah. Sure."

He dropped my hand, and my stomach dropped along with it. I hoped I hadn't said anything I'd regret later. I was relieved when he picked my hand up again.

"Hey, sweetheart, it's all right. Really. As Estelle Fagelman would put it, you can't be expected to dance at two weddings with one *tukas*," he said lightly.

"That's pronounced *tuch-us*, and thanks for understanding. Incidentally, I've been thinking of Estelle. I was wondering if we shouldn't discount her as a suspect. After all..."

Before I could continue we were joined by Jean Paul Altereit.

By definition, what is a dandy?

To me a dandy is an immaculately dressed gentleman, quick-minded, dapper. A man whose superiority over the rest of us mortal beings is unchallenged. The late actor George Sanders epitomized and glorified the ultimate dandy, and that morning the perennial dandy is exactly what Jean Paul brought to mind.

He wore an Armani three-piece khaki-colored suit, with a red pin-striped handkerchief neatly tucked in his pocket. A thick gold chain hung around his neck, and his shoes were Pierre Cardin's casual chic.

His hair, needless to say, was elegantly styled and in one ear was a small, gold moon-shaped stud.

Jean Paul had come a long way from that bakery in the Bronx.

We didn't waste much time in ordering; in fact, we got to the point almost immediately.

Jean Paul was the first of our suspects for whom Nick and I had agreed to lay our cards on the table, or some of our cards at any rate.

"Look 'ere," Jean Paul said, "I'm a beezy man. I come 'ere only because you tell me on zee telephone zat something about Michael's death, oh, how shall I say? Eet smells, *oui*?"

"*Oui*. That's right, Jean Paul," I said. "You see my friend here, Monsieur Comici, Nick, and myself feel that . . . well, based on certain factors, that is, we feel that Michael's death may not have been an accident."

"We think he was murdered," Nick stated bluntly.

"Murder?" Jean Paul shouted. Then, aware of the looks he was getting, he lowered his voice. "But zeez ees absurd. Really!"

He looked sideways at me as he spoke with Nick.

"I don't know what your interest ees in my former associate, but I believe mademoiselle 'ere 'as, oh, let 'er fancy get zee better of 'er?"

"I assure you, Jean Paul, we're talking of more than mere fancy," I said in haughty fashion.

"But why? Why would someone want to murder Michael?"

"We were hoping you could enlighten us," Nick suggested.

"*Moi*? But I don't see 'ow I could be of 'elp to you."

I recalled Jean Paul speaking with Tracy at some point during Michael's funeral service.

"Suppose you tell us what your relationship was toward Michael's ex-wife," I suggested.

"Toward Tracy?" Jean Paul's belly shook like jellied consommé beneath his vest, as he let out a resonant laugh.

"Ah yes, I see your train of thought, but I tell you truthfully, eet was for Michael zee romantic entanglements, zee leetle amours. As for me, I am basically zee man of beezness."

"And with Michael working at your salon, you'd done very well in business, isn't that so, Jean Paul?" I asked.

"Ahh, my dear, yes, I admeet eet. Michael, 'e was very good for zee beezness. Very good. Zee ladies een particular, shall we say, zey liked 'ees touch," Jean Paul conceded.

"Your losing Michael's services, would you consider that a big blow to your business?" Nick asked.

"Not really. Zee same people who came to Jean Paul's Salon before Michael's death, zey continue to come to Jean Paul's, no? Zat ees because zey know zat Jean Paul's, eet ees seenonemous with excellence," he bragged. "So you see, your 'ypothesees, eet ees incorrect. Zee beezness, eet continues to flourish, no matter whether Michael, 'e ees dead or alive!"

"Maybe," Nick said, "but when I was talking about losing Michael's services, I didn't mean through his death. I meant through the possibility of his opening his own salon and obviously taking his rather large following with him. That'd have been kind of leaving you holding the short end of the stick, wouldn't it?"

Nick removed a certificate from his pocket.

"And if he were actually planning to go out on his own," Nick went on to say, "as this business license taken out by Cole only a week before his death would lead us to believe, well, one might conclude that so far as you're concerned, Cole's death was timely, to say the least."

I'm not certain who was more shocked at Nick's ace in the hole, Jean Paul or me.

Jean Paul didn't respond immediately. Instead, he cooly reached for his pack of Gauloises.

"Smoke?" he said, offering the pack to Nick and myself.

I declined. Nick reached for his Luckys instead.

Jean Paul removed an unusual tortoise-shell lighter and took his time lighting a cigarette. Then he inhaled deeply before speaking, a somewhat melodramatic gesture, but what the hell, we're all guilty of theatrics now and then.

"I was afraid all this would come out when you began to ask questions about things that didn't concern you. I knew it the day I saw you in my shop," he said, pointing at me. "I thought to myself, that girl is a *yenta*."

I wanted to advise Jean Paul that his accent was slipping, but I held my tongue and allowed him to continue.

"Look, I'll level with you. Sure, I had an ax to grind with Cole. I had a lot of reasons for wanting to see that son of a bitch burn. Personal reasons as well as business reasons. I didn't like what he did to people. Brought them to the point of . . ." He didn't finish the sentence.

"And you're right, I was plenty pissed at him for wanting to open his own salon, not that it hasn't happened before. Lots of operators go out on their own, some make it, plenty don't. Not everyone's Jon Peter, you know."

"You were saying? About Michael?" I reminded him.

"Oh, right. So he wanted to open his own shop. I told him things were pretty bad for me just then. I have some debts, you see. Well, anyway, I asked him—*asked* the bastard, mind you—if he'd hold off on his own shop for another six months. Just 'til I got back on my feet again, you understand. He could afford it.

"But you know what that little fucker says to me? To me, the guy who took him in straight out of some fly-by-night beauty school in Van Nuys, he says, 'Why bother?

Once I open my salon yours will be as good as dead anyway.'

"Son of a bitch! I love that shop; it's my life. If he was murdered . . . and I'm not saying he was . . . but if he was, he had it coming to him. And I'm not the only one who felt that way, I'll tell you that much," Jean Paul said, stomping out his cigarette.

"As long as you've told us that much, why not tell us a little more?" Nick suggested.

"All right. You wanna start pointing fingers, I'd start with the person who had the most to benefit from Michael's death."

"And who would that be?" I asked.

"Don't tell me you don't know?" Jean Paul laughed. "Why his baby sister, that's who. She was the sole beneficiary of his life insurance policy. And he was insured for a few grand, he told me so himself. Now I'm not saying the kid did it, I only met her once and she seemed okay. But as long as you're pointing fingers . . . As for me, I was nowhere near Michael's place when he died."

"You weren't?" I prodded.

"No, I wasn't." He didn't elaborate and we didn't pursue it.

Our waitress came by shortly with our bill, which Jean Paul grabbed immediately.

"Eet ees on me," he insisted.

In return for his generosity, Nick and I tacitly agreed to overlook Jean Paul's brief and unconscious lapse into Bronxese.

Once more the gentleman, he excused himself politely to return to work.

"Eef I can be of further assistance, or should you learn anything more, please let us be in touch. *Au revoir.*"

With that he shook Nick's hand and kissed my own.

Jean Paul's exit would have done the consummate dandy proud, were it not for the fact that a dinner napkin had attached itself to the sole of his left shoe.

❧ ⟨ 15 ⟩ ❧

*Darwinian man, though well behaved, at best is
only a monkey shaved.*

W. S. Gilbert

"Great pancakes, Sue," Marc said on one rare Saturday
morning we had occasion to be eating breakfast together.

Marc and I were both making a concerted effort to be
kinder, or at least more civilized toward one another, than
we'd been in weeks.

In this spirit I had gone all out with breakfast that morning.

Crenshaw melon filled with fresh strawberries, link sausages, pancakes topped with powdered sugar and loganberry
preserves. Even the coffee was better than usual.

"Thanks," I said. "Plenty more where that came from."

"I'd better not," Marc said as he exhaled deeply. "I'll
have to jog an extra five miles tomorrow as is."

"For what it's worth, I think you've been looking rather
good lately," I told him, and meant it. "Didn't those jeans
used to be tight on you?"

"I don't know. I guess I may've lost a few pounds at
that," he admitted, embarrassed, I thought, because it was
so long since he and I had exchanged pleasantries.

"So. I suppose work agrees with you. How's that project
of yours coming along?" I asked.

"Fine," he said, bending down to pick up his napkin.
"We had been hitting a few snags, so if I've been a little
short-tempered lately . . ."

"Oh, that's all right," I assured him graciously, feeling

116

guilty about my own priorities lately. "We all have our days."

"What've you been up to lately?" Marc asked while leafing through the sports section.

"Nothing much," I replied.

Some instinct told me that it was better not to bring up Michael Cole. Or Tupperware. Or Nick.

"Working on another Kelly epic," I added.

"That's nice," said Marc, pleased that I'd given him the response he wanted to hear.

And so passed the morning.

No battles.

No recriminations.

No nothing.

Later that same morning Marc invited me to go horseback riding, an activity he knew left me cold. I declined, politely, explaining I was going to a Tupperware party that afternoon. I told him he was more than welcome to join me, knowing full well he wouldn't.

And so with care and courtesy, two modern, well-adjusted people adroitly managed to avoid spending a full day in each other's company.

I wasn't actually lying to Marc about the Tupperware. I merely neglected to say that I was not only going to, but giving the party as well. Truthfully, I had been scrupulous in giving my share of Tupperware parties, not wanting to disappoint Mitzi.

On this particular Saturday I was hostessing a Tupperware luncheon in Bel Air for fourteen Japanese businessmen. Having sold more than a thousand dollars' worth of Tupperware in less than two hours, I thanked them profusely, graciously expressing my heartfelt *arigatos* as I left to meet Nick in Westwood Village.

Nick had phoned me earlier, suggesting that we meet at

about two and take in some window shopping. As it turned out the man had more than windows in mind as his purchases included jeans, sweaters, shoes, and several pairs of argyle socks.

"Thinking of staying out here a while?" I asked.

"You never know."

We stopped at an Israeli falafel stand and ate and talked before shopping some more. Over my objections Nick bought me a pair of crimson sunglasses, a bikini, and a Panama hat.

We arrived at my home at 5:30 with three full shopping bags, tired, but content. Thankfully, Marc wasn't home; my time alone with Nick was becoming more precious by the minute.

"So where do you think Rosenbloom fits into all of this?" Nick asked out of the blue. It was the first time that afternoon we had talked about anything remotely related to Michael Cole. "I haven't the slightest idea," I admitted.

"Well, what would you think about giving the old boy a ring. Tell him how impressed you were with him. You know, flatter the guy if you think you can get something out of him," Nick suggested.

Why not, I thought. After all, a little "shuck and jive" might go a long way.

Nick and I weaved through traffic in Hollywood later that night, and as we approached our destination I found myself feeling apprehensive.

"Uh, I don't know about this, Nick."

"Not starting to get cold feet are you?"

"No, it's just, well what if Marc were to find out where I went this evening?"

"What if he were? Anyway, did you or did you not leave him a note telling him you were with Stephanie?"

"Yes, but..."

"All right then, she'll cover for you, won't she?"

"Yes, but Nick, it's so deceptive."

"It's for his own good. He wouldn't love to learn you were here, would he?"

"No, but still . . ."

"Don't worry so much. I heard it's bad for the sinuses."

"But what about Rosenbloom, or his guests?"

"In the first place, chances of your knowing any of Rosenbloom's guests are slim. In the second place, I can guarantee they'd be too wasted to ever recall having met you. And as for Rosenbloom himself, I strongly doubt that he would be foolish enough to tell Marc that he's invited you here this evening."

Feeling only slightly reassured, I walked out of Freddie's newly repaired car, holding on to Nick's arm as we left the parking lot.

"I wonder if they have postcards inside?" I asked Nick.

"Planning to drop a line to your mother? 'Having a wonderful time, wish you were here.' Something like that?"

I laughed at the thought of my mother receiving a card from Hollywood's one and only "Paradise Playground— An Adventure in Sensual Delights and Fantasy."

Paradise Playground was a rather new sort of "club" in LA. It had sprung up just about the time Plato's Retreat closed down, supposedly due to a zoning ordinance.

Like Plato's, Paradise Playground catered to one's erotic whims and sensual desires. Couples reportedly walked about nude or seminude, doing unmentionable things to one another behind closed or semiclosed doors. There were two major differences between Paradise and Plato's. For one thing, Plato's had barred any sort of alcoholic beverage, preferring natural juices and nectars, whereas Paradise permitted an assortment of imported wines and beers to be served on the premises.

Then too, Plato's policy on club membership was exceedingly liberal compared to Paradise's insistence on a more selective, almost exclusive clientele.

My first impression of Paradise Playground was that I'd walked onto a movie set. The tropical motif was authenticated by palm trees and by the calming roar of numerous waterfalls.

Along the entire west wall an intricate mural depicted Adam and Eve sharing an apple, and bliss, in the Garden of Eden.

Facing us directly was a huge, winding staircase, not unlike that upon which Rhett Butler had carried his Scarlett. I wondered just how many women had been carried up this particular staircase and if any had voiced a fraction of Scarlett's reluctance. Not likely. Were *Gone with the Wind* written today, Scarlett would be trying to reach multiple orgasms while Rhett made his way to Canada to avoid the draft.

"Does this bother you?" Nick asked.

"Does *what* bother me?" I asked, coolly, as I watched men and women partially draped in towels, walking hand in hand into different rooms.

"C'mon," Nick said, smiling, "let's have a look around before we join Rosenbloom and friends."

I noticed immediately that we were being scrutinized, and it dawned on me with a sense of irony that it was due to our being fully clothed. I said as much to Nick.

"Well, I'm all for shedding these duds and rompin' in the buff," Nick offered, beginning to unbutton his shirt.

"Not here," I whispered. "Maybe they supply, uh, robes or something."

We hurried downstairs to the locker area, where both sexes, in various stages of undress, were supplied with bath towels.

"Sorry, no robes," the attendant smirked.

We found a rather secluded area and Nick began to undress. Sensing my discomfort he stopped.

"Say, Gypsy Rose, I'll meet you at the top of the stairs when you're ready, okay?" he sighed.

"Okay," I agreed, relieved though curious just how I was going to make it through the remainder of the evening. As I disrobed, I remembered my phone conversation with Rosenbloom and my initial reaction to his invitation for us to join him in celebrating a great literary coup on the part of his agency. I was excited at the prospect of Nick meeting Meyer, anxious to know his impression of the man. It wasn't until I had already accepted that Meyer told me where the party was to be held.

I carefully tied a knot over my breasts and, as it occurred to me that without a purse or pocket I couldn't carry so much as a lipstick, I gave myself a quick once-over in the mirror, then left to join Nick.

I didn't see him at once, and while I surveyed the rooms for him, I found myself approached by no less than four men in the span of six minutes.

A young Peruvian with horrendous body odor propositioned me in broken English, on behalf of his giggling wife. I told him I wasn't into making it with other women, whereupon he proceeded to proposition me on his own behalf.

Explaining that I had a thing about admitting foreign objects into my body, I quickly moved on.

I spotted Nick conversing, chummily, with two nude women. One, a platinum blond—obviously out of a bottle, judging from her ebony-colored pubic hair—was rather petite, with disproportionately stupendous breasts that swung like knockwurst in a butcher's shop when she laughed. Nick seemed to be supplying her with a steady stream of quips that kept her laughing.

The other woman I figured to be in her late forties. Though her blond hair was undoubtedly out of a bottle as well, she had cleverly had what was at one time referred to as a "cuff and collar job." Her breasts sagged only slightly, and she had a terrific pair of legs. Noticing her stretch marks, I wondered if her children knew where their mother was that evening.

I walked over to where Nick and his buddies stood.

"Hi, guy, what's up?" I asked casually, eyeing the bulge beneath his towel.

"Ah . . . June . . . Shirl . . . this is Susan."

June, the petite blond, was friendly enough, but certainly not nearly as friendly as Shirl, who tossed her arm around my shoulder and gently stroked my arm with her fingertips. I began to feel uncomfortable. And guilty about the pleasure I was deriving from her touch.

Nick must have picked up what I was feeling.

"Ah, I think Susan and I are going to have a look around before joining our friend," he explained, taking my hand.

"Catch you later, doll," said Shirl in a cigarette-and-whiskey voice, as she smiled at me.

"Sure thing," I replied.

"Having fun?" I asked Nick when we were relatively alone.

"It's different." He grinned. "C'mon, I want to show you the place before we join Rosenbloom and the others."

We stopped in front of a curtain-veiled room.

"What's in here?" I asked, suspiciously.

"Groupies."

"What?"

"Just boys and girls together, as the song goes."

"Ahh-hmm. Look, Nicky-boy, I don't think I want to watch. I'd feel like a common Peeping Tom."

"C'mon Susan," Nick urged. "There's nothing common about you."

I entered the red-lit room reluctantly.

There, on a half-dozen strategically placed mattresses, were masses of flesh linked together like sausages.

"Everyone here must work out at Jane Fonda's exercise class," I whispered to Nick.

"Get a load of that," Nick said, indicating a frizzy-haired girl, who, while being penetrated anally, was giving head to a man whose member was the size of a large zucchini. He, in turn, was sucking the breasts of a black woman who writhed with pleasure as she nibbled at the fleshy cheeks of the man penetrating the frizzy-haired girl. As my aunt Bea would say, "a good time was had by all."

"Isn't anyone afraid of catching a social disease?" I asked. "I mean like Herbie's or something?"

"Herpes."

"Right. Can we leave?" I asked. "I think I've seen enough."

"What? Oh, sure, kid, right away, something else, huh?"

"Wait, before we go any further, I must make a stop at the ladies' room," I said. "Please don't stray too far, I'll be right out."

The ladies' room offered all the amenities of home, and more. Combs, brushes, cosmetics, creams, hairsprays, blowers, even vaginal deodorants. There were five stall showers as well.

But what seemed to say it all was the water cooler, which had been filled with Scope mouthwash. I was about to laugh out loud, when I overheard a young lady sobbing to her friend.

"He promised he wouldn't leave my side all night, and I haven't seen him for the past hour!"

As her friends tried to comfort her with implausible rationales, the way friends will, I became overwhelmed with the pathos of the place.

"Ready?" Nick asked when I emerged.

"As I'll ever be. Lead the way," I said.

As it turned out, Rosenbloom's private party was held in a room labeled "Gomorrah." It was more lush than the others we'd passed through; almost like a scaled-down tropical jungle.

Rosenbloom's guests seemed to be enjoying themselves as they frolicked in or lolled alongside of one of the three Jacuzzis. Actually it was only one tremendous hot tub in the shape of a pretzel, so it seemed like three.

I spotted Rosenbloom almost immediately. He lay by the center tub, a towel and Felicia draped across his body.

"Susie, baby, glad you could make it. You remember Susie, Felicia?"

"What?" Glazed eyes looked out at me from hollow sockets. "Oh, yeah, for sure."

A casual glance at Felicia's body told me she took good care of it. Only two things surprised me. That she'd completely shaven off her pubic hair and even more surprising for a southern Californian, her body was stark white. Not even so much as a slight bikini mark.

"Meyer, I'd like you to meet a friend of mine, the writer I told you about, Nick Comici, Meyer S. Rosenbloom."

"So," Meyer said, "you're the guy who, you'll excuse the pun, is diggin' up all the dope on funerals?"

"I'm the guy. Say, Meyer, you mind if we sit down somewhere, you know, where we could talk?"

"Of course, of course," Rosenbloom said as he rose and tied the towel around his waist. Though short in stature, M. S. had a terrific body. Taut. Not an inch of fat on him.

"Felicia, be a good girl and bring us a pitcher of sangría, we'll be over at the table."

"Great place for a party," Nick said appreciatively, once we'd seated ourselves.

"Glad you like it," Meyer said, patting my knee. "You know, I'll tell you the truth, orgies aren't really my scene. Two broads at a time's my limit. But I can dig other folks gettin' into it, you know what I'm talkin' about? So, a client of ours writes a best-selling book . . . with incredible box-office potential, I might add . . . I figure, why not spring for a party and give the people what they want? I mean what the hell, it's deductible, right?"

"Right," I agreed.

"And I mean, let's face it," Meyer continued, "watching some of these young bodies rollin' around in the raw ain't too hard on the eyes, eh, Nicky? Say, you into girls or boys or both?"

"Girls." Nick laughed.

"What are you laughing? These days, you and me, we're in the minority," Meyer said.

"You must handle some lookers in your line of work," Nick observed.

"I do all right." Rosenbloom smirked immodestly.

"Yeah, Susan tells me Tracy Simms was one of your clients. She was some beauty all right. I ran into her at her ex-husband's funeral. Sorry to hear about her dying like that. So suddenly I mean," Nick said.

"I know what you mean; she had so much going for her. Matter of fact, we were coming close to closing a deal with her over at MGM. A remake of *Leave Her to Heaven*, with Tracy taking over where Tierney left off. Ah, I'm tellin' you . . . her flushin' it all down the toilet like that, throwin' it away the way she did," Meyer lamented.

Felicia placed the pitcher of sangría along with four frosty goblets on our table. Staring unabashedly at Nick, she was about to seat herself beside him when Meyer poured out a glass of sangría and handed it to her.

"Here you are, love. Why don't you take it into the sauna room; I'll be along in just a while," he said, flashing her a suggestive grin.

As flaky as Felicia was, she knew a dismissal when she

heard one. She looked away from Nick, and once again her eyes took on a glazed look.

"For sure," she said, pouting her blue-red lips. She turned to walk away.

Meyer couldn't resist smacking her bare bottom as she did so.

"Not much in the tits department, but she's got one fabulous ass, that Felicia has. Oh, excuse me, Susie," he added as an afterthought. "I hope I'm not offending you with my crass talk."

"Not at all; your language doesn't offend me, Meyer," I said.

"Glad to hear it," he replied.

Certainly no more than the rest of you, buddy.

"I find what you said before curious," Nick said.

"Oh, really? What was that?" Meyer asked casually.

"What you said about Tracy's having thrown it all away, implying that you've no doubt her death was suicide. Is that what you meant?"

Suddenly Meyer was on his guard. His eyes shifted back and forth as though he were watching a tennis match.

"I thought you were writing about funerals." He laughed nervously. "Why the questions about Tracy?"

Nick sighed. I had a hunch we were all in for another one of his bullshit explanations.

"I'll lay my cards on the table."

Nick's preamble to a lie.

"While it's true my initial purpose here in Los Angeles was to research material for my funeral piece," Nick explained, "I'd be lying if I told you that an inside scoop on Tracy Simms's death wouldn't be some feather in my cap."

"Ah, Mr. Comici, you've just restored my faith in man's deceptive nature. And I'd like to help you out. Really I would. Unfortunately, I'm as much in the dark about Tracy's death as you and Susie and your readers. I still can't get

over it. And why the hell did they have to cremate that
gorgeous body of hers?" he asked nobody in particular, as
he took a huge gulp of sangría.

"One thing I will say, and this is just my opinion, of
course." He paused before speaking and sipped his sangría
slowly this time. "Tracy's death was no accident."

"It wasn't?" I said.

"Nah, she had to have known what she was doing. I
don't know what was in her head, but she was far too smart
to let something like that happen without her meaning for
it to happen. Too smart," he repeated. "You know, there
was a chick with more than just looks. She had wit and
charm, when she wanted to use it. And a terrific business
sense. Yeah, she just had an uncanny gift for knowing what
was commercial and what wasn't. And she was usually
right. Tracy knew just what she wanted and how to set about
getting it. When it came to business ventures that is. Now
when it came to men, we're talkin' somethin' else again,
you know what I'm sayin'?"

I wasn't sure that I did.

"She made a habit of picking up strays—out-of-work
actors, struggling musicians, waiters writing the great
American novel—you know?"

"Where'd the hairdresser fit in?" Nick asked.

"Michael and Tracy were married before Tracy's name
became a household word, and before Cole had built such
a strong clientele. They really dug physical perfection, and,
well, hey, that's exactly what they found in each other,"
Meyer reflected.

"Hold on now," I said, "are you saying that they were
so narcissistic that they married mirror images of themselves?"

"Say, Susie, that's heavy. Real heavy. I think you just
hit the nail on the head, you know what I'm talkin' about?
That's not to say Tracy didn't love him. I think she did, at

least I think she thought she did. She was faithful to him at any rate, which is more than I can say for him, the prick."

"You didn't like Cole?" Nick asked.

Meyer answered softly, "Depends on your definition of like. I like pastrami, but it gives me gas. As for Cole, I admired his style. I admired his cool and his ability to get the chicks flocking to him the way they did. The guy had magnetism.

"On the other hand, I didn't dig what he did to people. Women especially. Cole was the kind of guy who'd as soon ruin a reputation . . . a dream . . . a life, as not."

"But for what possible gain?" I asked. "Money?"

"Oh, money, sure," Meyer agreed. "But also revenge, power, or usually just the pleasure he derived from seeing someone reduced to dust. I'm tellin' you, babe, Michael Cole was a prince among men."

"I gather his feelings towards you were mutual?" Nick ventured.

Again, the studied, careful response.

"I guess that would depend . . ."

"On what I meant by the word 'feelings'?"

Rosenbloom laughed and looked at me.

"I like this boy, Susie. He's sharp. Maybe you should think about trading in the Buick for the Ferrari, if you know what I'm talkin' about."

This time I knew exactly what he was talking about and that bothered me.

"I'll be straight with you, okay, Nicky? No. Tracy's ex didn't love me. Actually we got on fine until I encouraged Tracy to dump him. On the other hand, just 'cause we didn't love one another, didn't mean we hated each other either. There's no room for extreme emotions in this city. Today's enemy can easily be tomorrow's business associate, you dig?" he asked.

"Is that what you and Michael were to each other?" Nick asked. "Business associates?"

"That was only an example," Meyer snapped. Nick had hit a nerve and for the first time that evening, the conversation took a chilly turn.

We all sensed it.

"Hey, I'm sorry if I asked the wrong question," Nick apologized.

"It's cool," Meyer said, though it was anything but.

It was then that Meyer reached for a small gold case and opened it, smiling at me. He opened the case carefully, revealing a smooth layer of white powder.

"Know what this is, Susie?" Meyer teased.

"Sweet and Low?" I smiled back.

"She's beautiful," Meyer said to Nick. "Beautiful. Say, either of you care for a toot?"

"Uh, not for me, thanks," I said.

"Me neither, Meyer," Nick said, "but be my guest. I mean shoot, I don't give a hoot if *you* toot."

"Heh, heh." Meyer winked and closed his case. "Nah, I just thought you might, well, you know what I say, give the people what they want."

I wasn't sure, but I got the distinct impression Meyer was trying to bribe us.

"Anyway, I'm sorry I couldn't tell you more about Tracy," he continued in a more relaxed fashion. "I mean about how she died. Ah, that *was* what you were interested in, wasn't it, Nicky?"

Point scored for Rosenbloom. He didn't intimidate easily, which undoubtedly accounted for his success as an agent.

"Well, listen, Meyer, thanks for inviting us to your, uh, party," I said.

"Stick around, Susie baby, you too, Nick. At midnight we're going to have a former Dallas cheerleader pop out of a cake—fully clothed!"

As Meyer roared at his own wit, Nick eye-signaled me. It was time for us to leave.

Nick extended his hand.

"That's okay, Meyer, I gotta take Susie home before she turns into a pumpkin, or worse. So if it's all right with you, we'll just have a quick look around the rest of this place and then split."

"Suit yourselves." M. S. shrugged. "You're my guests, enjoy! And as for you, chickie-baby, you ever change your mind about doing commercials give me a ring, will ya? I'll get you goin'."

He winked at me.

"You'll be the first to know," I said honestly.

"Fabulous. You'll give my best to Marky now, won't you?" he leered, glancing in Nick's direction.

"Yes, of course I will," I replied.

With that, he smacked a big wet one on my lips; Nick and I turned and left the Amazon terrain behind us.

✄ 16 ✄

Oh ponder friend the porcupine; refresh your recollection,
And sit a moment to define his means of self protection
How amply armored he to fend the
fear of chase that haunts him
How well prepared
our little friend, and who the devil wants him!

Dorothy Parker

"C'mon, let's get our clothes and shove out of here," I said
once we were outside the door.

"Okay, okay. No rush," Nick said.

"I thought you said I'd turn into a pumpkin," I reminded
him.

"Yeah, well, it was one way of getting away from Rosenbloom."

"Terrific. But why hang around here any longer than we
have to? I don't get it."

"Oh, but you will," he said.

I was not at all prepared for Nick's sudden embrace. As
he kissed me, I felt a fleck of his tobacco on my lips.

It was no surprise that I sneezed, pushing Nick away as
I did.

"Wonderful," Nick sighed. "You must've caught cold
walking around half naked."

"No, it's not that," I explained. "It's just that I sneeze
when I'm in a tough spot. I always have."

"Uh-huh. And that's what I am to you, a tough spot?"

"Yes, now that you ask, that's what you are."

I felt my voice rising to an undignified squeak.

131

We were beginning to attract onlookers so Nick knocked on a door, and when no one answered, he opened it and pulled me in.

This was my first and only time in a mens' bathroom.

"I goddamn don't believe that after all we've been through together these past weeks, you find me threatening!" Nick said.

"Not you exactly," I said, looking at all the urinals that surrounded me. "And would you mind if we elevated this discussion by moving it elsewhere?"

"Me, the situation, what's the difference?" he said, totally ignoring my request. "I try to kiss her and what does she do? She sneezes! *Marone*!"

"Maybe she's allergic to you," a man chuckled from one of the stalls.

"I'm getting out of here," I said, walking out with Nick close behind me. I headed toward the lockers. He caught me by the elbow.

"All right. Hold it, hold it!" he said.

I stopped.

"I apologize if I threatened you. I just . . . I just wanted to kiss you so badly. I have for a while," he said sincerely.

"But here? In this of all places?" I said.

"You think with all the action going down in a place like this, anyone's gonna notice my kissing you?" he asked.

"It's not just the place," I said, playing with a strand of my hair.

"No? Then what else?"

"It's what would happen after the kiss," I said, taking a deep breath. "Look, I'll be frank with you."

"Be Susan with me."

"I'm serious."

"I'm sorry. Go on. You were being frank."

"Nick, face it. There's a lot of chemistry going on between us, a lot."

"I'll buy that," he agreed.

"And in a place like this, with private saunas and private rooms, well it's all so conducive to... to..."

"To making love? You're right. And at the very worst, we might have ended up making love to each other. Would that have been so very awful, Susan?" he asked.

"Yes. Yes it would have been. At least it would have been in a place called Paradise Playground."

"Oh? You mean to tell me if we were to drive down to my nice, respectable hotel room, where they supply clean sheets and a continental breakfast and all the privacy in the world, you mean to tell me then that would be all right? Is that what you're saying?" he challenged.

"Nick, I told you, the place is only a part of the problem."

"I thought so."

"For one thing, I don't have my diaphragm with me. Practical, but there it is!" I declared.

"Well, we could manage, you know. I'm ingenious when it comes to these things," Nick said.

"You're missing the point."

"No, I don't think I am," he said seriously.

"Try to understand what I'm saying, okay? I don't know how things are going to turn out between Marc and me, but my going to bed with you is just going to confuse the issue, for now at least," I said.

"That's right, Susan, dangle the carrot with promises of things to come," Nick said with more than a little bitterness.

"Nick."

"Hey, I don't want to confuse you. I guess I just thought that you were feeling the same way about me as I do about you. I must have misread the signals."

"You didn't. I suppose I'm just not into cheating," I responded feebly.

"And just what do you think you're doing now, baby?" Nick asked. "You're cheating yourself out of experiencing something very special with a man who . . . who cares a great deal about you."

I tried to hold back the tears but wasn't too successful.

"Then that's my loss, isn't it?" I managed to choke out.

"I guess it is," he said, turning from me. "C'mon, let's go get dressed. I'll take you home."

Neither of us spoke in the car going home. Nick, because of frustration, disappointment, or what have you. As for myself, I was afraid that if I tried to speak, the tears would flow without ceasing, so I kept silent as well.

Nick saw me to the door.

"Look, I'm gonna be lookin' into some things the next few days. Research, you could call it. I'll let you know what I come up with," he said coolly.

"You mean you'll still help me piece this puzzle together?" I was surprised.

"Sure." He shrugged. "No reason not to."

An awkward silence before he continued.

"Just that now I guess it'll be more business than pleasure, you know?"

"Nick?" I pleaded helplessly, not knowing what to say to make things right again. I felt as though I was losing my best friend because of my own inability to face up to reality.

"'Night, Susan." He squeezed my hand and quickly got into his car.

An instant later his car had become just a small red dot in the moon-illuminated night.

✄ 17 ✄

*I don't think anything is ever quite the same to us
after we are dead.*

Don Marquis

I tried to put Nick out of my mind over what proved to be an excruciatingly long weekend.

On Sunday Marc and I saw *Evita*. He and the couple we went with, our accountant/lawyer, Peter, and his wife, Kristin, thought it was excellent. I myself couldn't get into it. Partly because I was preoccupied and also because my taste, as a rule, doesn't run to musical interpretations of South American revolutions.

As we were getting ready for bed, Marc commented on my mood.

"You didn't seem to enjoy the show," he said.

"What? Oh, it was all right, I guess. I just wasn't up to a show tonight," I admitted.

"Well, why didn't you say so before?"

"Why didn't I say that I wasn't in the mood for a show we'd gotten tickets for over three months ago?" I asked.

"Hmmm" was all Marc said. He'd begun his nightly exercise routine—one hundred sit-ups, thirty push-ups, and two hundred deep knee bends.

"Besides," I added, while massaging Oil of Olay into my face, "I think the Olsens enjoyed it."

"Mmmm."

I got under the covers while he removed his contact lenses.

Thinking that maybe a little lovemaking with Marc would

refresh us both, I dabbed a drop of Opium behind my ears and on my wrists.

Marc slipped under the covers and shut off the light.

I think that he was as surprised as I was to find me nibbling at his ear.

"Uh . . . what's that for?" he asked.

"For nothing. Can't I just nibble on your ear? You used to like it," I reminded him.

"I know, it's just . . ." he began.

"I know, it *has* been a long time."

That night Marc and I made love to one another more fervently than we had in months. It was reminiscent of our earlier years together. And yet when we were finished, when we turned from each other with a soft good night, I felt emptier than ever.

I knew then that it was over. After eight years, we had nothing more to give each other than our bodies. But who would be the first to say so aloud, I wondered.

Exhausted from thinking, I sought escape by falling into deep sleep. Like Alice, I tumbled into my own private Wonderland.

There I was at the H. R. Funeral Parlor, an onlooker observing all that was taking place around me. And yet it was as though I weren't there at all; people were treating me as if I were invisible.

The mourners themselves were a preposterous assortment. It seemed that everyone I had ever known, even for a brief time, was present.

Mrs. Gluck, my third-grade teacher wore her hair, as usual, in a chignon. Her high-collared blouse was clasped at the neck with a cameo and I'm certain that I'd gotten a whiff of her Chantilly perfume as she dabbed her eyelids with a white lace hanky.

As my eyes moved along the pews, I was able to discern

childhood friends, my parents, who incidentally had wonderful suntans, and my baby sister, Eileen.

My editor, Fran, was seated off to the left. And sitting beside her was none other than a six-foot cockroach, dressed in a tuxedo no less. Kelly sat there crossing and uncrossing his many legs, putting Kafka to shame.

I was getting an uncomfortable sense of whose funeral it was they all attended. Since no one was aware of my presence, and I couldn't find myself anywhere else, I cleverly deduced that this was, indeed, the funeral of Susan Finkelstein, who died before she was able to shake her name.

I recall reading that a person who dreamed of his or her own death was a person near to insanity. I was prepared to buy that. In a morbid way, I was enjoying myself.

I noticed Mrs. Fagelman and Harry. Estelle was passing Danish among the mourners. God forbid someone should have to sit still for more than fifteen minutes without eating.

Ellen Bethune was sitting alone. Her soft brown eyes were luminous; Ellen, of course, would know the proper amount of tears to be spent on me.

Standing in the back of the room was Horatio Reeper, who was apparently delighted with the magnificent turnout. The room was filling up so quickly. Well, Reeper, I could have told you that I am, or rather *was*, a very popular lady.

I was somewhat surprised to see Marilyn Monroe seated beside Alison and Cinnamon. Alison sat quietly, wearing a kimono and in fact, looking like a fragile, China doll.

Meyer S. Rosenbloom sat with Felicia, in the first pew, left center. I don't imagine he'd take a back seat at any performance, funerals notwithstanding. Felicia chewed gum and every so often blew bubbles that would take off and float high into the air.

Seated on the other side of Meyer was Stephanie, in a seductive, plunging Stephen Burrows gown. She was talking and laughing animatedly with M.S., trying to get new representation at my funeral, of all places.

I spotted Marc seated two pews in front of Bucky and Gary and looked on in amazement as he popped Mallomar after Mallomar into his mouth.

Next to walk into the chapel was Tracy Simms. All eyes turned to her as she walked down the aisle wearing an exquisite bugle-beaded black jumpsuit. On her head was an emerald-jeweled tiara, which I was to recall vividly. I think even in my dream I felt slightly miffed at Tracy's stealing the show. After all, this was my day. It wasn't my fault she'd been cremated.

She sat beside Jean Paul, who removed his tortoise-shell lighter and lit two Gauloises, one for himself, one for Tracy.

It was then that I heard a harp playing, what else? "Happy Days Are Here Again." Suddenly the doors flew open. In a cloud of luminous mist stood Michael Cole, dressed in a shroud and halo. How he had made it through heaven's pearly gates is beyond me. He must have had something on St. Peter was all I could figure.

His shroud was spotted with dark brown stains and it was only when I thought back on it that I realized it was blood. I felt like shaking him. Saying, "Michael, for Christ's sake, they're all here. Charlie Chan couldn't ask for a more complete room of suspects. So who was it? Who killed you?"

But Michael's body disappeared as quickly as it had appeared and my attention was drawn to Nick.

Nick was seated in the first pew, right center, wearing jeans and a black T-shirt on which was printed "I ♥ NY." He sat between Shirl and June, his playmates from Paradise Playground.

As the harp music softened, I heard a familiar, nasal voice asking for everyone's attention.

Standing at the pulpit, behind a black draped coffin, was

none other than Mitzi Fynch. Her red hair was tied up in a pink ribbon and she wore a black mini-dress.

"Please, please," Mitzi's voice echoed, "if you'll just settle down and give me your attention."

Everyone yielded to Mitzi's obvious authority.

"We are gathered here at the H. R. Funeral Home," Mitzi began, "to pay our due respects to Susan Finkelstein ...beloved daughter, cherished friend...I can't say wife because she never got the ring...and, of course, devoted Tupperware saleswoman."

After the usual lauditory spiel, Mitzi closed by saying, "Yes, Susan Finkelstein will be sorely missed, though why she chose to stick her nose where it didn't belong, God only knows!"

"Amen," said Estelle. "Vy did she vant to open from a ken of ketapillars anyvays?"

"If there are no further questions or comments, we'll say our last good-byes to Susan Finkelstein," Mitzi continued.

With that she slipped off the black material and revealed a huge, opened, Tupperware coffin.

"You see?" Mitzi said joyously. "This way we're sure to lock in freshness!"

I looked into the coffin and was stunned to see my very own likeness made up to look like Eva Peron. As Mitzi led the congregation in "Don't Cry for Me Argentina," the lid closed on my coffin.

I must have called out in my sleep, because Marc shook me until I awakened.

"Why the hell would you dream you were dead?" Marc asked when I told him about my dream.

"I don't know. Maybe it was symbolic of my feeling not totally here sometimes. Or maybe it was a precognition, what do you think?" I asked.

Marc turned over and grumbled, "I think you could have

lived without that raw cauliflower tonight. You probably have indigestion. Good night."

I willingly accepted Marc's simple and safe rationale, rather than question whether or not my dream was some sort of psychic warning.

✄ < 18 > ✄

Life is like eating artichokes; you've got to go
through so much to get so little.

T. A. Dorgan

I arose the following morning with unsorted feelings. For
one thing, the nightmare I had had left me more unnerved
than I cared to admit. I was also very conscious of the fact
that I could not call Nick and discuss my anxieties with
him. And to top everything off, the realization that my eight-
year relationship with Marc was tumbling to pieces, left a
stale taste in my mouth.

True, things had been souring for some time. But all the
same, the human being is a complex creature who would
often prefer to cling to mediocre comfort than shoot for stars
and stimulation.

Confronting Marc with the problem was an event I didn't
look forward to.

I needn't have worried about it just yet. Marc announced
at breakfast he'd be flying to New York that afternoon for
a series of network meetings. Apparently he had mentioned
it earlier in the week; I'd forgotten, but didn't let on.

"So, how long do you think you'll be away?" I asked.

"Oh, not longer than a week; ten days tops," Marc said
while glancing through *Variety*.

"Marc . . ." I began, hesitantly.

"Yeah?" He looked up at me with those Lassie eyes of
his.

"More toast? Or maybe you'd like your coffee warmed.
Just take a second."

Having decided that "the big talk" could wait until he returned, I breathed easier and turned on my most domestic charm.

When Marc left I went back to bed and, like an ostrich, pulled the covers over my head, hoping that when I emerged again all my problems would be gone.

For the next few days I occupied myself by consuming unique varieties and vast quantities of food. When I wasn't watching the daytime soaps I found myself checking off late-night movies in the following week's *TV Guide*. The only living matter I saw was the fungus that appeared to be attaching itself to the dishes stacked in the sink since Marc's departure. My wardrobe varied from my plaid nightgown to my red chenille bathrobe.

To say I was in a mild state of depression would be quite the understatement.

Having changed the shelving paper in every conceivable cupboard, closet, and crevice of the house, I decided to jot down what I remembered of my rather bizarre dream. It was as good as any other way to fill my time.

I recalled Michael's bloody shroud, Tracy's tiara, Ellen Bethune's teary brown eyes, and Kelly's tuxedo. I remembered Jean Paul and Bucky and . . .

Of course!

Without giving it much thought, I picked up the phone and dialed.

I let it ring four or five times.

"Ellen?" I asked when she answered.

"With whom am I speaking?" she asked.

"This is Susan Finkelstein." I was grateful to have gotten Ellen and not the maid on the phone. "I don't know if you remember me. I'm Stephanie Groman's friend?"

"Of course I remember you, Susan. Um, what can I do

for you?" she asked. "I don't need any more Tupperware I'm afraid."

"Ellen, I'd like to meet you for drinks this afternoon. There's something important I want to discuss with you," I said.

"Today?"

"Yes, today. Say five-ish? At Murray's Place on Ventura?"

"Oh, I'm afraid that's out of the question, honey lamb, much as I appreciate your inviting me. See, I'm previously engaged as it so happens," Ellen replied.

"Ellen, I think you're going to want to hear what I have to say," I teased.

"Sweetie, nothin' you could say could make me have drinks with you today. Like I already told you, I have several previous engagements."

"I want to talk with you about little Stevie's father," I said.

"Why, whatever in the world does Frank have to do with any of this?" she asked, cool to the last inflection.

"It wasn't Frank I had in mind," I said, dropping the bomb.

The sound of silence was deafening.

"I'll meet you at five," she said, confirming my suspicions. I gave her directions to Murray's.

I listened to the dial tone for several moments after she hung up, certain that Ellen's magnolia tree had been shaken up more than she cared to admit.

As she entered the restaurant, I realized just how much Ellen reminded me of a heroine in a Tennessee Williams play.

She had on a soft shirred shirtwaist dress in a becoming shade of apricot. A diamond cluster clasped a simple but expensive strand of pearls around her neck. I half expected her to be sporting little white gloves.

With a wave I attracted her attention to where I sat at the bar.

"Over here, Ellen," I said, indicating the seat beside me.

"Well, now, isn't this...pleasant," she said, looking around her with some disdain.

"I figured it'd be easy to get to and, well, we'd have some privacy," I explained.

Why I felt it necessary to apologize for Murray's Place is beyond me, although Ellen's ultrarefined manner might have had something to do with it.

Though not Ma Maison, this was certainly a respectable establishment. Also, it was immensely comfortable and the food was superb. It was a restaurant frequented by many ex–New Yorkers; Bucky had brought it to my attention when I moved out to Los Angeles.

"Are you hungry?" I asked. It was 5:15 and I didn't know about Ellen, but I was ravenous. "The food really is rather decent," I understated.

Ellen removed a Benson and Hedges Menthol 100; she lit it and inhaled deeply. The lady was obviously not interested in food, and I wasn't going to order alone.

"Sue darlin', let's not pussyfoot. I had a million and one things to do when you phoned. To begin with, I never got over to Neiman-Marcus as I'd intended and I simply had to buy a wedding gift today, to say nothing of the fact that I was forced to cancel appointments to have my nails wrapped and my legs waxed. Why I even had to miss a date with my interior decorator!" she exclaimed.

A regular upper-stratum Erma Bombeck Ellen Bethune was.

"I'm sorry to have disturbed your busy schedule, really I am. But I thought, well, I thought you ought to hear what I had to say," I explained.

"What'll it be, goils?" said Murray from behind the bar. Murray has lived in Los Angeles thirty-five of his sixty-seven years, but he still clings tenaciously to his New York accent. He also takes great pride in tending bar in his own restaurant.

"I'll have a bourbon and soda straight up," I requested.

"Bourbon and soda comin' right up. And what about you, miss?" he asked Ellen.

"A mint julep please," Ellen drawled without batting an eye.

Murray's eyes narrowed as if to ask if this broad were on the level, but he went about preparing our drinks nevertheless.

I paid for them and suggested we move to a table to avoid Murray's scrutiny.

"All right, sugar," Ellen said, sipping her drink delicately once we were seated. "Suppose you tell me what this is all about?"

"Michael Cole was Stephen's father, wasn't he?" I asked.

"Why are you asking me? You're supposed to have all the answers. Isn't that why you wanted me to meet you here?" Ellen replied.

"Okay, forget the question; I'll rephrase it as a fact. Michael Cole was your son's real father," I confronted her.

She didn't respond, so I continued.

"I'm not sure when I first suspected. Probably I made some sort of a subconscious connection between you and Michael when I remembered seeing that porcelain heart at his station. After looking over your porcelain collection, I guessed it was you who'd given Michael the heart."

Ellen smiled, amused at the memory.

"I gave that to him five years ago. I didn't realize the bastard was so sentimental," she said.

"You pretended that you barely knew Michael, and yet I discovered that you'd lied about attending his funeral, which led me to believe that you actually knew him quite well," I said.

"My, my, my, Susie, you've been a busy little beaver, now haven't you?" Ellen said, while signaling Murray for refills.

"I'm just observant, Ellen. You see there was something else I'd seen when I was in your house. Something that stuck in my mind, but I couldn't put my finger on what it was until today," I admitted.

"And just what would that be?" Ellen asked as she paid for our second round.

"The eyes," I said. "It was the eyes. You and Frank have brown eyes. Even Roslyn has your color eyes, or maybe that of your first husband. But little Stevie's brilliant turquoise eyes, he inherited those and that ingratiating smile from his natural father. From Michael Cole."

Ellen looked directly at me, making up her mind whether to take me into her confidence.

"Michael and I were, well, we met each other five years ago," Ellen finally admitted.

I made myself comfortable, since I could tell from her tone that the liquor had mellowed her and she had decided to talk.

"He was, oh he was the most beautiful thing I ever did lay my eyes on." Her voice softened as she described Michael's physical beauty with near reverence. "His face . . . his body . . ." She sighed helplessly.

"Not that I ever expected anything to come of it. I mean, I loved Frank," she said in earnest. "I still do. Why he's been just wonderful to me and to Roslyn. He adopted her when she was no more than Stevie's age, and he's loved her like she were his own flesh and blood. Still and all, he wanted a son of his very own, but much as we tried . . . nothing," Ellen shrugged.

"And when you met Michael?" I urged, trying to keep her from digressing.

Slowly, she stirred her drink with a swizzle stick.

"When I met Michael I was in a slump . . . a depression. I felt frumpy, you know the feelin', sugar?" she asked.

Did I ever. I just didn't think someone like Ellen did, which only goes to show you.

"Now, I might have been only one of a million typical housewives living in the suburbs with my husband and child. But Michael made me feel, well, he made me feel special. I'm tellin' you, honey, that man sure as hell knew how to shovel the cow dung," Ellen said as she downed her drink in one gulp. She ordered another round for us both.

The bourbon was beginning to get to me. After all, I'd had hardly anything to eat all day and was now on my third drink.

"So Michael and I had a brief affair l'amour," she announced melodramatically, convincing me that Ellen, too, either followed the soaps or else she was a closet Harlequin Romance devotee.

"Where'd you go?" I asked idiotically. "Oh, I'm sorry."

"That's okay. We had to be careful because of Frank, you understand. So my house was out. And since Michael was married to a rather public figure at that time, he had to be careful about that as well. Any well-known place might have attracted attention, so we'd spend our afternoons at the 'ntlmtl,'" she mumbled.

"Where?"

"At the 'No-Tell Motel,'" she blurted out. "Oh Lord, I know it sounds dreadful, but I was with Michael and that's all that mattered," she crooned in a parody of herself. "What a little fool I was. And the affair burned out three months after it began, when I discovered that I was pregnant."

"What did Michael say when you told him?" I asked.

"Let's see, first he gave me the name of a little clinic as

I recall," she said, "for an abortion, you know. Then, when
I refused, he said, 'Well, then you'll just have to convince
your ol' man he's the papa, now won't you?' I'll never
forget how cruel he was. He laughed and said I'd probably
be doing Frank a favor, by making him feel virile. That
SOB knew that Frank had, well, that he had a problem."

"A low sperm count?" I ventured.

"Mmmm. I made the mistake of confiding in Michael,"
she admitted. "Anyway, Michael was right about one thing.
When Frank found out I was gonna have a baby he was
thrilled. Of course, he never had an inkling of what was
the truth. When Stephen was born I forced myself to think
of him as Frank's. Frank's and mine. And eventually, things
got back to normal for me. Kind of."

"So that was that," I said.

"Yes, that was that," she said softly, "until about six
months ago when I got a call from Michael. You know, I
thought that man was out of my life. I even found myself
a new hairdresser here in the valley, though truthfully no
one could give a henna rinse as good as Michael." Ellen
stated this quite matter of factly.

"I asked him what he wanted and he told me right
out. That monster . . . that fiend . . . that slime of the earth . . .
that . . ."

She was running out of epithets.

"He threatened to tell Frank about us, about Stephen,
unless I 'lent' him some money. Seems he was plannin' to
go into business for himself and was a little short of cash."

"You didn't pay him, did you?" I asked.

By her expression I could tell she had.

"What else could I do?"

"Couldn't you have been honest with your husband?" I
asked, knowing the answer even as I asked the question.

"Jesus H. Christ, girl! Either you've never been married
or you're just plain naive! I mean Frank's a dear, but he'd

never have stood for that. Never. Especially since he's decided to run for city council. If this came out, it'd mean a smear campaign. I'd lose him. And if I lost Frank, I'd lose everything.

"You know what I came from sugar?" she asked, lighting up again. "I grew up just a step above white trash. This, even though my daddy was quite an educated man. A schoolteacher he was. But I'll tell you somethin'," she slurred, "bein' a schoolteacher in a shit-kickin' town over a hundred miles from the nearest big city doesn't make you much money. Especially when you've got five kids to feed. We were piss-poor crackers, honey. That's what we were.

"I got married at seventeen to get out of the house, was pregnant with Roslyn at nineteen, and was divorced at twenty-three. Well, I didn't have diddly shit's worth of an education, so I became a waitress. Fact, I was waiting tables at a place in New Orleans when I met Frank. He'd come down on business, you see. Lord, I'd never met such a nice, cultured guy.

"We started datin' and before I knew it, Frank was proposin' and I was acceptin' and well, it was like a Cinderella story come true. He's always been an exemplary father, a good provider. He's given me everything I've ever asked for and much, much more.

"So you see, Michael hit a rather sensitive nerve when he called me. Because I had no intention of losing everything that mattered to me," she said fiercely.

Now that Ellen had loosened up and filled me in on her background, I began to understand a lot. Like, for instance, why the *genteel* life was so important to her.

Ellen Bethune's reward in life was that she had become what she so much aspired to be.

"So, I began paying him," she continued, "every two weeks I'd make an appointment with him and . . . and make a payment. Of course, I tried to Jew him down on his askin' price, but he said no dice," she explained.

"How much were you paying him?" I asked, trying to ignore her ethnic slur.

"Five hundred dollars every two weeks."

"Whew! That's a thousand dollars a month. Ellen, weren't you afraid of what Frank would say when he noticed the withdrawals in your account?" I asked.

"No, why should I have been? I often spend more than $1,000 a month on shoes and perfume alone," she said.

I thought of the time Marc hit the roof when I failed to record the $21.50 I had spent on a heating pad I'd purchased one month when my menstrual cramps became unbearable.

"Well, anyway, the week before...he died...Michael phoned to tell me he'd be wanting seven hundred dollars instead of the usual five," Ellen said. "I knew then there'd be no satisfying that leech. So I refused to pay him any more. And he threatened to send Frank photocopies of my checks," she said.

"He must have wanted that money very badly," I said.

Ellen suddenly let out a surprisingly loud hoot.

"Oh, sugar, it wasn't only the money! No ma'am. It was knowin' he had me under his thumb that gave Michael so much pleasure. See he got his kicks seein' other folks eat dirt, Michael did. And I got the feelin' I wasn't the only sucker payin' him off," she said.

"What makes you say that?" I asked.

"I don't know," she shrugged. "Something he once said, I guess. I was late getting a check to him one time and he chided me about not being nearly as punctual as another 'sponsor' of his. Somethin' like that."

Who else was being blackmailed by Michael Cole?

"Ellen," I said, "I don't mean to sound smug, but surely you've watched enough police shows, we all have, to know that blackmailers are like parasites. They never stop their bloodsucking until . . . until . . ."

I looked into my glass.

"Until they're killed. Is that what you were going to say?" she said, calmly smashing out her cigarette.

Clouds of smoke filled the air. I said nothing.

"Well, as it so happened, luck was with me. Michael died. And my secret died with him. Or has it, Sue?" she asked cautiously.

It took me a second or so to fully comprehend her meaning.

"Ellen, are you afraid that I'll betray your confidence? To Frank? Because if that's so, let me assure you I won't."

"What about Stephanie?"

Tell Stephanie, tell the world.

"No, not to Stephanie either."

"Hey, now c'mon, I know you're not asking me these questions for any financial gain, so would you mind explaining just what business all this has been of yours?" Ellen demanded.

"Listen, I know you're entitled to an explanation, but I just can't give you one right now. It's too long a story, believe me. Let's just say you've helped me put together some pieces to a rather complicated puzzle," I assured her. "Oh, one more thing. When was the last time you saw Michael?"

She stared at me before speaking.

"Why, the morning of, well, I do believe it was the day he died, as a matter of fact. Or the day before. I'm not really sure. It was a Friday, I know that. I'd made an appointment to see him, so I could pay him the seven hundred dollars he asked for," she said sweetly.

I looked at my watch. We had been talking for an hour and a half.

"It's getting late, I've got to get going. Ellen . . . I want to thank you. And to apologize if I've stirred up some painful memories for you," I said sincerely.

"Sure," Ellen said, waving off my apology indifferently.

I rose, awkwardly; she didn't make an attempt to move.

"Well, I'm leaving now, how about you?" I asked.

"I'll just sit here for a few minutes . . . do some thinking. You go on ahead, Sue," she advised.

It was with some misgiving that I left Ellen at the table nursing her fourth, or was it fifth, mint julep.

My eyes adjusted themselves to the bright light outside. It was nearing seven o'clock, but we were on daylight savings time and there were still several hours of sunshine.

The parking lot had been full when I arrived, so I had to park across the boulevard. I walked to the corner, pressed the traffic-signal button and waited at the bus stop for the light to change.

My mind was trying to absorb all that Ellen had said to me.

The bus stop was particularly crowded and I remembered having seen a sign for a church bazaar around the corner. Women were carrying shopping bags of clothing; children were clutching balloons and stuffed animals.

I can recall the bus pulling in.

The light was about to change.

A little girl dropped her giraffe, and I stooped down to pick it up.

Suddenly I felt hands on my back, but it was too late.

Whoever shoved me, shoved me hard.

I saw the bus pulling closer as I lost my balance and attempted to grab hold of a trash can, to no avail.

The trash can toppled over.

Everything happened so fast. People screaming and my body surging forward in the direction of the bus.

I saw balloons soar into the air.

And that was the last thing I remembered before everything went black.

❧ 19 ❧

I long to believe in immortality. If I am destined to be happy with you here, how short is the longest life. I wish to love with you forever.

John Keats, letters to Fanny Brawne

"She's coming to," I heard someone say.

"...Have to get the giraffe..." I muttered. I felt a dull throb in my head, as if I had a stupendous hangover.

"She's hallucinating," I heard a white shape pronounce.

"Maybe," a green form replied.

As my eyes began to focus, the bright lights above me and the white and green blurs around me began to take shape.

A hospital. What was I doing in a hospital, I wondered.

Then I remembered the bus.

But if I'd been hit by a bus I was certain that my injuries would be considerably worse than a severe headache.

"Sue...Sue, can you hear me?" Bucky asked, reaching for my hand.

"Bucky, what happened? How'd I get here? How'd *you* get here? Ow, my head!" I exclaimed.

The dull pain was beginning to sharpen.

"Take it easy, kid, you're going to be okay, right, doctor?"

He looked at a bald black man for confirmation.

"I'm Doctor Powell, Miss Finkelstein," the doctor said, addressing me. "You hit your head against the pavement rather hard I imagine, which would account for your slight concussion. But your eyes are no longer dilating, which is a good sign. So I'd say that except for a few nasty scrapes

154

and bruises and a very natural feeling of being shaken up, the prognosis for your recovery is excellent." He smiled.

He had a nice smile.

"Now, you may have a little difficulty sleeping for the next few nights. Probably begin feeling the pain as the shock wears off. So I'm just going to prescribe some medication to make you more comfortable."

"Buck?" My voice was weak. I didn't recognize it as my own.

"Yeah, Sue? I'm right here, honey," he assured me.

"What happened? I remember the bus . . . and then . . ." my voice trailed off.

"You're a very lucky young lady," said a police officer standing behind Bucky. Funny, I hadn't been aware of his presence before that moment.

"According to witnesses, you stooped down to retrieve something," he read from a pad.

"A little orange giraffe," I interrupted. My memory was returning in spurts.

"Yeah. Well, anyway, you must've lost your balance and grabbed for a nearby trash can just as the bus was pulling in. That trash can just may've saved your life. It rolled in front of you and stopped you from sliding right under that bus. The driver slammed on his brakes. Wasn't anything else he could do, it all happened so quickly," the officer explained.

"How'd you get here, Bucky?" I asked.

"The detective on duty happened to've been an acquaintance of mine. When the call came in he remembered my introducing him to a Susan Finkelstein some time back. Your description fit. So on a hunch he phoned me," Bucky said.

"A detective?" I repeated. Vaguely, I recalled meeting a quiet, stocky man more than a year ago, when Bucky and I were dining at a new Hungarian restaurant.

"Jesus, he must have some hell of a memory for names," I remarked, impressed.

"That's why he does what he does," Bucky agreed. "Anyway, I'm glad he phoned; I'd hate to think of you having to come to with no familiar face around. Say, I'll be right back, gotta make a quick phone call."

"Well, I'll be finishing up my report and moving on then," the policeman said when Bucky had left the room. "You sure she's okay, doctor?"

"She'll be fine," the doctor said, while applying a bandage to a cut on my right arm.

"Wait a second," I said. "Doesn't anyone want to ask me what happened?"

No one responded, so I continued.

"I remember now. I was shoved. Pushed. I felt someone's hands on my back," I announced.

Still no reaction.

"Don't you understand what I'm saying? Someone wanted me beneath that bus!" I cried.

This time, not only was there no response to my outcry, but I sensed by their expressions that no one in the room believed me. Not the policeman, nor the kindly doctor, nor his efficient nurse, who probably began to doubt my sanity as soon as I described the orange giraffe.

"It's true!" I insisted. "Why else would I suddenly lose my balance?"

The policeman looked at the doctor; he seemed embarrassed.

"Uh, Miss Finkelstein," Doctor Powell said, also appearing uncomfortable.

What were they having so much difficulty saying?

"Miss Finkelstein," he repeated, "when you were brought into emergency, we took a blood sample and I'm afraid that we detected alcohol in your system."

I started to protest, but he stopped me.

"Now, wait, while I agree the amount wasn't substantial enough for you to have lost control of your abilities, the fact that you appear to have consumed it on a relatively empty stomach would certainly account for...a certain lightheadedness on your part, which could have resulted in your losing balance," Doctor Powell finished up.

What no one said was that this too would account for the "hands" that I obviously had imagined in my near "stupor."

I could see it was futile to pursue it any further. At least not here. Not with Officer Breslin or with Doctor Powell. And certainly not with Nurse Killgallen, who, by this time probably thought my orange giraffe was merely symptomatic of DTs.

"I'm sorry to be so much trouble, you're right, of course," I conceded. "What time is it?"

"Eight-forty," said Nurse Killgallen, trying to muster some sympathy into her voice.

"May I go home, doctor," I asked.

"Certainly. You'll have a few more forms to sign, then your friend can drive you home," he replied.

"Thank you," I said.

The doctor was as good as his word. The shock began to wear off and, as predicted, I was suddenly conscious of a grenade going off inside my skull.

I needed this like a hole in the head. Very cute, Susan, very cute.

On the way home I blurted out the events leading up to my so-called accident, as I remembered them, including my revelation of Michael and Ellen's relationship and my subsequent confrontation with Ellen that afternoon. I finished by asking Bucky if he had any food on him.

"Food?" he repeated.

"I haven't eaten since breakfast," I explained.

"Well, I know of a great Austrian..."

"No, please, I just wanted something to snack on. To tide me over."

Bucky blushed and dug deeply into his pocket.

"Here, it's not much, but it's yours," he said, handing me a Three Musketeers bar. So Bucky, the gourmet, was a secret chocoholic after all.

"Think it might've been Ellen's hands you felt on your back?" Bucky asked.

I was gratified to know that at least he believed my version of what had happened.

"But why?" I asked, my mind not quite in fourth gear.

"Why? Why did you ask?" Bucky said. "Sue, my dear, might I remind you that you are the one person privy to a skeleton this lady had guarded so carefully that she was willing to pay for it to remain a skeleton?"

"But I swore to her that I had no intention of divulging her secret."

As I said this I realized that in my excitement I had already betrayed her confidence by telling Bucky what I knew. I made a silent vow to be more careful in the future, and I asked Bucky to keep what I was telling him to himself, though I knew he would do so anyway.

"And supposing, just supposing, that it was this gal who murdered her blackmailer, then killed the vengeful ex-wife who had known of their affair and dangled it in front of her?" Bucky continued. "Just suppose, mind you."

"Mmmm, it's a thought," I said pulling at my Three Musketeers bar, "I just can't see Ellen messing her dainty hands with murder. And such a violent murder at that."

"Self-preservation is a mighty strong motive, Sue," Bucky reminded me.

We pulled into my driveway and he asked if I wanted him to spend the night in Marc's absence.

I thanked him for his offer, but insisted I'd be quite all

right. I planned on taking a piping hot bubble bath and turning in for the night.

Bucky drove off, promising to phone and check up on me the next day.

I walked into my empty, dark house that evening and felt as though I had been away a month rather than just a few hours. I toyed with the idea of phoning Marc or Stephanie or Nick, and filling them in, but instead I poured myself a Tab and took the pills Doctor Powell had prescribed.

The pain began to subside by the time I stepped into the tub. Thinking about Marc, about Nick, about the bus that almost killed me, I began to work up a good case of self-pity.

Five minutes couldn't have passed before the doorbell rang. I let it ring two more times before grudgingly leaving the warmth and security of my bath.

I wrapped a robe around me and walked barefoot to the front door. "Bucky, I meant what I said . . . I'll be fine!"

But it wasn't Bucky who stood outside my door, it was Nick Comici.

He was holding a jar of jelly beans and a huge stuffed giraffe.

"Bucky," I stated.

"Bucky," he confirmed. "Say, would you mind if I put this down somewhere?"

"No, of course not. Come on in," I said. He followed me back into the house. I attempted to straighten my hair.

"Don't bother, it wouldn't help," he said, opening the jar of jelly beans.

"Thanks a heap." I passed a mirror; he was right. Damp hair dangled on my shoulders and the bruise on my right cheek was no longer a dull purple but had, in fact, changed to a striking shade of chartreuse.

"Well, you're the one who insists on frankness," Nick said.

"Please, Nick, can we call a truce? As you seem to have heard, today was not one of my better days," I said.

"I know," he said. He was being sincere. "And I'm sorry. C'mere and sit down."

I hesitated.

"C'mon," he sighed. "I promise not to ravish you, appealing as you may look."

I sat down on the loveseat beside him, and he turned me so that my back was toward him.

"I'll massage, you talk," he proposed.

So for the second time that night I took someone into Ellen's confidence, explaining the entire story of her relationship with Michael and their son.

"Now tell me," Nick asked, when I finished with Ellen, "do you want to talk about what happened to you today?"

I would have been willing to talk about anything at that point, so relaxed was I becoming as Nick's fingers worked their way all over my back, my neck, my shoulder blades. It felt wonderful.

But by the time I completed relating my story, I was tense all over again; I began to shake as I relived my moment of helplessness at the bus stop that afternoon.

Nick held me close and I didn't stop him. There was no reason to; it was exactly what I needed.

"You're going to be all right, baby," he assured me. "You're going to be all right. No one's gonna hurt you now, I'm here."

I began to cry. Softly. And then in periodic gasps. It was the first time I had allowed myself to let go that evening.

"My dream. It almost came true," I managed to sob.

"What are you talking about?"

"Just a few nights ago I dreamed about my own funeral.

Everyone I've ever known was there, even you. You had on an "I ♥ NY" T-shirt, and you were there with those two women from Paradise Playground."

"Well, then don't you see how ludicrous your dream was?" Nick said. "I don't even own an 'I ♥ NY' T-shirt!"

I giggled and he smiled. And then he kissed me. Lightly, he kissed my eyes and my nose and then my mouth.

He looked at me questioningly and I suppose my eyes must have given him the answer he wanted. When we kissed again, we kissed deeply and hungrily. It had been so long since I had desired a man as I desired Nick then.

We made love in the guest room that night, since Nick felt odd about our being together in the bed I shared with Marc.

At first I was nervous. The sensation of holding a man other than Marc was strange. After all, what had Marc's body become if not an extension of mine?

Nick's chest was not as broad as Marc's but his stomach was flatter and his bellybutton was an "innie" whereas Marc's was an "outie." At that point I stopped myself from making further comparisons; it was unfair to Marc as well as to Nick.

Besides, I wondered what was going through Nick's mind as he stroked my belly. Were my breasts larger or smaller than the last woman he had been with? Had her nipples been the same shade as mine? Was she young?

And then easily, very easily, as if nothing else had any relevance, Nick's body all at once became part of my own.

In fact, our lovemaking was so natural, it seemed as though we had been with one another a myriad of years.

When we were finished, Nick turned to me and laughed.

"Y'know, sweetheart," he said, "I just realized you were nearly hit by a bus today. So, if you'd begged off with a

headache tonight, well, you know it would have been perfectly understandable."

"Not on your life, Mr. Comici," I whispered into his ear.
"Not on your life."

✄ 20 ✄

Seek and ye shall find.

Matthew 7:7

We slept late the next morning, after what proved to be an incredible, but tiring, night.

I awoke in a fetal position, my back spooned against Nick's body. The sensation was not unpleasant once I remembered where I was and with whom.

"Mmm," Nick murmured; he pressed against me and I felt his erection.

"Glad to see you're so awake." I laughed.

"How do you feel?" he asked. Sleep was in Nick's voice.

"Well my arm's still sore from the fall, but otherwise I feel good, no, great. Why? How should I feel?"

"Oh, I don't know. Guilt-ridden, remorseful," he suggested. "You know, I remember hearing this story about a Jewish man whose girlfriend asked that he bring her the heart of his mother as proof of his love for her. So the guy kills his mother, rips out her heart, and runs with it to his lover as proof of his devotion. And in his haste he trips, falls, and drops the heart, which was heard to ask, 'Did you hurt yourself, my son?'"

"Uh-huh," I laughed. "And I suppose Italian sons never feel guilty."

"Nah. We just go to confession and spill our guts."

Nick was nibbling at my toes when the lucite and chrome guest telephone rang.

"Hello?" I whispered into the receiver. I was in ecstasy.

"Sue?"

It was Marc.

"Mmm-hmm," I replied.

"You sound funny, is anything wrong?" he asked.

Nick began to massage the arch of my right foot.

"Oh no. No!"

"Good. Well I just wanted to let you know that things are going better than I anticipated. In fact, I wouldn't be at all surprised if I was in a new position within, oh, say, the next few weeks," his voice droned on.

I held Nick's head in my hands, caressing his curls.

"Higher . . . higher!" I pleaded.

"Well, of course higher," Marc said. "You don't think I'd consider taking a step down the ladder, do you?"

"Oh my God. Not now, not yet," I gasped.

Nick had worked his way up my leg and was licking my inner thigh.

"Jesus, I just knew you'd say that Sue," Marc said, not bothering to disguise the disgust in his voice. "I mean, for Christ's sake, have you any idea what this could mean for me? Why I could have this town eating out of my hands. Now tell me, Sue, would that be too, too hard for you to swallow?"

"Mmmmm. No, not at all," I said guiding Nick's erection into me.

"Sue? Sue you haven't been listening to a word I've said. Isn't any of this penetrating?" Marc asked.

"Oh yes, yes it is!" I breathed deeply.

"Well, look, we'll discuss the promotion when I get home, which, by the way, will be a week from tomorrow. I'll be flying into Burbank Airport," he informed me.

"I'm going to come," I whispered.

"That's sweet of you to offer, Sue, but it's really not necessary."

"I'm coming . . ."

"Don't be silly. I'll take a cab. Listen, somebody wants

to use the phone so I've gotta run. Anything you've got to say quickly before I go?" he asked.

"Ah . . . ah . . . ah . . . Nooooo," I sighed.

"Okay then, take care, I'll uh, see you soon."

"This is fantastic," Nick said.

We were finishing our cheese omelettes while relaxing in the Jacuzzi.

"Mmm, every inch of my body needed this," I said, allowing the friction of the water to knead my feet.

"Every inch, huh?" Nick asked.

"C'mon, you know what I mean," I said.

"Yeah. Look, Susan, I think we should talk," Nick said.

"About what?"

"About what happens now, that's about what."

"I think I'm going to have to talk things out with Marc, if that's what you mean. I'll do it as soon as he gets back."

"When he gets back? You can't be serious."

"Of course I'm serious. Nick, I can't very well tell him about us over three thousand miles," I explained.

"No, I guess you can't. He'd probably go into a gay bar and punch out the first guy he saw. But what about us?" Nick asked.

"What do you mean?"

"Ah, Susan, stop avoiding issues. I want to know where we stand. I mean if and when we grope our way out of this 'whodunnit' we seem to have gotten ourselves mixed up in, I'd like to discuss our future together. Of course, you'll have to move back to New York, and then we'll have to . . ."

"Wait. Wait. Wait. Backtrack. What's this about my moving back to New York?" I asked.

"Well you can't expect me to move out here," he laughed.

I didn't laugh with him.

"C'mon honey, I work for a New York–based magazine. Be realistic."

"Ever hear of *LA Magazine*, or of *New West*? Both excellent publications I might add," I said.

"Hey, what is this? I thought you were the unhappy transplanted New Yorker, longing to return to her roots?" Nick asked, surprised at my defense of Los Angeles.

Had the issue not been raised, I would have been quick to agree with Nick's description of me.

But as it was, I learned something about myself that day.

With all our jibes about plastic LA living, our jokes about the superficiality of its people, and our complaints about its lack of sophistication, the majority of us born-and-bred New Yorkers, us diehards, really liked—no loved—living in Los Angeles. I knew I did.

I enjoyed the open spaces, was partial to wide-aisled supermarkets. I'd become comfortable with the relaxed dress code and appreciated walking out in mid-January to find my car was not buried under blankets of snow.

The small theaters around town satisfied my cravings for off-Broadway productions and if my longing for rain became unbearable, San Francisco was an hour's plane ride away.

I realized then that once I stopped thinking of Los Angeles as New York, once I began to accept it on its own terms, this city could finally become my home.

Besides, what was a town, any town—Portland, Baltimore, Boise—if not your work, your friends, your loved ones?

No, the seeds of my discontent were not being nurtured by the Los Angeles life-style, as I had assumed, but rather by my life itself. I understood that now.

"I thought so too," I finally replied in response to Nick's question.

"Baby, don't you get what I'm sayin'? This man here, he's just not cut out to be what they call bicoastal, you know? This man is Nathan's. He's Joe's Clam Bar. He's even Yona Schimmel's Knishes. But what he's not is bean dip and guacamole. Say, I don't even like avocados!" Nick pleaded.

"You could learn," I said.

"I could learn. Susan, Susan, what are you doing to me?"

"Nothing yet," I smiled, walking my foot up the inside of his legs.

"Hey, that's unfair coercion," he said.

"All right then, I'll stop."

He held my foot.

"No, we'll just pick up the conversation some other time, how's that?"

"Fine by me," I agreed. "What's on the agenda for this afternoon?"

"I think you should take it easy today," he said.

"Oh no, Nick, please," I begged. "I'm okay, really I am. I'll go batty if I have to stay in this house all day." .

"Okay, but when I say you've had enough, you've had enough, agreed?" he asked.

"Agreed, Dr. Comici."

"Good, then let's get dressed."

"Where are we going?" I asked, easing myself out of the hot tub.

Nick narrowed his eyes and in his best Conrad Veidt voice, he replied, "To ze scene of za crime, zat is vhere."

"Your German needs work," I said as we entered the house.

"I know. I've been meaning to brush up. . . ."

"This isn't going to work," I warned.

"Shhh. Just be quiet and let me handle things."

Nick and I were standing outside the manager's door of Casa de Dolce Vita, Michael Cole's former apartment house in West Hollywood.

Nick knocked again, and from the other side of the door

we heard a woman's voice shouting, "I'm coming, I'm coming."

A bony woman in her early fifties opened the door slightly.

"Yes?" she said through a chained door, looking first at Nick and then at me. When she spoke I noticed her soft black moustache, covering what appeared to be a perenially tight-lipped grimace.

"Uh, Mrs. Polchik, I phoned you the other day? About the vacancy?" Nick reminded her.

"Oh yeah, yeah, I remember," she said, opening the door. Our being prospective tenants gave us the privilege of a glimpse of her brown-toothed smile. "But I think I told you on the phone, Mr. . . . ?"

"Beaumont."

"Beau . . ." I started. Nick squeezed my arm, tightly.

"Yeah, well, I think I told you on the phone, Mr. Beaumont, I don't know how you heard about this vacancy . . ."

She waited for an explanation, but upon receiving none, she continued.

"But like I told you, it won't be available till the end of the month and that's not for another week or so. It's being painted and all. The former tenant, he, well, he had to leave kind of suddenlike and he didn't give no notice. But see, he was paid up through July. Funny, but how was he to know . . . I mean . . ."

"I understand, Mrs. Polchik," Nick smiled. "But the little woman here had her heart set on seeing it, you see."

I growled beneath my breath.

"Well, I'm not sure it's right," Mrs. Polchik was considering it. "I mean this guy who was livin' there . . . A hairdresser he was, but no pansy that's for sure . . . Anyway, he left his belongin's here. His sister, she was supposed to be pickin' it all up, but she hasn't been by yet."

"Oh, we'll be very careful not to disturb his things," I assured her.

"I don't know," she wavered.

"You'd be doing us a terrific favor," Nick said as he greased her palm with a ten-dollar bill.

"Well, seein' as how it seems so important to your Mrs. here, and I don't see as it'll be hurtin' no one, why not?" she relented. "After all, the place'll be ready real soon."

As Mrs. Polchik rode up in the elevator with us, I looked around at my surroundings. Like many older apartment houses in West Hollywood and elsewhere, this had obviously been quite posh in its time.

While it wasn't by any means run-down, the chipped mosaic tiling, the dried out fountain in the lobby, the once-plush-but-now-faded carpet in the corridors, were all signs of its former splendor.

Mrs. Polchik unlocked the door and let us in.

The tremendous apartment was furnished simply but well.

Mostly modern, some art deco. The red acrylic dining room set was one I had seen in Design Research. Some of the furnishings in the room were covered with sheets, and cans of blue paint could be seen beneath a stepladder. Cartons of books and records explained the empty shelves.

"Nice and roomy don't you think?" Mrs. Polchik volunteered. "Excuse the mess, but like I said, it won't be ready for another week."

"Very nice," Nick said. "May we see the bedrooms?"

"Sure, but it's really only one bedroom. The other room is more like a den, you know? The landlord, he likes to call it a second bedroom," she explained.

The master bedroom was nearly as large as the living room. Here too, were cartons everywhere, mainly of clothing.

Hanging from the ceiling, above the water bed, was a circular mirror. The walls were covered with hundreds of framed photos, all nudes.

Noticing our noticing, Mrs. Polchik felt she had to explain.

"I never interfere with the tenants' private lives. So long as they pay their rent and don't make trouble," she sniffed.

"That's very liberal of you, Mrs. Polchik," I assured her, relieving her of any responsibility for Michael's erotic tastes.

"Yeah, well," she mumbled. "It's all coming down. Tomorrow!"

Stephanie's recollection of Michael's bathroom had been accurate. In addition to the rubber safety guards at the foot of the tub, there were metal safety rails on all the walls surrounding it.

Odd. On the face of it, Michael may have had everything and everyone under control, but obviously here, in the privacy of his own bathroom, he too had fears.

"Well, I guess that'll be all," Nick said.

"But you haven't seen the rest of the apartment," Mrs. Polchik said. She was actually disappointed.

"Uh, yes, well, we've another appointment, so we really must be going."

"So what do you think?" Mrs. Polchik pressed us as we walked down to the elevator.

"To tell you the truth, Mrs. Polchik, I don't think the tub is big enough," Nick said. We were waiting for the elevator to arrive.

"Not big enough? For what? Don't tell me you bring rubber duckies in with you?" She cackled at her own joke.

"No, but you see, Mrs. Beaumont and I do enjoy bathing together," he replied as the elevator door opened.

Nick and I stepped in, leaving Mrs. Polchik with her mouth wide open.

"Well, I never!" she snapped, finally.

"Oh, you should try it, Mrs. Polchik. You should try it," Nick said as the doors closed on her.

"She didn't leave our sides once," I said on the way down. "What a waste."

"Oh, I wouldn't be too sure of that," Nick replied.

"What do you mean?"

"We're gonna come back here and look around for ourselves."

"Oh, really? And just how do you propose we gain entry? Through the window?" I suggested.

"No need. I made an impression."

"Yes, I saw that. That's why I don't think we'll be able to get within ten feet of Mrs. Polchik again," I replied.

"Who needs her? I was talking about this kind of impression," Nick explained, holding up a piece of wax with the outline of a key imprinted on it.

"How did you...? When did you...?" I was astonished.

"Tricks of the trade, honey." Nick took my arm as we left the building. "C'mon, we've got to find a less-than-scrupulous locksmith."

Through Bucky's referral we found a locksmith downtown who didn't ask questions, and we had him make up a duplicate key to Michael's apartment.

By the time we returned to the Casa de Dolce Vita, it was five o'clock and people were returning home from work, so we didn't think we'd have difficulty getting into the building. As it turned out, the lock to the outside door was not even fastened securely.

Nick and I walked quietly past Mrs. Polchik's apartment. We heard a man's voice, probably Mr. Polchik's, call out, "Are you crazy, Dora? Look, there are some things a man likes to do alone. Now get out of the bathroom!"

Well, Mrs. Polchik, you tried.

Nick easily got the door open, and within seconds we were standing in the living room.

"Okay, now let's get organized," Nick said. "You poke around the kitchen, I'll have a look around here."

"This is so exciting," I said.

"Susan," he reprimanded.

"Kitchen. Gotcha."

There was nothing special about Michael's kitchen. Obviously eating wasn't one of his high priority activities. I opened the refrigerator. My own theory is that refrigerators usually tell a lot about a person.

But I was disappointed.

All I found there were a few beers, half of a moldy melon, a container of sour milk, and a few cartons of Dannon yogurt, probably also gone bad.

Michael's "junk drawer" was another disappointment. It was neater than most and told me nothing.

I noticed the kitchen wallpaper on my way out. It too was being painted over, in yellow. Too bad, since it seemed to have been put up fairly recently; in fact the smell of glue hadn't entirely disappeared.

Its sophisticated, erotic line sketches were rather explicit and ribald, to say the least, and I could see why Estelle Fagelman had been offended by it. She'd be pleased to know that a coat or two of canary yellow #4 paint would soon make the wallpaper nonexistent.

"Susan, wanna come here a sec?" Nick called from the bedroom. "I think I found something."

I walked in to find him holding an old pair of jeans he'd removed from a carton. He was rifling through Michael's wallet and held up two checks.

I looked at the first one and recognized the green rolling hills motif and the Bambi-like deers. The check was Ellen Bethune's.

"Seems like Miss Peach Blossom decided to pay the seven hundred dollars after all," Nick observed. "It's dated

June twenty-sixth, the day Cole died; he never got to cash it."

"Well then, if Ellen paid him off that day, she probably would've continued paying him off. Wouldn't that let her off the hook?" I asked.

"It would seem that way, not that she's sorry he's dead. Or maybe she gives him the check, they have a fight, she inadvertently kills him and then hurries out without retrieving her money."

"You really think it happened that way?" I asked.

Nick shrugged. "I think that when you get down to it, the additional two hundred dollars a week was chicken feed to her, considering just how much she had at stake."

"Is Ellen still a suspect?"

"Let's just say she's dropped in the charts," Nick replied. "Matter of fact, I find the other check a hell of a lot more fascinating."

He handed it to me.

This check was also dated June 26. It was made out to Michael Cole in the amount of $2,000 and the signature at the bottom of the check was that of M. S. Rosenbloom.

"What does it mean exactly?" I asked.

"I don't know, but I sure as hell intend to find out. C'mon," he said.

We were halfway across the living room when we heard the key in the door.

Without making a sound, I followed Nick to a nearby table; it was covered with a huge sheet. We crawled under and waited.

The doorknob turned and the door itself opened.

I almost sneezed, but Nick quickly pinched my nose.

Curious as to the identity of the intruder—intruder? Wasn't that the pot calling the kettle black?—at any rate, we slowly lifted the sheet an inch and were surprised to see Mrs. Polchik.

For some reason she was the last person either of us expected to see, even though she was the only one who had any reason to be in Michael's apartment.

She headed straight for the kitchen, and we heard the refrigerator door open immediately. Shortly thereafter, she walked out of the kitchen and out of the apartment carrying two bottles of Heineken.

Once we were certain she'd left, we got up from under the cover.

"Let's get out of here," Nick said, pulling me to my feet. As he did, I lost my balance and reached for what was nearest me. Unfortunately, it just happened to be the stepladder on which a can of paint began to tip precariously.

The can tumbled over so quickly that in a matter of seconds I became a head-to-foot human canvas.

"Ahgh!" All I could do was make choking sounds.

"Shhh."

"Shhh? Shhh?!" I repeated in a harsh whisper. "Look at me, Nicholas. I look like an Andy Warhol painting!"

"I see," he said, calmly wiping my face with a rag. Then he heaved me over his shoulder and headed for the door.

"Susan dahling, peacock blue is irrefutably your color," he said.

Nick was still carrying me as we waited for the elevator.

"Don't you think this looks kind of strange?" I asked.

"Not necessarily," he said. "This is Hollywood, isn't it?"

I saw his point.

Paint notwithstanding, I didn't look half as strange as some of the people getting out of the elevator. In fact, if truth be told, I'd say I looked more bourgeois than most.

✄ 21 ✄

A man's palate can, in time, become accustomed to anything.

Napoleon Bonaparte

Nick would have preferred driving directly to Rosenbloom's agency—Rosenstern, Rosenbloom, and Rosencrantz, Inc.—but I insisted we make a pit stop at his hotel so that I could, to coin a phrase, freshen up.

The hotel clerk stared at me. I can't say I blamed him; I'd have stared too. The paint had dried quickly on my body and clothes, and peacock blue was turning my blond hair a putrid army olive.

Fortunately the paint was water-based so most of it washed out in the shower. At least instead of army green it became a cheerful shade of chartreuse, thereby matching my swollen cheek.

I changed into one of Nick's T-shirts and rolled up a pair of his jeans. While I wouldn't have won any beauty contests, at least I was clean. My arms and face were still splattered with blue paint, however, and Nick had some on his face, from having carried me. He changed too.

"Ready?" he asked. "Let's go. It's a quarter past six; I just hope Rosenbloom's a late worker. Susan, what are you doing?"

"Putting on lipstick. I don't want to walk into his agency looking drab," I replied, blotting my lips. "There. Now I'm ready. How do I look?"

"Very glamorous, very 'undrab,' but do you really think the lipstick was necessary? Your face is beginning to look like an artist's palette," Nick said with the utmost tact. He grabbed his Yankee baseball cap as he shut the light out and we left the room.

The receptionist at Meyer's agency was, to say the least, well endowed. She must have been a D cup, easily. When I was fifteen I stuffed my bra with toilet paper to simulate the same effect, but my mother insisted that I literally stop making mountains out of molehills.

"Do you have an appointment with Mr. Rosenbloom?" she asked Nick as she looked me up and down. With a sense of futility, I pushed a stray lock of hair behind my ear.

"Oh, no, but if you'll just tell him that Nick and Susan would like a few minutes with him." Nick flashed his most charming smile.

It worked.

"Oh, all right," she replied, smiling herself, as though it was her whim alone that determined who did and did not get through to the Rosens—stern, bloom, and crantz, respectively. And to a great extent, I suppose it was.

I didn't have time to give her much more thought before Meyer bounced into the lobby.

He was carrying a monogrammed attaché case in one hand, and extended his free hand to us. He glanced briefly at my blue speckled arms and face, but said nothing.

"Nick . . . Susie. Why didn't you call first? We could've made plans for dinner or something."

His eyes shifted swiftly from Nick's to my own, and he licked his lower lip every so often in a nervous manner.

"As it is I've got to rush off and, uh, meet with a heavy client. They don't give you a chance to piss around here, you know what I'm talkin' about? Heh-heh. Look, I'll tell you what, Nicky, why don't you and Susie-Q here give me a jingle and we'll have lunch some time real soon, huh? How's that grab you?" he asked.

Before I could respond, Nick slapped Meyer on the back. "Sounds good to me, Meyer, baby."

Meyer slapped Nick's face playfully. "I like this boy," he said.

Before leaving, he planted another big wet one on my lips.

"Sorry I gotta split so fast, Susie, but money's the name of the game, you know what I'm talkin' about? *Ciao*," he called out as the door closed behind him.

"Nick, why didn't you ask him?"

Noticing the receptionist listening attentively to our every word, we stepped outside the office.

"Did you feel his palms?" Nick asked when we were no longer within earshot.

"Sure I did. They were clammier than usual, but so what? Stephanie tells me a lot of agents have sweaty hands."

"Not like his. And d'you see how nervous he was about rushing out of here on time?" Nick asked.

"I saw that he was nervous, but on time for what?"

"Good question. Let's go find out just where he was rushing off to," Nick suggested.

We waited for Meyer to zip his Porsche out of the garage before getting into Freddie's Mustang.

"Nick, how are we going to follow anyone in a bright red car like this?" I asked.

"With a lot of difficulty," he said as we shot out the garage door dramatically. Unfortunately, we had to back up to pay for validation before the guard would let us through.

"Validation," Nick grumbled as we drove away.

Following any car in Los Angeles rush-hour traffic is hard enough, but attempting to do so along Sunset Boulevard was madness.

We lost him a few times and at one point discovered we

were following the wrong Porsche. But once we left the boundaries of Beverly Hills we managed to stick with him unobtrusively.

When he turned off onto the side streets, Nick kept a greater distance, although, contrary to what screenwriters might have us believe, it's unlikely that the average driver would have any idea if someone were following him.

The streets we rode down began to take on a familiar aspect. As though I'd ridden this route. With Nick. And fairly recently at that.

"Nick, do you know where we're headed?" I said suddenly as it came to me.

"Yep, I sure do," he replied, "and I don't get it. For the life of me I just don't get it."

"What in the world would Meyer Rosenbloom be doing visiting the H. R. Funeral Home at this time of day?" I said.

We parked our car eight car lengths behind Meyer's, then we turned off the ignition and waited.

And watched.

Meyer got out of his car jangling his keys. He hurried up the stairs of the funeral parlor and looked around before placing a key into the door.

The entire scene was unreal. Meyer S. Rosenbloom, renowned agent, sneaking into a funeral parlor. With his own key, no less. It didn't make sense.

Once we saw Meyer shut the door behind him, Nick and I rushed toward the building. The place was just as I'd remembered it, only now it was dark. Dark that is, with the exception of one, weak ray of light that shone sporadically through the crack beneath the door.

We tried the door but Meyer must have locked it from the inside.

"Don't funeral chapels have side entrances? You know, where they bring the bodies in or something?" I asked.

"Let's hope so," Nick replied. "We're on to something now."

There was a side entrance, but it too was locked. Nick was trying the doorknob one more time when it occurred to me that the H. R. Funeral Home was only a few feet from the building next to it. Their roofs nearly touched.

"What are you suggesting, Susan? That we go up to the roof next door and jump onto this roof in order to gain entrance? Is that what you're suggesting?" Nick asked.

"Well, sort of. But I was kind of thinking that maybe one of us could do the actual jumping and then maybe let the other one in?"

"Not a bad idea. I'll wait for you right here."

"Okay, okay," I said, "we'll both go."

We walked into the apartment building next door and took the stairway to the roof. I recall wondering why anyone would want to live next door to a funeral parlor; it wasn't even as though it were in Santa Monica, where apartments are under rent control and are snatched up regardless of *what* they're next to.

The distance between the roofs, which had appeared to be so negligible from down below, looked much greater from a closer perspective.

"Maybe if we knocked, Meyer would just let us in the front way?" I suggested, hopeful.

"C'mon, this was your idea in the first place, remember?" I remembered.

"Besides, it's not so bad, really," he assured me. "Look, I'll tell you what, I'll go first. I've had more practice. My friends and I used to do this for kicks in the old neighborhood."

"You must've had a precious childhood."

"And! One . . . Mississippi . . . Two . . . Mississippi . . ."

At the count of three, Nick was over on the other side. "Nothin' to it," he said. "Ready?"

"Not really, but here goes."

By holding my breath and jumping up as far as I could, I managed to get to the other side, where I landed right on Nick and tackled him to the ground.

"Was that necessary?" he coughed.

"Sorry, are you all right?" I asked.

"You'd make a hell of a quarterback, y'know that?" he remarked, kissing me. "C'mon, let's go."

Quickly, we ran down the steps leading to the front lobby. The light I had seen from the outside was coming from within the chapel itself. From the way it dimmed and flickered, I guessed its source to be a candle.

Nick opened the doors to the chapel very slowly.

Meyer was nowhere to be seen.

I was about to speak, when Nick pointed out the lights flickering beneath the curtain up front.

Strange, I hadn't noticed that curtain being drawn the last time I was here. But then this whole thing was odd.

"Uh, Nick, this could be embarrassing. I mean Rosenbloom might be praying back there, who knows? Don't you think we're intruding?" I asked.

"I'm an investigative reporter, remember? I intrude for a living," Nick replied. "Ah, come on, we've gotten this far, don't bail out on me now."

Our rubber-soled tennis shoes permitted us to glide down the aisle in silence.

"And whatever you do, don't sneeze," Nick warned.

"Terrific. Why'd you have to say that?" My nose began to tingle at the very suggestion.

We were standing at the right wing of the platform. When I heard Meyer moaning softly on the other side of the curtain, I knew that my curiosity had gotten the better of my sense of propriety.

Nick moved the curtain aside a fraction; a fraction was enough. Actually, it was *more* than enough.

Until that evening I'd thought I had seen everything. But this topped it all.

Crouching with his back toward us, was Meyer S. Rosenbloom, in the flesh. In fact, in nothing else but the flesh. He was stark naked, his clothing neatly folded on a nearby stool.

And yet this alone was not what made my eyes pop out. Nor was it what caused Nick's lips to curl in disgust.

Rather, it was what Meyer was crouching over that got to us.

Laid flat out in a teakwood coffin was the cadaver of a thin brunette, who, had she been alive, would have been thirty, thirty-five years of age. Her breasts had to have been injected with something; they swelled like balloons.

She was dressed in a pink satin bra and matching panties and wore a garter belt and mesh stockings, as well. The body had been made up heavily as had her face, with an almost grotesque application of eye makeup. Rouge and lipstick alone, however, could not disguise the icy-blue pallor of her skin or lips.

For a brief moment she reminded me of someone.

The black hair. The chalky face. The hollow eyes. The blue-tinged lips. So . . . so like whom?

Felicia! Of course.

Oh-ho! So that was it! This then was Meyer's attraction to Felicia. Her uncanny resemblance to a corpse. My mind took a morbid turn and I began to speculate as to whether Felicia played other "death" games with Meyer. For all I knew, she allowed herself to be bathed in ice-cubes.

I placed my hand on Nick's shoulder and he jumped slightly; this was spooking him as well.

Meyer removed the dead woman's undergarments and placed them alongside of his own clothes. He then lifted himself on top of her and began ritualistically to fondle her breasts with one hand and his member with the other.

I turned away at that point, but Nick continued to watch, disgusted, yet fascinated all the same.

I heard the creaking of the teakwood box, and could make out Meyer's "lovemaking" sounds, if you will, take on a more passionate fervor.

Sounds of slapping and panting now accompanied his moans. And the moaning grew louder. And louder.

And then it stopped.

A soft sigh followed; it all happened within a matter of seconds.

"I think he's finished," Nick observed. "Boy, talk about your minute men."

"I wonder how it was for her?" I whispered back.

"Shhh."

"Who's there? That you, Reeper?" Meyer asked.

He quickly dismounted and grabbed his jeans, blowing most of the candles out at the same time. Only a few still flickered.

Nick stepped forward, I followed.

To say Meyer was flabbergasted would be putting it mildly. Even in the dim light we could see his eyes dart between the two of us, making him look like a cornered mouse.

No one spoke. Each of us was embarrassed in our own way.

A look of panic swept over Meyer's face as he turned toward the coffin and then back to us. His expression seemed to question just how much we had witnessed.

It must have been apparent from the looks on our faces that Nick and I had seen it all.

Meyer looked at Nick with tears in his eyes. For a second I thought he was going to cry out loud.

"Look man, this isn't what you think," he pleaded. His voice was hoarse with fear.

"No?" Nick replied. "Well tell me something, Rosenbloom, you bring all your dates here?"

Meyer looked at me, then looked away and threw his hands up in despair. He swallowed hard.

"All right!" he finally shouted. "All right, it *is* what you think. So what? What's the big, fucking deal? You think I don't know other people who're into their own kinky trips? I mean everybody gets their jollies some way, right? Animals, snuff flicks, defecation, body painting . . ."

He stated this last kink while looking directly into my blue-splotched face.

"Say, hold on, this isn't . . ." I began, defensively.

"Sure, babe, sure it isn't," he smirked. "Nothing's what it appears to be right? Listen, you don't have to explain your actions to anyone, and neither do I."

"No one's saying you do," Nick said quietly.

His manner seemed to soothe Meyer.

"Okay, you want to talk? We'll talk. But, uh, would you mind letting me get my shit together? Collect myself, you know? I'll meet you in the back of the chapel in a few minutes. Just give me a few minutes," he requested.

We did as he asked.

"What do you suppose would make a man get into that?" I asked Nick as we waited for Meyer.

"Beats me," Nick replied. "Maybe she encouraged him."

In a few minutes Meyer loped down the aisle with a renewed air of confidence. It was remarkable how quickly he'd been able to compose himself.

He seated himself in the pew in front of us and turned to face us both.

"I know what you're thinking," he began. "What's a guy like me, a guy who could get a date with any chick in town, what's a guy like that doin' makin' it with a stiff?"

He forced a laugh and shook his head.

"Okay, let me try to explain. So that you'll understand where I'm coming from, you know?"

He exhaled before going on.

"I've gone out with so many broads in this town I couldn't guess how many. What can I tell you? Some guys bag deer, I'm into beaver myself. All right, granted, some of them were dogs. But most? Most were really foxes, you know what I'm talkin' about? Not bad for a kid who went through school being fixed up with everyone's piss-faced cousin." He laughed.

"And then the kid does good in Hollywood. Real good. And suddenly there are women hangin' all over him all the time. Great, no? Or at least it should have been. Only thing is I'm not sure whether they're hangin' on to Meyer S. Rosenbloom the man or Meyer S. Rosenbloom the agent." In that moment I genuinely pitied the man.

"Sometimes I think they put up with the old Meyer for what it was worth to them. I get the feeling they're laughing at me.

"It used to drive me bananas worrying about it. I was a regular basket case, so help me. It got so bad I became, uh, I became..." he struggled.

"Impotent?" I suggested helpfully.

"Yeah, all right," he acquiesced, "for lack of a better word. And then one night I was at this party? A real swingin' deal, you know what I'm talkin' about? And some chick was floating so high on something, she made herself up to look like a corpse. Stripped down to the bone and just lay there on the floor without moving a muscle. So for the hell of it, I figured, okay, why not try to get it on with, you know, a corpse. Shit. It was worth a try; I wasn't scoring any better with the live wires.

"You know something? It turned me on. Swear to God it did. I mean I really got off on it. Three times in fact.

And that from a guy who, if I'm gonna be honest, hadn't been able to get it up in over a year."

"What happened then?" Nick asked, totally engrossed.

"Well, I figured, this being a town of actresses, I'd just get hold of an actress who could play the part of a corpse," he replied.

"Where'd you advertise, in the obituary columns?" I asked.

"Cute, Susie, but you know I didn't have any problems. I knew lots of broads who'd dress up and make like a kangaroo if I promised them a screen test. And finally I found one who fit the role to a tee," Meyer said.

"Felicia?" Nick asked.

Meyer nodded.

"Only trouble was her body was too warm at room temperature, so I'd make her take a cold shower before she got into bed," he explained.

"But why, Meyer?" I asked.

"I don't really know the answer to that one, Susie. Maybe it gave me a feeling of total control, I don't know. Oh, I'm sure there's a lot of deep-rooted Freudian crap at the bottom of it all, but I'm no shrink," he said.

"Did you ever consider going to one?" I asked.

"Once," he admitted, "but the guy I went to liked little boys. So I got to wondering whether we all didn't have our own sexual deviations. You know, there's probably a primitive tribe in Africa where kissing is looked on as a perversion for all we know."

"Truth is, Meyer," Nick said, "most of us just fantasize."

"So? I act out my fantasies. Is that such a crime?" Meyer demanded.

He had a point. But where did one draw the line, I wondered.

"Besides, who could it hurt?" he continued, pointing to

the front of the chapel as he spoke. "These broads are dead, for God's sake."

"Have you ever thought how her loved ones might feel if they knew?" I asked.

"Her husband for example?" Nick said.

"Well, it wouldn't be like she was cheating on him," Meyer rationalized. "But I can see what you mean. No, I guess I never gave it much thought."

"By the way, how'd you progress from Felicia to the real live thing? Or, in this case, the real dead thing?" Nick asked.

Meyer sighed. "I confided my, um, preference to Tracy and Michael one time. They were still together and there was a time we were pretty close, you know?

"Well, it so happened Michael knew this guy, Reeper. Some of his clients had attended services here. Michael said for the right amount of money and a fifty percent cut, he could arrange for me to . . . you know, get the real thing, whenever I wanted.

"At first I didn't think I could go through with it but then I figured, why not? I mean, shit, I wouldn't have looked for it, but here it was being tossed in my lap."

A poor choice of words on Meyer's part, I thought.

"So the deal was set. I'd pay Michael a thousand dollars a month for him to set me up with, say, oh, one to two bods a week. That'd be five hundred a month for him, clear profit. And for me, well, I figured it'd come out to a little over a hundred a broad, which is what you'd pay for a decent call girl these days," Meyer explained.

There seemed to be no limit to his crudeness.

"Let me get this straight," Nick interrupted, "Reeper would get five hundred dollars in the setup and Cole would get the same for just getting the two of you together. Acting as, uh, well, an agent, if you'll excuse the expression."

"That's okay," Meyer assured him. "Look, I've had to

negotiate enough deals that died in the making, to make the comparison valid, you know what I'm talkin' about?"

"What did Reeper do for you exactly?" I asked.

Here, Meyer became a little reticent.

"Ah c'mon, Meyer, you told us this much," Nick pointed out.

"All right," he said finally. "Reeper made up a key for my use. By the way, how'd you two get in? I thought I locked the door behind me."

"It's a long story," I said. "Go on with what you were saying."

"All right, so he made up this key. Then when a chick came in that met my specifications . . ."

"Which were?" Nick asked.

"Oh, between sixteen and forty, say, good bod, nice tits, though of course that could be fixed," Meyer replied.

How do you like that? Even after death, the criterion of a woman's sex appeal was the same as in life. I suppose then this was the ultimate meat market, surpassing the most action-packed singles' bar around.

"Then I'd tell Michael how I'd like them, um, embalmed," Meyer continued. "What I'd like them to be wearing. What kind of underwear that is. He'd pass it on to Reeper and when one came in he thought I'd dig, he'd contact me through Michael, who'd either call me or get in touch with me through Tracy."

"So you never contacted Reeper directly," Nick said.

"Never even met the guy till recently," Meyer said. "I'd just give Michael the money and things were always left according to my instructions. Once Reeper collected his money he'd leave the key under the mat."

"I'm just curious. I mean, from a purely physical standpoint," Nick began.

"How is it?" Meyer smiled. "Is that what you want to know? Well, of course, one has to simulate a lot. You know, use lubrication of some kind for one thing. But with the right imagination, what can I tell you? It took a stiff to make me stiff you might say, heh-heh. Now do you mind if I ask you a question?"

"Go right ahead," Nick said.

"How'd you find me out?"

"Uh, well, as a matter of fact, we didn't," I admitted.

"I don't dig it."

"Nick?"

"Look Meyer, it's like this. Susan and I just happened to walk in on you at, well, at a hell of an inopportune time it seems. You see, we followed you here; we got in through the roof," Nick said.

"Followed me? But why?" Meyer asked.

"To ask you about this," Nick explained, removing the check he'd found in Michael's apartment.

Meyer looked at the check and handed it back to Nick.

"How'd you get hold of this?" Meyer asked admiringly.

"Two thousand dollars is not one thousand, unless, of course, you paid a month in advance, which I strongly doubt," Nick said.

Meyer removed a package of chewing gum from his jeans and offered it to us. I declined, but Nick thanked him and for a while they just sat there unraveling paper and chewing.

"Believe me," Meyer finally said. "I was less than pleased about the increase in payment. I even called him . . . the day . . . the day he, uh, died. At the shop. I told him he was asking too much. All right, another hundred or two I could maybe understand, but to double the figure like that?"

"What did Michael say?" I asked as it dawned on me that I had possibly been witness to the very conversation he described.

"Say? What would he say? The bastard laughed."

I was sure now that it was with Meyer that Michael had been speaking that morning.

"We had some words, I think I told him what he could do with himself, you know, but in the end I coughed up the extra grand," he admitted.

"But why?" Nick asked. "I mean, couldn't you deal with Reeper directly by then?"

"Oh, it'd gone way beyond that," Meyer explained. "Cole hinted that he might leak the story of my 'peculiar tastes,' as he put it, to the gossip columns if I tried to cut him out of his percentage. And he would have too, that shithead!"

"Well, with everything you hear, would that have been such a scandal? I mean these days, and in this town, especially?" I asked.

"You bet your ass it would. Necrophilia is not one of your more acceptable aberrations, Susie baby," Meyer informed me. "Besides, the rules—or should I say lack of them—that apply to actors don't necessarily hold true for those of us who *really* wield the power.

"My name's my bread and butter. I like to keep it untainted. Smelling sweet. Like a 'rose-in-bloom' you might say."

He smiled at what he thought to be a brilliant quip.

"When did you get the check to him?" Nick asked.

"Oh, I dropped in on him later that same day. He knew he had me. Of course, I didn't think that it'd be the last check I'd be giving him," he said with the utmost sincerity.

"Well, if this check was never cashed, how is it you're still here?" Nick asked.

Meyer grinned and tapped his head. He was beginning to enjoy his own narrative.

"I didn't know what happened to the check, but I stopped payment on it the Monday after Michael, uh, met his maker.

"Now, you may think it callous of me to be thinking about money at a time like that, but look, life goes on, you know what I'm talkin' about?

"Then I arranged to pay Reeper through Tracy. His five

hundred dollars just like before. I actually saved five hundred when Cole conveniently dropped out of the picture. Tracy had no objections. I've done a lot for her. Besides, to tell you the truth, I think she got off on it. Got her out of her own space.

"And Reeper was cool. Oh, except maybe at Michael's funeral service. You had him a little uptight, you know. He thought you were with the *Enquirer* or something, and that you were on to our little game. Told me later he slipped you a C note to keep you quiet. The shmuck! I can imagine what you must've thought," Meyer said.

"I didn't know what to think," I confessed. "How'd you manage when Tracy, well, when Tracy died?"

"I finally phoned Reeper. Told him I never wanted to be seen meeting him in public, not even at a funeral. I'd pay him in cash, leave it in a locker I rented at LAX, and for a little extra consideration, like a few more girls and my own personal key, for instance, so I could come and go as I pleased, I arranged to pay him the thousand dollars a month. Why not?

"I figured I'd let him keep Cole's cut, oh, and I threw in a small role in a new film I'm negotiating. Even promised him points."

This last remark of Meyer's struck me as being very ironic. Actually the entire evening was a sort of study in the macabre.

"Okay, kids, now if there's nothing else," began a man who was used to dismissing people, "I'd be eternally grateful . . ."

"Meyer, Tracy was murdered," Nick cut in.

If he was shooting for shock value, he failed; Meyer's response was anything but surprised.

"Yeah, I know" was all he said. He rolled his wad of gum into a ball, and popped a fresh piece into his mouth.

"You know?" I said.

"Well, I didn't want to mention anything the last time we spoke, but it occurred to me that the papers said they found traces of ludes and vodka in her blood," Meyer said.

"So?" Nick said.

"So Tracy was allergic to hard liquor. Made her throat itch. She'd never pour herself anything but champagne, imported at that. Even if she were killing herself. I knew Tracy would never think of leaving this world uncomfortable."

"Well, if you suspected, uh, 'foul play,' why didn't you go to the police?" I asked.

Meyer looked more embarrassed than I'd seen him look all evening.

"Heh-heh, first thing you know my name would be dragged into it and well, you know...Let's just say it wouldn't have been tasteful for me to have gotten involved."

Tasteful? I hadn't realized Meyer knew the meaning of the word.

I could only guess that he was lying to cover up his involvement in Tracy's death, or he was simply a spineless son of a bitch; neither possibility seemed unlikely.

"Well, that's about it," Meyer concluded. "If I've shocked you provincial people with my sordid account, I sincerely apologize."

"Shocked? No, I'd say educated might be more appropriate. All the same, Meyer, if you want to insure the fact that that rose-in-bloom continues to smell sweet, I'd give up these charming carcasses; it's against the law. And I'm kind of an ethical person about some things." Nick shrugged.

"I like your style, Nicky." Meyer breathed a sigh of relief. "Besides, you're right. Maybe I'll go back to actresses, it's cheaper."

"Atta boy." Nick patted him on the back. "This'll be our secret, now that both Michael and Tracy are dead."

"Tracy. Poor Tracy," Meyer sighed, shaking his head

mournfully. "Cremated yet! You know I never got to first base with her when she was alive, but something tells me that maybe..."

Nick and I were already out the door, leaving Meyer to erotic reflections about Tracy Simms and his many other girl—or should I say ghoul friends.

✂ 22 ✂

*Murderer: One who is presumed to be innocent
until he is proved insane.*

Oscar Wilde

Friendship is an umbrella from the rains of trouble.
Fortune found inside my crumbled Joy Fung cookie

It was Nick's idea that our friends be introduced to one
another so that we could add yet another dimension to our
ever growing relationship.

As it turned out, it proved to be an excellent idea.

Bucky and his lover, Gary, and Stephanie and her doctor-
boyfriend, David, joined Nick and myself for dinner at
Borden's, a western-style barbecue joint renowned for its
ribs. For hours we exchanged stories and drank beer while
the voices of Willie and Waylon serenaded us from the
jukebox.

Stephanie yanked us up to the dance floor one by one
so that she could teach the newest dance step, kicking saw-
dust beneath her three-hundred-dollar western boots in the
process, a cowgirl with panache.

When we left Borden's Nick suggested we all pile into
David's Eldorado in search of the ultimate dessert. After a
half-hour debate as to what actually constituted the ultimate
dessert, it was agreed upon that we'd go to my house where
we'd at least be assured of good coffee.

Not surprisingly, the subject of Michael Cole's death
came up during the drive back.

It was Nick who suggested we cast our ballot for the "suspect" of our choice. Of course, David and Gary had to be filled in somewhat.

To the best of my recollection we each had a favorite candidate.

Nick himself pointed the finger at Alison. The motive? As he so delicately put it, "one hundred grand ain't hay." One hundred thousand dollars was the figure Mutual of Omaha had disclosed as having been the amount for which Michael was insured; Alison was the sole beneficiary.

It was David's opinion that Alison's friend, Cinnamon, had killed Cole because all the shampoo and hair spray he used was contaminating our waters.

While I thought that showed imagination, I was more inclined toward Jean Paul. After all, as Tracy had said, "love kills," and the business Jean Paul had built and loved was being threatened by Cole.

Stephanie's vote went to Meyer S. Rosenbloom. Her reasoning was that since the firm of Rosenstern, Rosenbloom, and Rosencrantz, Inc. turned her down for representation last spring, it would serve one of them right to hang for displaying such a phenomenal lack of insight.

"More coffee, anyone?" I asked.

"I'll have a bit more, thanks," Nick replied.

I looked at him curiously.

Having located a basket of knitting at the foot of the couch, Nick was busy scavenging through odds and ends of yarn. He satisfied himself with the red and blue makings of a sweater and began to knit. Claimed it helped him concentrate.

Gary settled himself at the piano and began playing old favorites. The subject was still Michael Cole's murder, for by now there wasn't the slightest doubt in our minds it was murder. Suddenly, the music stopped and Gary asked, "What about Ellen Bethune?"

"What about her?" Nick replied.

"Couldn't she be our murderess?"

"That's a sexist word, Gary," Stephanie remarked. "Try getting away with Jewess or Negress in this day and age."

Gary continued innocently hypothesizing that Ellen Bethune might have had a fling with Cole she didn't want her husband to find out about. "Maybe she was paying him off."

"Hate to poke a knitting needle into your hypothetical balloon," said Nick, "but even if that were true, don't you think she'd have paid off rather than resort to murder?"

"Or told her husband outright?" David concurred. "The guy would have taken her back for, say, her one indiscretion. I know I would."

"Would you dear?" Stephanie purred.

"Of course, uh, why do you ask?"

We tossed about some other ideas, Stephanie finally suggesting that Estelle Fagelman *kvetched* Michael to death and that's all there was to it.

Nick was laughing at this when the door slammed shut.

"I . . . oh, I'm sorry. I didn't realize you'd have company," Marc said, his eyes quickly surveying the room.

And I hadn't expected Marc to come home just then either. He wasn't due back for another two days, and I hadn't counted on his arriving ahead of schedule.

He glanced with disdain at Nick, who, though he continued knitting, looked up to meet Marc's eyes.

"A sweater," Nick replied to Marc's unvoiced question.

"Right. Uh, Sue? May I please speak with you in the kitchen?" Marc asked.

"Look, Sue," Marc began, tearing voraciously into a box of Mallomars.

"Marc, before you say anything, I want to remind you that I had no idea whatsoever you'd be coming home tonight. And besides . . ."

"Whoa, hold on, Sue. You know, I'm not exactly the monster you seem to be making me out to be these days. Contrary to what you think, I wasn't going to come down on you for having guests, though I admit our taste in people, like everything else it would seem, is decidedly different.

"But for Christ's sake, this is your home as much as it is mine. I was just going to say that I'm beat, and I hoped you wouldn't think it rude if I didn't join you and your friends," Marc said.

I can't recall feeling much more ashamed of myself than I did standing in my kitchen that evening. For one thing, it hadn't even occurred to me to invite Marc to join us.

He was right. I was making him out to be some kind of monster, whereas in truth neither of us was guilty. We were merely two people who were mismatched and now found ourselves in monstrous circumstances.

"I'm sorry," I apologized. "Of course you're not a monster, and I'm sorry if I've made you feel as though you were. Marc?" I began.

He brushed my cheek tenderly with the palm of his hand.

"Not now, Sue. I really am tired you know." He smiled. "We'll talk in the morning. No, better make it over dinner. I've got a ten o'clock meeting tomorrow."

With that, he walked out of the kitchen.

The group was disbanding when we entered the living room.

"Please don't go on my account," Marc said, holding up his hands.

"That's okay," Bucky assured him. "We were just leaving."

Stephanie leaned over and kissed my cheek.

"Sorry if the shit's hit the proverbial fan because of us," she whispered.

Nick took Bucky's right arm and Gary's left, and as he walked out the door, turned back to Marc.

"Be seein' you around, huh?" Nick said.

Marc just shook his head pityingly and waved him an exhausted good night.

✂ ❮23❯ ✂

*Life is a tragedy for those who feel, and a comedy
for those who think.*

Jean de La Bruyère

Tradition had always dictated that whenever Marc and I
quarreled, the restaurant in which we chose to make up
indicated who won. Typically, when I played the martyr,
we would inevitably wind up in an English or American
establishment noted for its prime ribs.

On the other hand, when Marc wanted to make up with
me, we dined in more exotic surroundings, usually a Med-
iterranean restaurant of my choosing.

So fixed was this scheme of things, it had become a sort
of private joke between Marc and myself.

With this in mind, I was surprised the following evening
when Marc informed me that he had made dinner reser-
vations at Dimitri's, an Armenian restaurant we'd discovered while driving north up the coast highway.

I'd been fully prepared to explain, over a thick porter-
house, why we would have to dissolve what was left of our
relationship.

Mr. Dimitri seated us personally.

"Ah, it is nice to see you both again."

"Nice to see you too, Mr. Dimitri," Marc said.

"So, you come here to celebrate something special maybe?
Hah? You finally tying up the knot? Hah?" He grinned.

"Uh, no, Mr. Dimitri. We're not, uh, tying the knot," I
said, looking at Marc as I spoke.

"Oh well, I bring you a wine list anyhow," he said, the epitome of discretion. "Or maybe you prefer ouzo, hah?"

"Ouzo would be fine," Marc assured him.

Dimitri returned to take our orders and serve us with a bottle of ouzo and an appetizing assortment of grapeleaves stuffed with lamb, phyllo pastries, feta cheese, and other delectable goodies.

"You let me know when you ready to order, hah?" he said, rushing off to reprimand an incompetent busboy.

"Sue," Marc started in somewhat hesitantly, "what I've got to say isn't going to be easy."

Right then I knew that whatever it was would be easier for him than me.

"But I think it has to be said," Marc continued solemnly.

Good for you, Marc, I thought to myself, I'm glad one of us has the guts to get the ball rolling.

"All right, here it is. We've been going at each other for the last, oh, what would you say, for the last three months or so?"

I'd have said the last year, but that was irrelevant.

"Go on," I said.

He took a big gulp of ouzo and then bit down and gasped.

"Jeez, I forgot how strong that stuff is."

"Finding the courage to say some things is never easy," I philosophized sympathetically as I sipped the strong licorice-flavored liquor. I was seeking my own strength at the time.

"I don't know what went wrong," Marc continued. "Well, not exactly. What I mean is, I'd always accepted the fact that you've never loved me as much as I've loved you, Sue, but they say that's the way it is in most relationships. Tipping of the scale or something.

"But we'd always been compatible with one another, more or less. Wouldn't you say so?"

"More or less," I agreed. God, I thought, why is he dragging this out? What was the point?

"Well, I've always believed we were, that is, until lately. Lately I've come to realize that whatever it is you've been looking for in a man, I'm not it."

I began to protest, but Marc took my hand.

"No, no, let me finish, please. Now I just said that I'm not what you're looking for in a man and that's the truth.

"Maybe you find me more demanding than most. You need, or at least you think you need someone with more, how should I put it . . . *savoir faire*? Someone more impulsive . . . more . . . Oh, I don't know, but you see what I'm getting at. Maybe I'm just a little too straight or stuffy for you. I've disappointed you, and for that I'm sincerely sorry. And yet you've still wanted to marry me. I could never figure out why," he admitted.

Everything was suddenly sad, so very sad. The sweet, pungent scent of ouzo, the song coming over the stereo. I recognized the voice as that of Ari San, a Greek singer known for his bittersweet love songs. I looked into Marc's big forlorn eyes. More than ever they looked like those of a puppy. A betrayed puppy at that.

And betrayed by whom? By a friend. Someone he trusted. I felt sure that what he was leading up to was some sort of eleventh-hour appeal. A desperate attempt to keep us together at any cost. Even marriage if it came to that.

Oh, I would have given anything not to have hurt Marc then. But it was too late for us to salvage anything. Couldn't he understand that? This was it. I had to tell him about Nick.

"Marc . . ."

"Sure, I know I'm not what you desire in a man," he repeated.

"Marc, please stop. You couldn't make me feel worse than I already do."

"But then, you're far from what I desire in a woman, Sue."

I was wrong. About his not being able to make me feel worse, I mean. He could and he did.

"Which is why...which is why...I..." He sucked hard on an olive pit.

Idiot! Susan Finkelstein, you've been a prize idiot!

Any halfway observant fool could have seen that Marc's ramblings were not those of the "betrayed" but rather those of the "betrayer."

How strange to think that moments before Marc's revelation, I felt, well, almost remorseful. Sorry that I couldn't give Marc the love he was rightfully entitled to.

Now here he was assuring me that he was getting that affection with or without me. I'd gotten my comeuppance, that was for sure, and it hurt.

However distant Marc and I had grown, a part of him was still in me. I know it was illogical, but it pained me to discover that someone could make Marc happy where I had failed, though in effect this is exactly what Nick had done for me.

All those nasty questions began to gnaw at me.

Who? Where? How?

Out of the corner of my eye, I watched a *zoftig* belly dancer entertain the tables with her suggestive movements.

I turned my attention back to Marc.

"Tell me about her," I said.

Marc looked relieved at what appeared to be my calm resolve. Actually, what he was witnessing wasn't resolve at all, it was numbness. It was as though I had become a third party, an onlooker if you will.

Now I was curious more than anything else.

"Sue...Sue...Sue, you don't want to hear..." Marc said.

"Oh, but I do. Please, Marc. What's she like? When did you meet her? I want to know," I assured him.

He sighed.

"I don't know where to begin," he began. "I met her on the court a few months ago."

"What court? When were you in court?"

"Not *in* court. *On* the court. The tennis court. At the club."

"Oh, so you met her playing tennis?"

"Not exactly."

"Well, what exactly?"

"Dee Dee runs the tennis pro shop."

"Dee Dee. That's her name, Dee Dee?"

"Her name's Diane McGuire, but she likes to be called Dee Dee."

"Oh. How old is Dee Dee, Marc?"

"For Christ's sake, Susan, what difference does it make how old she is?"

"That young, huh?"

Not only was I to be tossed out of Disneyland, but there went my remaining "E" tickets as well.

"I wasn't aware that any of this was supposed to make me feel better. What does she look like, or shouldn't I ask?"

"You shouldn't, but I'll tell you because you did. She's blond, she's petite, she's . . . oh, I don't know, this is silly."

"It's not silly," I said.

"It is too. The point is not what she looks like, it's how . . . it's how she makes me feel," Marc stated.

"And how *does* she make you feel?" I asked, in a voice so soft it surprised me.

"Good about myself. Not like I'm some kind of schmucky jock, that's how."

I tried, unsuccessfully, to ignore the barb in Marc's last remark.

"So you met Dee Dee while playing tennis, jumped the

net and it was L-O-V-E, huh?" I sipped my drink. "I'm sorry, that was stupid of me."

Marc didn't debate the point.

"Do you . . . do you see her often?" I asked.

He shrugged, embarrassed.

"We've been seeing each other on and off, a few nights a week for the past few months. I, uh . . . I took her to New York with me," he said, though his words were barely audible to me.

How funny. How so, so funny. I was too absorbed in my affair with Nick to appreciate or care that Marc was having a fling of his own.

And yet it was so obvious, I thought in retrospect. All the telltale signs were there. They were practically spat out at me.

His evasiveness when I inquired about his project. His longer work hours. His defensiveness, followed by moments of guilt-motivated tenderness.

Even his sudden obsession with a diet and exercise program. Why, he'd begun exercising himself into better shape and renewed vim and vigor all for young Dee Dee.

It made sense now.

"I showed her a snapshot of you. She . . . uh . . . thinks you're very attractive," he remarked, trying to soften the blow.

"Swell." I lit a cigarette. I toyed with the idea of disclosing my relationship with Nick, but I could see no point in subjecting Marc to the same pain and humiliation I had just experienced. So I kept quiet and took his hands in mine.

"Thank you for understanding, Sue," he said gratefully. "You've been remarkable about all this. Really."

"Mmmm. Well, where do we go from here?" I asked.

"We'll have Peter go over the paper work with us, I've already discussed it with him," Marc informed me.

So Peter and Kristin knew. What was it that they said about the wife always being the last . . . blah, blah, blah?

"We'll divide everything fairly . . . the house, everything. I wouldn't want you to think I'd cheat you," Marc added, concerned.

"Of course not, Marc. I know you're fair. I'd never think you'd cheat me," I assured him.

Ha! How ironic my words were, since the issue of Marc's cheating had been the inspiration for our very conversation.

"Have you given any thought to where you'll be living?" I asked, shifting uncomfortably in my seat. This entire discourse was beginning to take its toll on me.

"Uh, well, for the time being we'll stay in Dee Dee's apartment in Brentwood. But, well, Dee and I have been looking in Malibu. She loves the water . . . likes to surf and all, you know."

I had to ask.

"But of course, as I said, that won't be for a while. Not until . . . until we're married this winter," he said with some difficulty.

Dee Dee Beaumont. Not bad. Nor surprising either.

Nothing would have surprised me at this stage of the game.

"I see," I said, quietly.

It was then that I thought of Nick. Nick in his Yankee cap, playing his dumb harmonica. Nick carrying me into an elevator, the two of us drenched in paint.

It was the memory of those images that enabled me to say with the utmost of grace, "Marc, I really and truly wish you and Dee Dee all the happiness in the world. You're a good man, and you deserve the best. We all do."

"Thanks, Sue," Marc said. "It means a lot to me to hear you say that. I've got to tell you, I've dreaded this evening, but you've made it easier for me, you really have. And who knows? Everything may turn out for the best all the way around. Maybe now you'll be able, finally, to find the man of your dreams and go for it."

"Maybe." I smiled.

Dimitri returned for our orders to find Marc and me in a tearful embrace.

"Ah, that Ari San, he sing for lovers, hah?" Dimitri sighed.

✂ 24 ✂

Birds are entangled by their feet, men by their tongues.

Thomas Fuller

Marc dropped me off at the house after dinner, explaining that he'd be spending the night at Dee Dee's.

"Don't you need to come in for anything? I mean a toothbrush? Something?" I asked.

"No, that's okay. I, uh, have whatever I need over there."

He wasn't kidding.

"I'll come back for the rest of my things when, well, whenever it's convenient for you," Marc told me.

"Sure. Well, Marc, I guess it's good night. Or maybe I should say good-bye," I said.

"You know, Sue, I hope that one day, you and Dee Dee can get to know each other and, well, maybe we can all be good friends," he said, optimistically.

"Maybe. Some day. But in the meantime, better not send me a wedding invitation, okay? I'm not prepared to be that civilized just yet," I replied.

"I understand."

"Good."

We hugged each other, and then I watched Marc Beaumont zoom out of the drive and out of my life for good.

I was barely in the house when the phone rang. As I went to pick it up in the kitchen, I wondered who would get custody of all nine of our phones.

"Hello?"

"Hi, it's me. Nick. You don't sound too great, everything okay?"

"This you can tell from one hello?"

"Hey, I'm a sensitive guy, what can I tell you? So, what's wrong?"

"In brief? Marc and I split up."

"You . . . say, that's fabulous, or isn't it? I'm sorry, kid. I guess that was kind of a shitty thing for me to say."

"Don't worry about it. After an evening of listening to shitty things, I've become callous."

"So, you're feeling down. Full of doubts. Well, that's to be expected. Are you alone? Want me to come over?" Nick offered.

"Yes I'm alone, but no honey, don't come over. I think I'd prefer being alone tonight."

"Anything you say. But remember, I'm just a phone call away, so if you need me, just whistle. Oh no, I take it back. The switchboard closes at eleven-thirty; if you need me after that, you're gonna really have to whistle."

I laughed.

"That's my Susan. Look, I'll let you go in a second. I just called to ask if you could do me a big favor tomorrow."

"What's that?" I asked.

"My cousin Freddie called tonight. Seems he's entering his wheels in some kind of hot-rod race, I don't know. Anyway, here's the thing. I gotta get Freddie's car down to him sometime tomorrow."

"Where do I fit in?"

"I'm coming to that," he replied. "I'm going to need a ride back from San Diego, so I was wondering if maybe . . ."

"You want me to follow you down in my Toyota and that way we can drive home in one car," I finished.

"Whaddya say?"

"Of course I'll do it. That's not such a big favor."

"Well, I know it's a drive."

"Nonsense."

"Oh, hey, that's terrific of you, Susan, really. I mean

it. You're the salt of the earth. And wait till you meet Uncle Mario and Aunt Camillia. You'll love 'em."

"But will they love me?"

"You kidding? Aunt Camillia can't wait to meet you. She started cooking her special sauce yester...uh..."

"You creep. You knew I'd say yes. Salt of the earth!"

"That's because I know what a truly wonderful woman you are."

"Uh-huh. Don't worry, the deal's still on. What time should I be ready to leave?"

"We'll get an early start. That way we can spend the day, how's that grab you?"

"Sounds fine to me."

"Thanks, and, um...all kidding aside, I know what it's like, breaking up with someone you've been with for so long. Doesn't make any difference who does the breaking. It hurts just the same. So if there's anything I can do," Nick said.

"Just be there for me, that'll be enough."

"You got it sweetheart. Say kid, did I ever tell you I love you?"

"No, Nick, you never have."

"Remind me to tell you the next chance I get."

"Right. 'Night, Nick."

"'Night, Susan."

Dinner with the Comicis was a feast. The ravioli was hand rolled, the Parmesan just grated. Even the minestrone soup was prepared with vegetables from Mario's own garden.

The care that Nick's aunt put into her cooking and his uncle into his garden was evident in the caring and warm way they treated people.

I was immediately welcomed into the fold by everyone except Aunt Camillia's somewhat ornery mother, Theresa, but even she relented by the day's end when I presented her with a Tupperware muffin pan that I'd discovered in my car.

Naturally we couldn't make the two-hour drive back to Los Angeles without an assortment of cold cuts, fruit, candy, and half of an amaretto cheesecake.

In addition to this, Uncle Mario bestowed upon Nick and myself matching "his and her" watches, whose alarms, when set off, buzzed out "Stars and Stripes Forever."

I was truly touched by the gesture and assured him I'd treasure it.

Nick and I were both rather quiet during the drive back to Los Angeles. Nick, no doubt, was recalling to himself one of the many stories Uncle Mario had told at dinner.

My mind began to drift back to the subject closest to my heart and one that seemed to occupy both my waking and sleeping hours. Michael Cole's murder.

It was almost like that game we used to play, *Clue*. We'd hop from room to room eliminating Colonel Mustard and Professor Plum as suspects and the candlestick as a weapon. I even recalled the intricate ways in which each room was designed, with great attention to detail. Why even the wallpaper . . . the wallpaper?

Suddenly I was back in Michael's kitchen. What was it Estelle had said about his wallpaper? That it was disgusting.

Of course, Estelle must have been referring to the new paper, which was indeed risqué, no denying that. But how was that possible when she said that her encounter with Michael was the first she'd seen of him in ages?

Estelle Fagelman was lying.

She must have visited Michael's apartment recently. Why had she lied?

No. I still couldn't see Estelle killing Michael simply because Alison had planned on moving in with her brother. That was pretty farfetched.

Unless, of course, Estelle suspected there was more at stake. But what? Alison was Michael's sister, or half sister at any rate. Was that it? Did Estelle believe there was more at stake than a mere brother-sister relationship?

If there were some "unnatural" attraction between Alison and Michael, it would certainly explain a lot. Tracy and Alison's deep-rooted hatred, for one thing, and why the thought of Alison moving in with Michael would bring an elderly woman with vague suspicions to the point of hysteria. And possibly murder?

Upon hearing my revelations, Nick wasn't nearly as startled as I thought he would be.

"All right. I think maybe, just maybe, mind you, you might have something," he conceded, down-shifting into third, "but I've had enough experience making premature assumptions before checking out facts. So, we'll have to check it out.

"Speaking of checking out, I was planning to check out of my motel and move my things on over to your place, if that's all right with you?"

"Great, but what am I supposed to do in the meantime?"

"For one thing, stay out of Estelle Fagelman's way, in case you were getting any bright ideas. Apricot, please."

I passed him an apricot and began peeling myself a tangerine.

"Nick, do you realize we just demolished this entire basket of food?"

"Increased sexual appetite," Nick explained, shifting my left knee into neutral.

Nick awoke early the next morning, showered, and left to go about his itinerary while I was just beginning to stir.

Awaiting me on the dining room table was a fresh fruit cup and a vase that held a single, long-stemmed rose.

I decided to surprise Nick, in turn, by baking him a chocolate scratch cake, something I hadn't done in ages.

I looked through my recipe book and picked up an egg. The phone rang just as I cracked it into a bowl.

I assumed it was Stephanie, since we'd planned on having lunch that day. I was wrong. It was Fran, wanting to know how *Kelly's Family Tree* was progressing. I promised her I'd have the first draft into her no later than Wednesday of the following week. I told her about my breakup with Marc, and she said she was sorry to hear it. Her tone was less than convincing.

The doorbell rang while I was still on the phone.

"Ooops, Stephanie was probably trying to get through and couldn't. I've got to run, Fran. Talk to you later.

"I'm coming," I called out, wiping off my eggy hands.

I opened my door to the unexpected faces of Estelle Fagelman and Harry Singer.

"I hope ve're not distoibing you or nothing," Estelle said.

"Uh, no, of course not. I was just starting to bake and . . . well, come on in, please," I said, after they had already stepped inside.

Estelle insisted they join me in the kitchen so that I could continue with my baking.

I made them tea and went back to my eggs.

"Nice place you got here," Harry commented, with approval. "You rent?" He sipped his tea while sucking on a sugar cube, just as my grandfather used to do.

"Uh, no . . . it's mine . . . well, at least half of it is. That is to say, I share, or at least I used to . . . I . . . no, Harry, it's not rented," I said finally.

"*Kein na hura*, you must have paid a pretty dollar for it," Estelle observed, looking at me inquisitively.

I merely smiled and reached for the sifter.

"Here. You do the eggs, let me do that," Estelle said, beginning to sift the sugar before I could stop her.

"End d'vay you decorated it, it's also very nice. Tasteful. Not too *ungepotchked*. Right, Harry?"

"Right," Harry agreed, slurping his tea. He was a regular suction cup, Harry was.

"Mrs. Fagleman, Estelle, I appreciate your helping me bake and I'm glad you like the way I've fixed up my house, but surely you had something else on your mind when you came here," I said, beating the eggs vigorously.

By this time Estelle was creaming the butter into the sugar.

"You're right, dollink. I came here to talk vit you about Mickey," she said.

"Essie!" Harry warned.

"Sha! Herry, don't nudge me. Dis is why I came, so let me tro it from my chest, nu?" She handed him an apple and a knife. "Here, enjoy."

"What is it you wanted to tell me about Michael?" I asked.

"I vant you should know det I understood you vas more interested in Mickey den in selling your plastic bowls. Em I correct?" She winked.

"Is there something in particular about Michael you think I'd be interested in knowing?" I asked cautiously while greasing two baking pans.

"Enough beatin' around the bush," Harry said. "Get to the point, Essie. Don't make such a *tsimmes*."

"Herry's right," Estelle said. "Vat I came to say is just dis. You maybe are tinkin' det Mickey, det no-goodnik, he didn't die by eccident. Det maybe somevone killed him. Vell, I came to tell you you're right. He didn't die by eccident. He died by poipose," Estelle said. "You see, I killed det *schtunk*. Vould you mind pessing me d'spet-chula?"

"Essie!" Harry shouted, piercing the apple so fiercely that pieces of it flew into the air.

The greased baking pan slid out of my hands and onto the floor.

"Sha! I know vat I'm doin'!" Estelle admonished Harry, staring at him sharply. "Let me be."

"But we ..."

Another look from Estelle stopped him mid-sentence.

"Good. Now you vant to hear my confession?" Estelle asked me. "Maybe your Italian boyfriend he should hear it too?"

"Nick's not here. I'm alone," I replied, biting my tongue as the words came out. Never let the suspect know you're alone.

"But I expect him back soon," I added, "very soon."

She shrugged indifferently and continued creaming the butter as she spoke.

"Oy, vhere do I begin. You know already vat I tought of det sveetheart," she sighed, referring to Michael. "Vell I told you vat happened vhen I saw him at his beauty parlor, didn't I?"

"You spit in his face," I remarked.

"I soitenly did." She nodded proudly. "But vot good vill det do, I taught to myself later. It bothered me all day, gave me indigestion. To think of Elison end det bum ... oy!"

"Living together?" I asked.

"Nu, vat den? Remember, Mickey and d'friends he brought around, dey vasn't so hotsy-totsy."

Estelle then, worried only about Alison's being exposed to Michael's undesirable life-style in general and apparently had no suspicions of anything more specific. I can't say the same for myself.

"So I decided to give it anotter go," Estelle continued. "I vent to visit Mickey det very night."

"I drove," Harry confessed, his mouth full of apple.

"All right, all right. My accomplice here, he drove me. Anyvays, I valked into Mickey's apartment ..."

"The door was open?" I asked, suspiciously.

"Eh . . . I picked the lock," Estelle said.

"*We* did," Harry quickly added.

"Yeah, ve did. So I . . . ve . . . looked around. I heard d'vater runnin' in d' shower end . . . end so I charged into d'betroom . . ."

"You weren't embarrassed?" I asked, as her story began showing more holes than I'd have to have in my head to believe it.

"Emberrassed? To see Mickey naked, you mean? Vhy should I be emberrassed?" Estelle seemed surprised at the suggestion. "I used to bathe him myself, vonce."

"And then?"

"End den, ve argued. I slepped him in d'face end he, eh, slipped. *Shoin*. Finished. So, let them arrest an old lady. I'll find vat to do, yet, in d'vomen's penitentiary," Estelle assured me.

"Why didn't you phone the police in the first place, if this all happened the way you said it did, Estelle?" I asked.

"I . . . eh . . ." she began.

"She's protecting me; I pushed him on poipose," Harry insisted, belching up his apple.

"Vat's a metter, ve don't heve enough problems? I say I slepped him!" Estelle said.

"And I say I pushed him!" said Harry obstinately.

"He vas slepped!"

"Pushed!"

"Slepped!!"

"Pushed!!"

"Stop, stop," I interrupted. "All right, he was slapped, pushed, whatever. And you were both in on it. Did you two also kill Tracy Simms?"

Estelle and Harry stared at each other, confused.

"The point is, you're both lying. Neither of you had

anything to do with Michael's dying. So suppose you tell me what you're trying so hard not to tell me," I suggested.

I watched them hedge, debating about what to do.

Finally Estelle handed me the mixing bowl, wiped her hands, and sat down.

"Tell me, vot vill you do if you find d'von who killed Mickey? End Tracy too? I hed no idea, mind you, det she too vas . . . Vell anyvays, vot vill heppen to d'guilty party?" she pleaded with her eyes.

"I guess that would depend on the circumstances," I said, honestly.

She sighed.

"It's Alison you're protecting, isn't it?" I guessed.

Estelle nodded.

"She couldn't heve known vat she vas doin', I'm tellin' you," she told me.

"Maybe it was wotchamacall, sudden insanity," Harry proposed.

"Estelle, did Alison admit to killing Michael?" I asked.

Estelle shook her head in the negative. "She didn't say, end I'd never esk."

"Then how do you know?"

She put her hand up.

"It's true, det night Herry end me ve drove to Mickey's house. I taut maybe I could talk some *sechel*, some sense, into his head.

"So ve drove to his apartment. Ve let ourselves into d'building, no problem. I tink maybe someone should call d'menager by d'vay. D'security in his building, it's not so secure, if you cetch my meaning," Estelle said.

Didn't I know?

"Ve got up to Mickey's door. I knocked. No von answered. I hoid d'vater runnin, like I said, so I took a chence end tried d'door. It vasn't locked neither.

"Henry end me ve looked around to see from vhere d'vater

was spillink. Ve looked in d'kitchen end den . . . end den, ve saw vater comin' from d'betroom," Estelle informed me.

"I thought maybe the toilet was leakin'," Harry interjected, "until we walked in."

"*Vey es mere*, I'm tellin' you, such a sight like det I've never seen before. End I seen plenty," Estelle clucked mournfully, as she emptied the chocolate batter into the pans. I didn't stop her, thinking that perhaps it was therapeutic for her to help bake.

"Blood all around, everyvhere. Feh! In d'tub, over d'tiles, on d'floor . . . it splattered."

She described the scene vividly all the while she spooned out the rich, brown concoction.

"End Mickey, even *he* should rest in peace, he vas lyin' dere in d'middle of it all. I'm tellin' you it vas disgustink!"

"We didn't touch him or nothing," Harry assured me. "No sir, we didn't touch him or nothing else in the room. Estelle wanted to at least clean up the blood . . ."

"Ah, such a mess," she explained, licking the spoon before placing it in the sink.

"But I said, 'No, Essie, don't be such a *balabuster*, we don't need a housekeeper now.' I insisted we call the police," Harry said.

"Det's right. Det's right, he did," Estelle confirmed.

"So I went to the phone and started to dial," Harry explained, "but then Essie stopped me."

"Why?" I asked Estelle.

"Because of someting I found lying on d'betroom floor. A comb, made of seashells. I saw Elison vearing von like it ven she came to visit me a few days before. End den I recalled her tellin' me det she vas going to see Mickey det night. Vat could dey heve fought about, I vondered.

"I didn't know vat hed heppened, but I knew she vas dere. End I didn't vant my Elison she should get mixed up vit no police," Estelle said.

"Did you ever question her about it?" I asked.

"No. I...I...gave her back d'comb a few days later. She tenked me...pretended everyting vas all right. She didn't say nothin' else, so I didn't mention vhere it vas det I found it. I didn't know about Tracy den," Estelle said, sobbing softly.

"Enough!" Harry said, placing his arm protectively around Estelle. "She's gone through enough aggravation all these weeks, worrying that someone would loin the truth. I'm glad you know, I am. But I'm tellin' you, you and your boyfriend are gonna have a hard time proving anything."

"I appreciate your coming here," I said to Estelle. "I know it can't have been easy for you, but maybe it's all for the best."

"Maybe. Maybe it takes an ill vind to blow your het off. Maybe you can talk vit Elison. Find out vat heppened. Help her," she pleaded, looking up at me suddenly. "You're closer to her age, maybe she'll talk vit you. Please, go talk vit her, end tell her...tell her how much I love her. I alvays vill, no metter vat. Y'know to err is human, to forgive, it's a *mitzvah*," she paraphrased.

"But Estelle, I couldn't possibly..."

"Oy, Susila, please, please," she begged, taking my hand in hers.

What could I do, Nick?

"All right," I sighed. "I'll go see her this afternoon."

"God bless you, dollink. C'mon Herry, ve better get out from under her shoes," Estelle told him.

I walked them to the door, where Estelle turned and kissed my cheek.

"Maybe you vant I should stay and help vit d'frostink?" she offered.

I assured her it wasn't necessary, and watched as she and Harry left my house.

* * *

I removed the cake from the oven and left it to cool while I changed into a pair of jeans and a sweater. I wasn't at all sure I was doing the right thing, but after all, I had promised Estelle. So while I frosted the cake, I put in a call to Alison.

"Hello. Save the Whales. Cinnamon Blake speaking."

"Oh, hi, Cinnamon. This is Susan Finkelstein. Is Alison there?"

"Alison hasn't come in yet, Susan. Is there something I can, like, help you with?"

"No, that's all right. I just thought, well, if she's going to be around, I'd like to talk with her. It's important."

"You mean come down here?"

"Uh-huh."

"Well, let's see, she should be in about three, three-thirty, I'd say. In fact, she's probably on her way. You're more than welcome to come in and wait for her."

"Good idea. I'll do that."

"For sure. Say, is anything the matter?" Cinnamon asked.

"No. Not exactly. It's only that Estelle . . . oh, never mind."

"Say no more. Estelle Fagelman wants you to see that her Alison's in the best of health. Taking her vitamins, the whole *megillah*," Cinnamon guessed.

"Something like that," I replied vaguely.

"I didn't even know you knew Estelle."

"Mmm, we've met. Uh, Cinnamon let me ask you something," I said, as a morbid thought popped into my head. "Has Alison been herself lately? I mean, since Michael died?"

"For sure. Well, of course, she'd, like, taken his death pretty badly, but after all, that's only to be expected, right?"

"So you haven't noticed any serious changes in her character, say?"

"No. Oh, except as I said she's been kind of tired the past week. And maybe a little quieter than usual. You know, like nothing seems to be very important to her these days. That the kind of stuff you mean?" Cinnamon asked.

That was exactly the kind of stuff I meant, but not wanting to alarm Alison's friend, I just told her I'd be down as soon as I could get away. I hung up praying that Alison's remorse would not cause her to do something rash.

Quickly, I left word with Stephanie's service, canceling lunch and promising to call back and explain. Then I phoned Nick at his hotel.

"I'm sorry, ma'am, I'm ringing his room but there's still no answer," the operator apologized.

"May I leave a message?"

"One moment. I'll ring the reception desk."

After what seemed to be an eternity, a man's voice answered.

"Hello. I'd like to leave word for the party in room 227? It's very urgent. Tell him Susan phoned and that I saw Estelle and Estelle's protecting Alison, whom I suspect . . ."

"Lady, let's not have "As the World Turns" here, all right?"

"Right. Just tell him I'm rushing off to Marineland to make sure the butterfly doesn't snap off her own wings!"

✂ < 25 > ✂

Depend on the rabbit's foot if you will, but remember, it didn't work for the rabbit.

R. E. Shay

I pulled up to the cul-de-sac alongside the entrance to Cinnamon and Alison's office, and squeezed my Toyota between a monstrous Oldsmobile and a blue Chevy. How I planned on getting out of that spot was something I neglected to consider. I was already very late, having gotten a late start.

"Door's open," Cinnamon called out to me when I knocked. "Hi, I hope you don't mind my eating in front of you, but like, I didn't get to eat lunch and it's getting close to dinnertime," she apologized as she wolfed down a big bite of her sandwich.

"Oh, no, not at all."

"Would you like half?" she offered. "It's zucchini and natural peanut butter on honey-wheat."

"I'll pass, thanks." I looked at my watch. "It's after four. Alison hasn't been in, I presume?"

"You presume correctly. She phoned to say she was running late, but she'll try to make it here as soon as she can."

"Are you worried?" I asked.

"Worried?" She laughed, reminding me of *Mad* magazine's infamous Alfred E. Newman. "No. Why? Should I be?"

Cinnamon looked ready to be worried at a moment's notice if told that it was expected of her.

"Not necessarily," I said, purposely evasive.

"Look, Susan, be straight with me. If something's wrong and it concerns Alison, I think you should tell me about it. Maybe I can help?"

"Well..." I wasn't sure it was ethical to confer with Cinnamon over Alison's state of mind, particularly since what disturbed me was largely conjecture on my part.

"Hey, sometimes it's easier to talk in, like, a more relaxed setting," Cinnamon said. "I'll tell you what. Have you ever been inside Marineland?"

"Marineland? Uh, no, I guess not. I've been to Seaworld," I volunteered, "but no, I've never made it to Marineland. Or to Knotts Berry Farm either, for that matter."

"Well, c'mon then, that's where we're going. It's closed now," she said, glancing at her watch, "but I'll get us in."

"Isn't it kind of late? I mean I don't expect the fish will be biting at this time of day," I joked.

"It's never too late to enjoy the wonders of the sea, Susan," Cinnamon reprimanded. "I'll just, like, leave Alison a note. Tell her where we'll be."

We quickly left the office and got in her car. I held my breath as she backed it out sharply.

Hearing me gasp she said, "Oh, is that your car next to mine? Don't worry. I didn't touch it."

Maybe not, but as we headed the short distance toward Marineland, I couldn't help glancing back at my Toyota just to make sure it was in one piece.

We had been in the cold-water tank exhibit for over an hour, and in all that time Cinnamon had never shut up.

She was a walking-talking nonstop lecturing tour guide, and I was her private audience. I would have excused myself but I kept expecting Alison to show up any minute.

I had already learned as much as I'd ever want to know about the eccentricities of the lemon shark, the cowfish, and the threadfin, and by this time even Cinnamon was beginning to take on fishlike features.

"And now we come to the Pacific octopus. Something else, huh?"

I watched the large creature as he cartwheeled along on his blue-red tentacles. To think I may have eaten the poor beast's mother so nonchalantly in any number of sushi bars around town.

"Exquisite," I agreed.

"And smart," Cinnamon said. "When he feels threatened the octopus ejects an inky secretion, something like a dense cloud, you might say. That way he paralyzes the sense of smell of pursuing fish, giving him time to make, like, a quick getaway. Far out?"

"Clever," I agreed, as we walked out the door. It was getting late, and even the few employees who were there had begun to leave for the day.

We visited the killer-whale tank and then worked our way past the Baja Reef and on toward the walruses, which Cinnamon insisted I see before going back to the office.

"I enjoy the Baja Reef," Cinnamon confessed. "Sometimes I come out here and rent a wet suit and snorkel and just swim along with all the beautiful fish. Like, it makes me feel beautiful too," she said, waddling alongside me.

I tried to imagine Cinnamon's stocky body in a wet suit, but all I could picture was Aunt Bea in her orange-and-black flowered bikini.

"Cinnamon, I think it's time we talked about Alison," I suggested, finally.

"What about her?" she asked.

"All right. Now, I don't want to frighten you, but you did mention some changed in her behavior lately. Has it ever struck you that Alison might, well, want to take her own life?"

"Alison commit suicide? God no! Why would she? God!"

"Relax, Cinnamon. I was just asking," I said.

I realized that I would have to use the indirect approach with Cinnamon lest she become completely hysterical.

We were approaching the walrus tanks; I heard a bellow beneath us that sounded like that of a wild elephant.

"That's Faruk," Cinnamon explained. "He lives over in that area with his wife, so to speak. Her name's Petulia. And over here are their neighbors, Woolfy and Priscilla."

So familiarly did Cinnamon talk about these four-thousand-pound sea lions, she made it sound as if Faruk and Petulia and Woolfy and Priscilla enjoyed the pleasures of suburban domesticity together.

Faruk's bristly whiskers made him look something like a conductor on the Atchison, Topeka, and the Santa Fe.

"Cinnamon. How much did you know about Alison's relationship with Michael?" I asked.

"I told you. She loved him very much," she replied impatiently.

"As a brother, and nothing more?"

"I'm not sure I follow."

I thought for a while about the best way to broach the possibility of Alison's incestuous love for Michael. A love so passionate that it may very well have caused him to die by her hand.

I looked down into their lair and watched Faruk lovingly nuzzle up to Petulia. Warm-blooded mammals. How different were they from man?

The fact of the matter was that these particular mammals were among the most vicious in the whole sea-world community.

According to the sign, the Pacific Walrus . . . or the *Odobenus rosmarus*, as it was technically referred to, consumed at least one hundred pounds of clams and mussels a day and used its sharp tusks to spear its food.

"If you're suggesting that there was something, like,

weird going on between Alison and Michael, you're wrong!" Cinnamon snapped.

"Cinnamon, let's be honest with each other. You must know as well as I that Alison was planning to move in with Michael."

"She was planning no such thing," Cinnamon insisted.

"Yes, she was. What's more, I have reason to suspect that they were, well, in love."

Cinnamon looked as though she were going to be sick.

"I'm sorry. I didn't mean to spring that on you the way I did," I apologized, placing my arm around her.

"Love?" She shook my arm off. "Love him? He was a pig. Nothing but a pig," she hissed.

"Look, it's getting late . . . you're distraught," I said. "Maybe you should let me drive your car back to . . ."

It was then that it hit me.

Cinnamon's car.

The blue Chevy. The bumper sticker . . . Save the Whales.

I'd seen the car before. I was positive that it was the one that had nearly pushed Nick and me off the road on our way back from Jean Paul's that afternoon.

It was Cinnamon's car we had seen. But how was that possible?

Cinnamon claimed she hadn't returned from New York until the morning of Michael's funeral.

Her first time east of West Covina she had said. But wait, that didn't make sense either. If that were her first time back east, as she professed . . . My thoughts were splintering in a million different directions.

"Cinnamon? Did you say you'd never been back east before your trip last month?" I asked.

"That's right." Cinnamon looked up sharply.

"How is it then that your grade school was letting out when you got word of Kennedy's assassination? That would make it close to three o'clock Eastern Standard Time."

"So?"

"So in West Covina it wasn't even noon."

She sighed. "All right. So kill me. I exaggerated. It wasn't my first time back east. So what does that prove?"

"Nothing. Not a single thing. But why lie?" After a moment I said, "You know the way you observe fish, Cinnamon? Well I guess you might say that I'm an observer of human nature."

"Are you?"

"Yes, I am. And as an observer of human nature, I've noticed that people frequently use little lies to embellish even bigger lies. Especially when those bigger lies can mean the difference between having an alibi or not." I was gambling.

"Alibi? What are you talking about, alibi?"

"You were never in New York last month. In fact, I'd wager you were here all the time. Nick and I saw your car. How'd you get Alison to back your story, Cinnamon? Did you frighten her to death?" I asked.

A metamorphosis took place as the homey girl I had spent the afternoon with was suddenly transformed into a pillar of confidence and undefiable strength.

"What Alison did for me, she did because she loves me."

Love kills.

"And did you kill Michael because you loved her?"

"Of course I did," she admitted serenely, as though it were foolish of me to have asked, "but it wasn't murder. It was an accident. What *he* was scheming to do with Alison was horrendous. Imagine! His own sister!"

"But surely Alison..."

"Alison would have gone along with anything that pig wanted," Cinnamon replied, adding sadly, "I don't know why, except that she idolized him. She didn't tell me about her plans to move in with him, but I had my suspicions. When I knew for sure what it was she was intending to do,

I confronted Alison and she admitted it was true. I nearly died. Alison said it was what Michael wanted and that it would be all right. She said she planned on moving out of our apartment fairly soon.

"But I wouldn't hear of it. I knew Alison was going to see him later that night. So I called Michael, said I'd be over earlier, to talk with him. I told him it was important. When I got there, I rang but he was in the shower. He couldn't hear me. Then I remembered a spare key Alison had given me to Michael's apartment when she apartment-sat for him one time last year. I used it and let myself in.

"God, I was so angry! I . . . I walked right into the bathroom! I couldn't wait to give him a piece of my mind. Michael saw it was me and laughed.

"He said if I were a *real* woman he might have gotten excited. The pig!"

"Go on," I said.

"I told him to keep his slimy hands off Alison. That she was too good to get mixed up in his filthy life. He told me to get out. I said I'd leave, but that it was *me* Alison needed."

"What was his reaction?"

"He screamed at me. Claimed Alison could never be happy with a 'frustrated dyke,' as he so eloquently referred to me."

Cinnamon's story made me think that Alison was in a no-win situation; her alternatives were altogether slim.

"Then he told me he'd forbid Alison to have anything more to do with me once they moved in together," she said, her expression one of sheer panic, "and that we'd see each other again over his dead body."

Truer words were never spoken.

"That's when I, like, lurched for him. I pulled his hair . . . so he pulled mine . . . so I bent back his fingers . . . so he slapped my face . . . so I kicked his balls . . . so he grabbed his groin, thereby causing him to slip in the tub and crack his piggish skull wide open," Cinnamon concluded neatly.

So, in the final analysis, Michael had gotten it in the balls.

"I ran out real fast, like, I don't even think I locked the door. When I got home . . . I . . . I broke the news to Alison. Shit! That was the hardest thing I ever had to do. What a bad scene.

"She got hysterical. Called me all kinds of names. Threatened to go to the police. But then she calmed down and realized it was an accident and that going to the police wouldn't do anything but drag our names through the mud. Besides, with Michael gone and Estelle getting on in years, I was all she had left in the world."

Poor Alison, talk about victims.

"So I held her close and she cried straight through the night. In the morning we agreed that we'd wait until Alison was officially notifed and, in the meantime, I'd lie low. Alison would say I'd been in New York should the question ever arise. And if anyone was concerned, and I doubted too many people would be, Michael's death would go down as having been an accident."

"What went wrong?" I asked, as I listened to the walruses flip their fins below us.

"Tracy. That's what went wrong," Cinnamon declared. "Seems she'd also planned on visiting Michael before Alison showed up. To bring him some legal papers or some other such bullshit. Anyway, he mentioned to her that I was coming by so they'd have to make it another time."

"How do you know all this?"

"Tracy told me herself. The morning of Michael's funeral she whispered to Alison that she'd guessed the truth about how Michael died. So I called her later that day, and we talked. She suggested I drop in on her some time so we could discuss my 'precarious situation' she said. That cunt!

I don't think she was going to blackmail me. In fact, I thought she may've been bluffing about the whole damn thing," Cinnamon said.

"Then why . . . ?"

"She just wanted something to hold over Alison's head, that's why. Tracy despised Alison, you know. Always has, because Alison was the one and only thing that pig ever cherished."

"So you went to see Tracy just before Nick and I got there."

"Oh, for sure! See, I wasn't even going to keep our date but then I heard you say you were planning a chat with her, and I couldn't take a chance on what she might tell you, now could I?"

Reasonable. I just hoped, though, that our going to visit Tracy hadn't been the catalyst that resulted in her having died.

"Was Tracy's death also . . . um . . . an accident?" I asked.

"Looked that way, didn't it?" She smiled, smug at her accomplishment.

"Uh-huh."

"Uh-huh. I didn't even bother phoning. I just sped over to Tracy's and walked right in. See, her door was open. So anyway, she yells out for whoever it is to come on up; I don't think she was too discriminating, if you get my drift. I went up to her bedroom and found her at her vanity table, an obvious place for that cow to be, since she was just about the vainest bitch on two legs. I remember she was wearing her bra and panties and these, oh you know, these spike heels . . . fuck-me shoes!

"So anyway," Cinnamon continued, "she was surprised to see me at first. Real surprised. I mean she knocked over a whole bottle of perfume, that's how much I caught her off guard. Then she starts to get back, like, her confidence? Goes into this whole rap about how she knows I had something to do with Michael's death, since he had told her I'd be dropping by that night.

"So I tell her she couldn't prove a goddamned thing, and she says she'd never have to, because what she suspected would be enough to make Alison's life a living hell and that would be more than enough satisfaction for her."

"So?" I helped her along.

"So what could I do? I showed her the gun I'd brought with me and told her she'd better listen very carefully. She didn't believe I'd use it, you know. She even laughed. She shouldn't have laughed, Susan."

I wanted to assure Cinnamon that by all means, should I ever find myself on the wrong end of a loaded pistol, I would never, ever, laugh.

"So I said," she continued, "I said, 'Start walking down the stairs, you cunt,' and then she knew I meant business. She admitted that she didn't know anything, she was guessing. But by then it didn't matter. I pointed to a bottle of vodka and told her to help herself to a drink. She started to bitch, but I held up my revolver.

"Then I tossed her some Quāaludes, made sure she took them all and led her out to the pool. By now, I had her begging me to call a doctor. She said her throat was beginning to tighten up on her.

"I laughed and told her a nose, ear, and throat guy wouldn't be any use to her now. Funny?"

"Very."

"I thought so. Anyway, we walked down to the side of the pool. I told her to strip, which she did. I'll say one thing for the lady, she was built like a brick shithouse.

"You might even say that Tracy embodied the single quality most men look for in a woman," Cinnamon scoffed, "not that that was her fault."

"So anyway, I waited until she got drowsy, left her glass and the empty bottle of pills by her chair, and then I pushed her into the pool," she stated simply. "God...she didn't even struggle. It was, like, pathetic, y'know? And then I just waited."

"You waited?"

"Waited for her to die," she explained.

Was I hearing correctly? Was the girl who devoted her entire life to saving whales and seals and the like, the same girl who was telling me she complacently looked on while another human being lived out her final hours, simply because it was expedient?

"You screwed around with Freddie's car!" I accused.

"Who the hell's Freddie?"

"The red Mustang we drove up in. You did something to it."

"Oh, that. A minor adjustment. I'm pretty good with mechanical things," she said modestly. "I knew when I met you and your friend that you suspected something. Nick, with that stupid survey of funerals business. I wanted to do something to scare you off.

"Alison talked me into recording that idiotic warning at low speed. I told her it was dumb. That it wouldn't discourage you if you were really determined to learn the truth."

"It did scare me," I confessed.

"It did? Well, that's good. At least it served some purpose," Cinnamon said. "So anyway, when I saw you go into Tracy's house, I guess I got nervous and messed with your car. I thought maybe you'd come across something incriminating inside, but, of course, that was silly of me."

"Of course."

"It wasn't until after Tracy died that I realized the extent you were willing to become involved in finding out what actually happened," Cinnamon said.

"Did Alison know? About how Tracy died, I mean," I asked.

"No," Cinnamon admitted, "the papers wrote it up as a suicide and I didn't see any reason to burden Alison with the truth. See, I could have let you find out about Michael's death, I mean, it was, like, an accident, sort of. But Tracy's death was murder. And well, Susan, you must see my difficulty there.

"I wanted to get you alone. You know, without Nick. So I waited outside your house. God, I waited for three days and you didn't come out. How could you stand being cooped up for three solid days?" Cinnamon asked.

"I'm a writer, I'm used to solitude," was all I said. I should explain my former state of depression to this lunatic?

"Oh. Well anyway, you finally did leave the house. I followed you to some bar on Ventura Boulevard," she said.

"You tried to push me under a bus," I stated with sudden horror as the realization hit me.

"And you'd think that would have stopped you," Cinnamon clucked, sounding like Aunt Bea when one of her children had disobeyed her. "But no, you and Nick continued prying. Prying and suspecting everyone."

"I'm not the only one who suspected the wrong person."

"Huh?"

"Estelle Fagelman. She's under the impression that Alison murdered Michael. You see she found a comb on the floor she believed to be Alison's, but it was yours, wasn't it?"

She nodded. "It must've fallen when he grabbed my hair. Alison! Oh, my God, poor Estelle, what she must be going through!"

Poor Estelle? Estelle isn't standing in an isolated marina, seven feet above four deadly walruses and one foot from a deadly young lady such as yourself, Cinnamon.

It was then that I became aware of just how alone we were. Only Cinnamon and me. And the four walruses.

"Carnivorous." The word shot up at me, and I recalled how the walrus used its tusks to attack its food.

"Oh, I get it," Cinnamon said. "She thought Alison killed Michael and that in a fit of self-recrimination, she might take her own life. So that's why she sent you out here. To stop her."

"Well, actually the suicide theory was my own," I admitted.

"God, Susan! Were you ever off the track!" she said, removing a .38 caliber pistol from her purse.

"Tell me about it!"

"You know I had a feeling you were up to something when you phoned today. So I called Alison and told her not to bother coming in today."

"Not coming? But you wrote a note. I saw you . . . you . . ."

"That's right, I lied. As a matter of fact, I've been lying to you all day. So what are you going to do, kill me?"

"I was just about to ask you the same question."

"Oh no, Susan, please. I'm not going to kill you!"

"Well, I must say you're being sensible about this Cinnamon," I said, breathing easier.

"I don't have to. They'll do it for me," she said, pointing to the walruses. "Did you know that for the past three hundred years, man has been the walrus's greatest adversary?"

Cinnamon didn't have to tell me that. I could have guessed that an unexpected visit from one Susan Finkelstein would not be well received by Faruk and friends.

"Of course, it will have to look like an accident," she said.

This woman was mad!

"I'll just say you came out here to visit Alison and thought you'd have a look around," she explained. "So you could, like, help your reporter friend with his article, say. Given your inquisitive nature, you snuck in after hours and climbed over the fence to take some pictures. You slipped and fell in. Your body, or at least what's left of it, won't be discovered till morning."

"Nick wouldn't believe that for an instant."

"It'd be his word against mine. He couldn't prove a thing, Susan. Not a thing. If he mentioned Michael and Tracy, well, so what? There's no proof there either. Let's face it, my hands are clean."

"Oh yeah? Well, how could I have been taking pictures if I don't even have a camera?" I challenged. Spoken too soon.

While pointing her gun at me, she managed to rummage through her huge purse and come up with a 35mm. Canon.

"Here you go," she said. "Put it around your neck."

"You thought of everything."

"Just put it around your neck," she repeated, still pointing the gun. "I don't want to have to shoot you."

"No, you'll just leave the grisly task to your fishy friends," I said, putting the camera around my neck.

"Susan, has anyone ever told you you have a tendency to overdramatize? Now, turn around and . . . okay, let's have it."

"Have what?" I asked, innocently.

"Cut the crap. The film, let's have it. I saw you shoot and if you don't mind, I'd rather this little episode weren't recorded for posterity. Now let me have it," she demanded.

Out of sheer desperation I had snapped the picture thinking that even if I were to die, I would have at least left behind absolute proof as to who my murderer was.

It seemed now that I wouldn't even have that slight satisfaction.

"No!" I clutched the camera stubbornly and stupidly on my part, considering the fact that she did have a gun. But I wasn't prepared to die without a struggle.

As Cinnamon and I grappled over the camera, she managed to press a lever thus dispatching and exposing the film.

"Are you satisfied?" she asked. "Okay, put it back in the camera, Susan, and no bullshit this time or I'll do the next shooting. And not with a camera!"

I loaded the useless film back into the Canon. Since she held the gun straight at me, I saw no point in not doing as I was told.

"Good," Cinnamon said. "Now climb over the fence."

Reluctantly, but not knowing what else to do by now, I climbed the fence as she instructed, my knees shaking all the while.

I slid down.

"Try harder, Susan," Cinnamon suggested, raising her revolver.

Once again I climbed up, holding on tightly, as I shimmied down the other side onto a narrow ledge.

The bellowing that ensued caused me quite literally to wet my pants.

At this point, the only thing preventing me from becoming the walruses' dinner was the fact that I clung tenaciously to the barbed-wire fence, keeping my footing on the ledge.

"Good. Now lower yourself off the ledge."

"And dangle like a yo-yo from the fence? Are you nuts?"

"Let's not get into name-calling," she suggested. "Just do it!"

"What are you going to do now? Smash my knuckles?" I asked when I had lowered myself to Cinnamon's satisfaction.

Bright, Susan. Give the lady suggestions, why don't you. This broad knew her business, she didn't need any assistance from you.

"That won't be necessary. You must realize you won't be able to hold on to this fence all night. Your hands will get tired. And when they do . . ."

"So you're just going to watch me die, that it?"

"I watched Tracy die," she rationalized.

That's true, she did. My hands were beginning to hurt.

"Do you think Alison could condone this?" I asked, trying to combine psychology and Jewish guilt. "She'll hate you for it."

"Alison will believe what I tell her," Cinnamon replied.

I looked into the tank below. Into the murky water. The walruses were restless, barking and bellowing in anticipation of my fall.

Maybe someone will come along, I thought. A night watchman, perhaps. At any rate, my other option was Cinnamon's pistol, which seemed a surer threat. At least if I could manage to hold on, I'd have some control of my destiny. Short as it might be.

I wished I had sensed the danger I was in and could, like the octopus, have ejected an inky secretion of my own to aid my speedy getaway.

The wire cut into my left palm, and I winced with pain.

"Five minutes and you're already squirming. How much more of this pain can you take?" Cinnamon asked. "Huh, Susan, how much?"

The girl would have put Tokyo Rose to shame.

I tried to get a better grip and almost lost my hold completely in the process. The walruses went crazy.

My left hand was raw and bleeding now, but I thought of those tusks, how they used them to tear into their food. I held on tighter.

"Relax, Petulia, it's not soup yet!" I called out.

"It's amazing that you can still retain your sense of humor at a time like this," Cinnamon marveled.

"When I'm scared, I joke." I sneezed.

"Bless you."

"And sneeze, thank you."

"You sneeze when you joke?"

"No, I sneeze when . . . skip it. Why do I have to explain anything to you?"

"You don't. In fact, why don't you just shut up and die?"

I was willing to comply with the former, but not the latter.

Not yet.

For a few seconds there was total silence. Even the walruses were still.

And then the sound of footsteps broke the silence.

In the far distance I heard Nick's voice.

"Nick," I gasped. "Nick, I'm over . . ."

"Shut up," Cinnamon warned, "or I'll shoot you and then your boyfriend."

And I believe she would have.

Cinnamon was alarmed at this sudden, unexpected turn of events. As if to regain control, she quickly hurdled the fence and crouching on the narrow ledge, pointed her revolver inches from my head.

The footsteps came close, but soon receded.

Cinnamon relaxed, and then suddenly stiffened.

"What was that?" she demanded.

What it was, was exactly 7:00 P.M. and my watch began buzzing out "Stars and Stripes Forever."

I could have kissed Uncle Mario then and there; never was a gift more appreciated. The tank acted as an echo chamber and reverberated the sound, increasing its volume by several decibels.

"Over this way." I heard Nick shout out to someone.

We heard the running and I held on for dear life.

Cinnamon looked up as Nick and Alison charged in our direction.

Frightened, she aimed the gun at Nick and was about to shoot when Alison blocked the way.

"No, Cin, no! Enough!" she cried out in a voice louder

than I had ever imagined possible. "You'll have to shoot me too!"

Cinnamon hesitated, then tossed the revolver into the walruses' den. Slowly I eased myself onto the ledge, then scrambled back over the fence, dropping to the other side as Nick and Alison raced toward us.

I fell into Nick's arms and clung to him as fiercely as I had clung to the wire fence moments before.

As Alison stared at her friend accusingly, Cinnamon remained on the ledge clutching the fence; she appeared impervious to her surroundings.

"Tracy! You killed Tracy, Cinnamon! And that was no accident!"

"For you, I did it for you Alison," Cinnamon's voice choked out. "She threatened to hurt you, baby. I couldn't let her hurt you."

She broke down, sobbing hysterically.

"And I suppose you killed Michael for me too?"

Cinnamon was startled. "Oh no! No, no . . . you know that was an accident. I told you it was!"

"I'm not sure of anything you tell me anymore," Alison said with uncustomary bitterness in her voice. "I only know that you killed Tracy. And you killed my brother. And I loved Michael more than anyone in this world. I loved him more than you, Cinnamon. Why, you're nothing more than a cold-blooded murderer. You're revolting!" Alison screamed. "I despise you. And you'll pay for what you've done. I'll see that you pay for it!"

Cinnamon's devastation was complete.

"Alison . . . don't . . . please!" For one second, Cinnamon lifted her arms to plead her case.

It was one second too long.

Helplessly, we watched as she lost her balance and fell; we heard the bellowing and the splash.

And the screams and crunching that followed. Blood

spurted up as though a geyser had been hit. And then, all at once, it was quiet once again. The walruses had not been disappointed after all.

I threw up.

✂ EPILOGUE ✂

All's well that ends well.

William Shakespeare

We waited for the ambulance and special police task force to arrive.

"She on something?" a policeman asked Nick, as they lifted Cinnamon's remains into the coroner's van.

"Nah, she just climbed over to talk with them before we could stop her. Thought she had a unique rapport with walruses," Nick replied, significantly.

"I getcha." The cop nodded appreciatively. "Well, there's not much one can do in a case like this. Uh, I'll need a little more information. Maybe the young lady here? When she feels up to it, of course."

"Alison?" I said softly. "Alison, do you think you can answer some questions?"

She stared at me blankly.

"No use, she's in shock," Nick said. "Her brother died a few weeks ago. Now her roommate...the kid's been through a regular holocaust these past few weeks."

"That's all right. I understand," Officer Batista said. "Just some paperwork that has to be taken care of. Nothing that can't wait."

"Good. I'll go down to police headquarters, make a statement."

"Appreciate it. Is there a next of kin to be notified?"

"I don't know about Cinnamon. Alison will have to fill you in when she's recovered. But as far as Alison herself is concerned, I'll phone her godmother," I offered. "She'll

239

come down to the hospital. In fact, I'm sure Alison will be wanting to spend a lot of time with her from now on."

"Thanks," he said. "Well, like I say, there's nothing more to be done. Sorry you folks had to witness this here. Pretty gruesome night for you, I imagine."

Officer Batista had said a mouthful.

Nick had come down to Marineland in Alison's car, which one of the policemen thoughtfully offered to drive to the hospital where Alison was to be treated for shock.

We drove back to the city in my car. Actually Nick drove, since my body was still akin to Jell-O.

I described to him the events that had led up to Cinnamon's holding me at gunpoint.

"So as it turned out, Tracy didn't know anything for certain the day she asked me over. She probably just wanted to pump me to find out what I knew," I surmised.

"Which, indirectly, led to Cinnamon's killing her," Nick added. "What's ironic about this whole business is that it was Meyer's call to Michael that initially started you thinking he was murdered. And as it turned out, that call had nothing to do with Cole's murder."

"Maybe not, but look where it led us," I pointed out.

"Incredible. Absolutely incredible," he remarked.

"But that's what happened. Now, how did you manage to team up with Alison?" I asked.

"Oh, that. Well, I went to Estelle Fagelman's, figuring you'd have tracked her down, totally disregarding my advice."

"Ah, but it was she who tracked me down," I reminded him.

"I know, she told me about your talk. Incidentally, I'm expecting one hell of a chocolate cake for dessert tonight. Anyway, she told me about asking you to have a heart-to-heart with Alison. So I rushed over to her place. Hell, I figured if she killed Tracy and Cole, what was to stop her from killing you?

"When I got to her apartment she was alone. I asked her if she'd seen you, she said she hadn't. Then I asked her where her roommate was, and she told me Cinnamon had called and told her it was a light work day, not to bother coming down . . . that she'd have things under control."

"Did she ever!" I remarked.

"I didn't so much as mention Cole's name, but without Cinnamon by her side to bolster her, Alison became completely unglued. Told me what she knew of the way Cole had died. But she insisted it was an accident. That her friend Cinnamon ordinarily wouldn't hurt a hair on anyone's head."

"Let me tell you, that Alison's some judge of character," I said.

"Anyway, I asked her what she knew about Tracy Simms's death, and she very innocently told me that Tracy had committed suicide. I figured either this girl could win an Oscar or she really had no idea what was going down. I gambled on her genuine naivete. When I told her we suspected that whoever was responsible for Cole's death was in all probability responsible for Tracy's as well, Jesus, she fell to pieces!

"So, I let that soak in while I called my hotel for messages. That's when I learned where you were. And with whom! Susan, I swear to God I could've killed you!"

"That was already being taken care of," I reminded him.

"Right. Well, I grabbed Alison and we flew out of her apartment. She offered to drive, said she knew of a shortcut. When we got down there, we saw the note Cinnamon had left for Alison."

"She didn't intend for anyone to see it, you know," I said.

"Yeah? Well, we did. We parked inside Marineland and started looking everywhere. It's a big place, you know."

"Why didn't you call out to us?"

"We didn't want to upset Cinnamon. In her frame of mind, who knows what she'd have done. You know, once I actually thought I heard you call my name. Say, you think maybe I'm psychic?"

"No, I did call your name, but Cinnamon's gun was very persuasive in shutting me up," I said.

"Thank the Lord for uncle Mario's crazy gizmos, huh?" Nick grinned.

"You're not kidding. That watch saved my life. I don't know how much longer I could've held on."

"Well, it's all over."

"Yes, it is. By the way, I'm glad you didn't go into detail with the police in front of Alison."

"Nah, when we make our statements to the police we're gonna have to go into it, though."

"About Michael?"

"About Michael, about Tracy . . . the whole crazy story, if they'll believe us. The truth's gotta come out sooner or later."

"Uh, what about our having discovered Tracy's body? Are we going to tell them about that?"

"Sure, if anyone asks," Nick said.

"You know I feel kind of crummy about our lying to Cinnamon about the article you promised to write. You know, on the seals and whales and their mistreatment," I reminded him.

"Who was lying? I fully intend to write that article. Okay, Cinnamon happened to be a nut-case in her private life, but she worked for a very worthy organization. Oh no, I'm writing that article, all right," Nick said firmly.

"That's terrific. In fact, I think you're pretty terrific. And, uh, Nick? There's something you told me to remind you about the other day."

"Oh, yeah? What was that?"

"You said to remind you to tell me you love me."

"Right. Susan . . . I love you."

"I'm glad, because I love you too, Nick."

"I know," he said, giving me a big, sloppy kiss.

Then he made a sharp U-turn and pulled into the parking lot of a twenty-four-hour supermarket.

"Wait here," he said. "I'll be right out."

Ten minutes later he returned to the car carrying a huge grocery bag filled to the brim with avocados.

"Nick, are you crazy? You must have two dozen avocados there. Nobody eats that much guacamole," I said.

"Three dozen," he corrected, getting into the car. "I thought I'd better get a head start on California living."

ABOUT THE AUTHOR

Vivian Rhodes is a successful young writer who received her M.A. from Syracuse University in the Newhouse School Department of Television/Film. *Groomed for Murder* marks her debut as a talented novelist. Vivian lives with her husband in Los Angeles.